I0763743

THE CAMIGAS SCARF

THE CAMIGAS SCARF

Crone

BOOK THREE

ALDER ALLENSWORTH

Edited by Robin Cain.
Cover illustration by Nupu Press.
www.nupupress.com

This is a work of fiction. Names, characters, places, and incidents are either the product of the author's imagination or are used fictitiously. The views expressed in this book are solely those of the author and do not necessarily reflect the views of any of the women who have carried the scarf, the administrators of the Facebook group *Camigas: A Buddy System for Women on the Camino,* or any of the individuals who participated in bringing this book to fruition.

ISBN 979-8-9900189-4-5

The Camigas' Scarf

Dedicated to all of the Camigas who walk The Way.

Acknowledgments

My gratitude goes out to the Camino de Santiago, the people of Spain, and people worldwide who support and maintain this magical place where the impossible becomes possible.

To Gigi Mashburn, finder of the scarf. She embodies the spirit of sisterhood. Listening to the scarf, she blessed it and sent it on its way. To Annie Herman for showing me the purpose of the scarf. And to every scarf carrier and all the women who choose to walk the Camino.

To Lorena Gaibor, Caroline Loder, and Jenna D'Amore (*in memoriam*), who created and maintain a safe, supportive place for women who walk the Camino through the Facebook page *Camigas: A Buddy System for Women on the Camino,* and for graciously permitting me to use the name the Camigas Scarf.

I especially want to thank Jenna McKenna, who read the original rough draft and encouraged me to give voice to the scarf and passion to my characters. And to the Tampa Writers Alliance, whose members read my drafts month after month, gently taught me writing techniques, and cheered me on when I wanted to give up.

I am honored to have the beta reader Shoshana Kerewsky, who made wonderful suggestions and encouraged me to believe in the work.

My mentor, Beebe Bahrami, guided me along the way with her knowledge of the Camino and the sacred feminine. We enjoyed a glass of port and several dinners while on the Portuguese route. Readers may want to check out *Camino de Santiago: Sacred Sites, Historic Villages, Local Food & Wine* (Moon Travel Guides), and keep an eye out for her upcoming guide to the Portuguese route.

I would have been lost without the *Village to Village* guide by Matthew Harms, Anna Dintaman, and David Landis, and the Camino Ninja app.

Not just women have touched this book. Gerry Hudson Martin read the first complete draft, corrected my punctuation, and my memory of key places along the way.

Four women jumped in to make this book possible and bring it to life when I was at my wits' end with revisions: Robin Cain and Marian Woyciehowicz Gonsior for their astute suggestions and editing, Kim Narenkivicius for the beautiful layout, and Nupu for creating the cover with her art.

To Ben Ritter, who supports my dream of making this trilogy a reality and cheers me on when I walk the Camino de Santiago.

To LifeWave technology for keeping this old body moving and quickly recovering on the Camino Portugués.

And most importantly, *the scarf.*

Introduction

The Camigas scarf has been passed from Camiga to Camiga in solidarity with their pilgrimages. The term Camiga was coined in 2015 when a small group of women came together to support women walking the Camino. Ca stands for Camino, and in Spanish amiga means female friend.

The Camino de Santiago is one of the few places in the world where a woman can go, walk alone on pilgrimage, and feel safe. In March of 2015, that sense of safety was shaken by the death of a young woman named Denise. The perpetrator was found and convicted. In response, the Facebook page *Camigas: A Buddy System for Women on the Camino* was created so women who want to participate in the pilgrimage have a safe place to connect with other women and plan their Caminos. At this writing, the Facebook page has over 37,000 members.

I have so much gratitude for Lorena Gaibor, Caroline Loder, and Jenna D'Amore (*in memoriam*) for seeing the need women have for a buddy to embark upon such an arduous pilgrimage. They gave me their blessing to use the term *Camiga.*

The origin of the scarf goes back a little further. The story began in 2010 when Gigi walked the Camino Francés from Saint-Jean-Pied-de-Port, France, to Santiago de Compostela, Spain.

Along the way, she met a young American woman in a small town who was working in Spain as an au pair. The young woman was so happy to hear English being spoken that she joined them for the evening. She missed the last bus back to her employer's house, but Gigi made sure she had a safe place to stay. The next morning, she left early to catch the bus and left her scarf behind. Gigi rescued the scarf and carried it with her, hoping to connect with the young woman again. This never happened.

Seven years later, in the fall of 2017, I was getting ready to walk my Camino. I worked with Gigi and asked her if we could have lunch. I wanted to learn all I could about the Camino before I left. Gigi brought me three gifts: a palm frond cross that had been blessed, four euros to buy a cup of café con leche, and the scarf.

As Gigi prepared for our lunch, she opened the drawer where she kept her Camino gear and hiking clothes. In the back of the drawer was the scarf. She pulled it out and, as she stroked its soft fibers, memories of her Camino came flooding back. She had the distinct feeling that it needed to go back to the Camino, though she did not know why. She knew she had to give it to me to take back.

Gigi has the reputation of being connected to a higher power. I did not question her wisdom. I took the scarf and completed the entire five-hundred-mile Camino Francés with it around my neck in October and November of 2017. I appreciated the warmth of the scarf as fall turned into winter. The Camino was not easy, but knowing I had the support of the other Camigas, Gigi, and the scarf, I made it to Santiago.

Annie, a woman from my local area, saw me posting about my Camino on the Camigas Facebook page. She messaged me and asked to meet for lunch so I could assist her in preparing for her Camino. I took my pack loaded with everything I had carried. Sharing the contents item by item, I reminded her that less is better, since she would have to carry everything across Spain.

I pulled out the scarf and told her its story. She leaned in and met my gaze, and it was written all over her face that she wanted to take the scarf back to the Camino. Reluctantly, I offered her the scarf. She accepted immediately. It was hard releasing this piece of yarn. The scarf had served me well. It was around my neck the morning I walked into the square in front of the Cathedral of Santiago, completing my five-hundred-mile Camino. The scarf had been my constant companion and support. It held both the joyful memories and the hardships. But what was I going to do with a scarf in Florida? So I handed it over.

It was wonderful following Annie and the scarf on her Camino. I cheered her on through messages and photos shared online. When I saw pictures of her standing in front of the cathedral in Santiago wearing the scarf, I knew it had found its purpose and why it had to return to the Camino.

Annie's friend Donna was getting ready to walk the following year, and Annie passed the scarf on to her. As of this writing, the scarf has accompanied Camigas on seventeen Caminos. Each Camiga passes the scarf on to a woman who has been called to walk one of the ancient paths to Santiago, continuing a tradition of support for women and pilgrimage.

The Camigas Scarf Trilogy follows the journey of three women: a mother, a maiden, and a crone. Each character is fictional, as I could not do justice to the experiences of the Camigas who have carried the scarf. I did not want to intrude upon the personal reasons that draw women to walk the Camino.

Women of all ages, races, cultures, religious persuasions, and backgrounds walk the Camino for many reasons. The Camino is a place of reflection and growth. The experiences of each character in this trilogy were created in my imagination and shaped by interviews with women on the Camino, stories and Facebook posts, and my own Camino experiences. Any similarity to a real person is purely coincidental.

Each book highlights a different Camino route. The historic places each woman experiences are authentic to that particular route. I have taken care to research each route, as well as walk them myself. Some albergues have changed names and owners and may not be found on the Camino today.

Book One follows Helen, the mother, as she embarks upon a life-changing pilgrimage, starting in Saint-Jean-Pied-de-Port. She struggles across the Pyrenees to Santiago de Compostela and discovers a light within herself.

Book Two follows Valerie as she heads to Spain to walk the final one hundred kilometers of the Camino de Santiago, seeking to heal her fragile heart. A chance encounter with mesmerizing blue eyes leads her off course and onto the rugged 833-kilometer Camino del Norte.

Book Three follows Dot, our wise crone, burdened by grief after losing her husband and worn down by life's responsibilities, as she embarks on a solitary journey up Portugal's west coast to Santiago de Compostela. Much to the dismay of her adult children, she discovers that at the age of seventy-nine, she is far from too old for adventure.

It is fun to be part of the sisterhood of the scarf. It has become part of my Camino journey. The scarf carried me through the Camino Francés at the age of sixty. I was called to walk the Norte at sixty-seven, and I walked the Portuguese at sixty-eight. I believe LifeWave photobiomodulation technology has given me the energy, strength, stamina, and focus to complete these routes and write these books.

Thank you for following the scarf's journey. If you have never walked a Camino, I hope this trilogy inspires you to embark on this life-changing pilgrimage someday. And if you have, may this trilogy inspire you to cherish the memories of your journey forever.

BOOK III

THINK LIKE THE CRONE

Dot

Love like the Mother
Dance like the Maiden
Think like the Crone

- Stenciled on a jar of homemade Sangria
that was given to me by a wise crone.

CHAPTER 1

LISBON

I grab the soft fabric around my neck.

"Scarf," I whisper, "we're here."

I don't want anyone to think I'm one of those old ladies who talks to herself, but I suppose I've become one. I giggle, fluffing my short, curly hair. The silver has taken over the gold, but it's still thick and curly. Roy always said it was one of my best features. I sigh, then square my shoulders. My eyes fill remembering him.

I unbuckle my seatbelt. I'm uncertain—I want to start my pilgrimage, but I also want to stay wrapped in this cocoon of safe steel.

Whenever I froze in fear, Roy would run his fingers through my curls and say, "Dot, darling, the show must go on."

I can almost hear his voice beside me. It will always be with me.

I reach under the seat in front of me and pull out my toiletry bag, wiping my tears with the scarf. I check my documents, cash, and cards in the fanny pack at my waist. All there. Zipping it closed, I remember what my local pilgrims group told me—never let it out of my possession.

I move toward the aisle as a friendly, handsome, tall young man from the row behind me opens the overhead compartment.

"May I get your bag, *senhora*?" He speaks in perfect English with a charming accent.

"Yes, please. The bright orange one. My children want me visible if anything bad happens." I smile at him.

"Ah, the *Caminho*."

"Yes. Have you walked it?" I notice his fit build. He would definitely be an asset on the trail.

"A few of the stages on holiday."

"Would you happen to be on holiday?" I ask with a wink.

He laughs—such a lovely, rich sound.

"Oh, senhora, I regret to inform you I must go to work this week." He helps me put the pack on my back and nods toward the cabin door.

Oh, I'm holding up the line. I walk down the aisle. When we get inside the terminal, he gives me a bow and says, "*Bom Caminho.*"

Well, Scarf. I think I'm going to like Portugal.

I follow the crowd to the terminal exit. Just before the doors leading outside, I start looking for an information desk.

It must be nearby. Oh, there it is. I walk over to the desk and stand there for a moment. The young man is so focused on his computer that he doesn't even look up. Some things are international.

"Uh. Hello, *olá,*" I say.

Startled, he looks up. "*Sim*, may I assist you?"

"Yes, thank you. I'm trying to find the best way to get to my hotel. Well, it's a hostel called Hostel Lisbon." He pauses briefly, observing my grey hair and backpack. I can see the wheels turning. Aren't you a little old for hosteling? I'm sure his training wouldn't permit such a breach of etiquette.

"I know the one. Just a moment, and I will tell you the correct metro to take."

He pulls out a map, marks the hostel, and tells me where to catch the metro. Gesturing down a long corridor, he indicates I should go that way. This doesn't look very easy.

I smile at him, more confidently than I feel, straighten my shoulders, and tighten my backpack's belt. Accepting the map, I start down the corridor.

"Excuse me. I couldn't help overhearing. I'm heading to Hostel Lisbon. May I come with you?"

I turn. The voice belongs to a young girl. She sounds and looks American. About my grandchildren's age. I look around, and she appears to be alone. What are her parents thinking, letting her wander the world alone?

"Of course. We keep going down this corridor and take the escalator to the metro."

"Thank you. I have such a bad sense of direction. My name is Sydney. Are you walking the Caminho?"

"Nice to meet you. I'm Dot. Yes, I'm walking the Caminho."

"Me, too," she squeaks, looking scared.

"Follow me," I say, and step onto the escalator.

"If you don't mind me saying, you'll be easy to follow with that bright orange pack."

I laugh. "You're the second one who has noticed. It must be working. My children got it for me. They want to make sure my body is seen if I collapse in a ravine."

"Well, it will do the job," she replies. "Your children let you come alone?"

"And where are your parents?"

She begins laughing. "I'm twenty-four, you know."

"Since we're sharing, I'm seventy-nine. As Muhammad Ali said, 'Age is just a number.' I plan to walk into Santiago on my eightieth birthday."

As we step off the escalator, she stops walking and looks at me. "That's a birthday party I plan on attending. By the way, who's Muhammad Ali?"

"Never mind," I say while linking my arm through hers. "I think the two of us will manage just fine."

There are signs pointing to ground transportation and a kiosk. We join the line in front of the kiosk to buy our tickets. When we get to the front of the line, I hesitate; of course, everything is written in Portuguese.

The woman behind us taps my shoulder and offers to help. I buy a three-day pass because I plan to do some sightseeing before I start walking. Who knows if I'll ever come back to Lisbon? *Carpe diem.*

While we sit on the bench waiting for our train, I realize I haven't let my daughter know I've arrived. "Sydney, would you take a picture of me? I want my kids to know I'm safe."

"Of course."

I find a poster of Lisbon on the wall, arrange the scarf around my neck, and strike a pose. Then I offer to take Sydney's picture. Sitting down on the bench, I activate my eSIM. It works perfectly. I smile at the picture Sydney took of me. I look relaxed and confident. I send the picture and a message to my family.

I open Facebook. I promised the Camigas and Valerie I would post about the trip.

> POST: Camigas, made it to Lisbon! I'm at the airport metro station with my pack, my credencial, and exactly one working brain cell. The Scarf is proudly around my neck, announcing to the world that this pilgrimage has officially

begun. If you see a slightly dazed woman pretending she knows how the Lisbon metro works... that's me. Next stop? The city—and then the first yellow arrow. Bom Caminho!

I tuck my phone away, and there's a ding. I pull it out again and open Facebook. It's Valerie. She has replied immediately.

The scarf looks great on you. I hope it supports your Caminho as it did mine.

There is a warmth in my chest. Such a wonderful young lady. She chose me to carry the scarf.

The train arrives. Sydney and I hop on. We look at the map the man at the information desk gave us and compare it to the metro map on the wall. Metro lines are all over the place. I can't find one that matches the map.

Sydney glances over my shoulder. "Did we get on the correct train?"

My stomach tightens as we lean close over the map.

A young girl in torn jeans and tattooed arms asks in perfect English if she can help us.

"Yes, please," we say in unison.

I follow up with, "We are trying to get to our hostel, Hostel Lisbon."

She looks at our map, then at the map on the wall. After a few seemingly very long minutes, she says, "Sim, you must get off at São Sebastião, then get on the blue line to Restauradores. It is about a three-minute walk from there. Sim?" She points to the map that the information desk gave me, and sure enough, he had circled it.

Sydney and I exchange glances before looking at the young lady. She points to the wall map and shows us how many stops remain.

"*Obrigada*, thank you," I say.

"*Por nada.*" She goes back to checking her phone.

We count stations and watch for ours to come up. When it does, we quickly exit the metro, follow the signs to the blue line, and catch it to Restauradores. It's easy when you know how.

We get off at Restauradores, and the city overwhelms us. The traffic and people are rushing in all directions. I look at the map and try to orient us from the metro entrance to our hostel.

Sydney takes out her phone, Googles the hostel's address, and puts the map on Walk. She points across a huge intersection with six lanes of traffic feeding around a plaza. We have to cross this road. I start looking for a crosswalk and see one about a block away. We cross, then head back to where we started on the other side and see the name of the side road we must take. There are many small hotels and restaurants. That's where the stop must get its name.

Down two blocks and on the right, a few people are loitering in front of a door, smoking.

"*Peregrinas?*" one asks.

"Yes, we are pilgrims," I say.

"This is the hostel, 'Hostel Lisbon.'"

Sydney turns to me with her hand held high. "We found it!"

We high-five.

There is a sign that reads *Proibido Fumar* on the door, which is why they're standing outside smoking. What a relief—I don't think I could handle a smoky room.

We present our passports and pilgrim credencials. The credencial identifies us as pilgrims and allows us to stay at hostels. I keep calling them hostels, but I believe they're called *albergues* in Portugal.

We walk upstairs and pick a bunk. I spread out my sleeping bag to reserve it. I don't remember the last time I slept in a bunk bed. It's part of Caminho culture, so when in Rome—or rather, Lisbon... I giggle.

Sydney gives me a sidelong look.

"I was just thinking that I don't know when I've ever slept in a bunk bed."

"I'm an only child. I had my own room." She grins. "We'll get used to it."

"Will you watch my pack while I take a shower? I'll return the favor for you."

"Sure, but please take your valuables and passport with you. I don't want to be responsible for them."

"Okay." I glance at my pack. I don't believe the few items inside would tempt a thief.

I gather my clean clothes, passport, pilgrim credencial, credit cards, and money, and head to the shower. I'm glad I brought the Ziplock bag to keep everything dry.

I step out of the shower and look in the mirror. Time has not been kind to my elfin features. That's what Roy called me, his little elf. God rest his soul. I fluff my short curls. Smiling, my blue eyes sparkle. Mother told me that you look and feel your best with a smile on your face.

I gather my shower stuff and head back to our room, where I find Sydney talking to a young man. Her head is tilted to the side as she looks up at him, her blonde hair brushing her shoulder. There's a light in her plain face I hadn't noticed before—a faint blush on her cheeks.

"Dot, this is Sean."

"Pleasure to meet you. Where are you from?"

"I'm from Ireland. Are you walking the Caminho, too?" he asks.

"Yes, but I'll be a tourist for a few days first. And you?"

"Ah yeah, meself and me pal Ian are off in the morning. We've not much holiday time. And where would yourself be from then?"

"Meself is from California." I can feel the smile spreading across my face, and I wink at him.

"I'm from New York," Sydney chimes in.

I didn't mean to intrude on her. Sean is a handsome young man with olive skin, dark wavy hair, and eyes nearly as black as coal. He must be what they call the 'Black Irish.' I'm sure he's the one who caused that faint blush on her cheeks.

"Would you ladies fancy joinin' us for a bit o' dinner? Just meself, Ian, an' a couple o' other pilgrims we bumped into this afternoon from Brazil."

"We'd be delighted," I say, then look at Sydney.

"Me too—but I need to take a shower first."

"Ah, no rush at all. We'll meet in the lobby and walk over to a small place nearby for a bite," Sean says.

"Lovely." I turn to my bunk, rearrange my pack, and take my dirty clothes to wash in the sink. Then I hang them on a line in the washroom to dry.

We gather in the lobby and walk toward Plaza Rossio. It's just down the street from the albergue. I glance at our group. There are two young men from Ireland and four from Brazil, along with Sydney and me. Two of the women from Brazil seem to be friends, and the other two are a couple. The man in the couple leads the way. The group is speaking a mix of Portuguese and English, and even Sydney seems to be following along.

We walk back toward the busy road and turn left. The sidewalk leads us to a large plaza. Traffic splits to navigate around this open space. The bricks are arranged in a wavy pattern.

I carefully step onto the bricks, feeling a bit woozy. I really need to eat; the airplane breakfast wasn't very filling.

One of the women from Brazil turns to me and apologizes for leaving me out of the conversation.

"It's fine," I say. "I should have tried harder to learn Portuguese before I came, but I just don't have a head for languages."

"No problem," she says in English. "We'll help you."

"Obrigada."

We walk through the city streets toward an arch. Beyond it, the sun's afterglow illuminates another plaza by the River Tagus. The people of Lisbon are out in full force, enjoying the cool evening and strolling around. Children are playing what looks like a game of tag near a large column topped with a statue. We stop in front of the statue.

The kind Brazilian woman explains in Portuguese, then switches to English for me. "This is the statue of Pedro IV erected in 1870. He was also the first Emperor of Brazil.

"I didn't realize how closely your cultures are connected. There are so many people. Is there a special event going on?" I ask.

She laughs. "No, it is the *passeio*. It happens every evening, even in Brazil. The neighbors gather in the square to gossip." She smiles. "And the lovers meet at the café for a glass of wine and snacks." She points to a couple sitting at an outside table, sipping wine as if they are the only two in the world. "And the children play. Do you not do this in the U.S.?"

"No, we don't. I think it's lovely. My husband would have loved this."

"You are married?"

I hesitate. "No, widowed."

There, that's the first time I've said it. I turn to see our group at the other end of the square. I tell her that we must hurry.

The Brazilian man turns down a side street. We hurry to catch up with him. I sense his impatience as he tells us he has reservations at this very popular local restaurant. He stops in front of a plain door, opens it, and holds it for us, motioning for us ladies to go in first.

The waiter guides us through a cozy, dimly lit room to a table for eight in the center. A few smaller tables along the walls create an illusion of privacy. Exposed beams overhead give the space an ancient, rustic feel. The stone walls, marked by the patina of countless meals served here, add to the charm. The patrons seem unhurried as they sip wine and nibble on the juicy platters of beef and seafood before them. The aroma of charbroiled steak makes my stomach rumble, and I'm sure it can be heard above the noise.

The Brazilian man speaks quietly to the waiter as we take our seats. The waiter leaves and returns with several bottles of wine and glasses. We all toast to the Caminho. The wine is a full-bodied red port, the wine for which the country is named. Or is it the other way around?

"How did port wine get its name?" I ask.

The woman knowledgeable about the statue explains that port wine is made from grapes grown in the Douro region and is transported down the Douro River to the port city of Porto, which gives the wine its name. Portugal comes from the Latin Portus Cale, meaning "port" in a specific settlement. Portugal is a seafaring country, full of ports. King Alfonso I, in 1139, is credited with making the name official.

"We'll be walking through Porto in a few weeks," I say.

"Yes, that's correct, and we'll be drinking more wine," she says with a smile, lifting her glass to me. "*Saúde*, to your health. Now you reply, '*À vossa,*' which means 'and to yours.'"

We all pick up our glasses and say "*chin-chin*" as we clink them and drink, all while maintaining eye contact and nodding to each other. I could learn to like this.

True to her word, Sydney, sitting on my right, helps me with the menu. One of the ladies from Brazil says something to her, and she turns to me and translates. "She suggests we all order a dish, and then we'll get extra plates and share."

"That sounds delightful," I say as I take the last sip of my wine. The gentleman from Brazil, sitting on my other side, picks up a bottle and refills my glass. I pick up my glass and turn to him. "Saúde."

He picks up his glass and replies, 'À vossa.' Touching glasses, he smiles as we say "chin-chin". He turns to the woman on his other side and gives her a quick kiss. I see the ring on her finger when she gently touches his cheek with her left hand. My heart aches.

The food arrives, and what a smorgasbord. We begin with a delicious savory vegetable soup accompanied by a hearty, warm loaf of bread.

"This soup is the mainstay of Portugal, made of locally grown vegetables. You will find it everywhere," the Brazilian woman says.

The main course arrives, accompanied by extra plates for sharing. There are sardines in olive oil, pasta with pesto, porco preto (the meat from the pig that only eats acorns), octopus, mussels, rice, and a fresh salad. Every bite melts in my mouth. I'm in ecstasy from the countless flavors and the aroma of fresh garlic filling the room.

The server clears the table, and the man from Brazil

orders a Madeira to go along with the dessert known as *arroz doce*, or rice pudding in English. *Deliciosa.*

Replete, we collectively sigh as we sip our wine. I feel the warm comfort of being in good company. So far, Portugal is everything I hoped it would be.

One of the women from Brazil taps her wine glass with a knife. "Let's share our Caminho intentions."

"Intentions?" I ask.

"Yes, when you walk the Caminho, you walk with an intention," Sydney says.

The woman who made the suggestion says, "I'll start." She takes the hand of the man next to her and smiles. "Roberto and I are newly married. We were both widowed and found love again. We want to deepen our relationship on this pilgrimage." She then looks at Sean.

"I came for a lark and to be with my pal Ian," Sean says, then turns and smiles at the young man with brilliant red hair and a beard just starting to sprout, who is sitting beside him.

The other Brazilian woman, the history enthusiast, goes next, mentioning she has always wanted to explore her Portuguese roots. Visiting the Caminho will give her a chance to fully immerse herself in the culture.

Her friend speaks up next, saying she just went through a divorce and is struggling to accept the major life change it caused.

Now it's my turn. I take a sip of the Madeira, hesitate, and blurt, "I want to experience exquisite sex one more time."

A hush falls over the table. Everyone is looking at me.

Scarf, what have I done?

Ian breaks the silence, "I'll volunteer!"

"Young man, that's very kind of you, but I don't think you could manage it just yet." Oh, that didn't come out right either. "No offense, but you could be my grandson."

Sydney sighs. "I want that, too."

"And you deserve no less," I tell her. "Oh, my name is Dorothy, but everyone calls me Dot. I'm from California, and this is my first Caminho."

"Well. I don't think I can top that," Ian says, smiling at me. "My name is Ian, and I want to renew my faith in God. My father died of cancer when I was young, and I always blamed God. I want to find out who God really is."

Everyone is openly sharing. I feel like I have found a family here in Portugal.

We each pay our checks and walk back to the albergue.

Sydney walks beside me. "Everyone is leaving in the morning. I want to walk with them. Will you be upset if I go ahead? I know you plan on spending a few days here."

"Oh, honey. It's okay. You go ahead. I'll be just fine."

• • •

I wake up, and it takes a moment to remember I'm in a bunk bed in Portugal. There is the soft purr of a snore above my head; the others in the room are sleeping quietly. My head aches. My throat burns. I crawl out of bed to get some water.

I use the bathroom and wander into the breakfast room. I'm so glad that breakfast is included. I see Sydney and the two Irish boys finishing up their meal.

"Hurry, Dot," Ian says. "We're about ready to start walking."

"I can't. I don't feel well. I'm going to rest today. Besides, I want to do some sightseeing."

"No worries," Sean says. "They are really nice here, and a good rest will put you right. But we cannot wait; we must go."

"I understand," I say as I see Sydney hesitate. "You need to go. We'll stay in touch."

She breathes a sigh of relief. We exchange numbers.

"I'll see you in Santiago for your birthday party, if not before."

With that, we say "Bom Caminho," and I give her a quick hug. This must be the way of the Caminho—people walking in and out of your life.

The two guys and Sydney shoulder their packs and head out the door. I head to the coffee, orange juice, and toast. Maybe this will help. Maybe I'll start walking later. Maybe I'll go back to bed.

CHAPTER 2

CALIFORNIA

"Dot, it was a lovely tribute," the hospice nurse says, hugging me. "I'm so thankful for your support. I couldn't have kept Roy at home without you."

I smile, and when she steps to her left to speak to my daughter, I turn to the next mourner in line.

I'm thankful for the tent's shade as the Southern California sun beats down. The guests take their seats. The rest of my family and I move to the roped-off seats at the front beneath the canopy at the gravesite. I can't focus on what the priest is saying. He pulls me back by asking me to join him beside the coffin.

Roy wanted the whole big funeral and burial thing. I just want it to be over. The priest motions for me to take a handful of earth and let it fall onto the coffin. I don't think I can.

Karen and Karl step up beside me. My children have been my strength through this entire ordeal. We each pick up a handful of dirt and drop it on the coffin. The priest says the benediction as I brush the dirt off my hands. Then he leads us to the waiting cars to be taken home.

• • •

"Mom, did you do the deviled eggs?"

"Of course I did, darling. They're in the refrigerator in the garage."

That child of mine is micromanaging everything, but I don't know how I would have gotten through the past several years without her.

In need of a moment, I go upstairs to what used to be "our" bedroom and sit on the rocker by the now-empty bed. I've spent many hours here. I pick up my phone and check Facebook. So many wonderful old friends are reaching out to me.

There's a notification from Valerie. I've been following her Caminho. Fresh energy. Youth on an adventure. I still recall all the adventures of my youth. I'm not ready to hang up the hiking shoes yet.

I scroll and find her post. And there she is, waving that scarf over her head in front of the Cathedral in Santiago. I'm as proud of her as I would be of my own grandchild. I send a GIF of congratulations.

Karen calls up to me. "Mom, the guests are arriving."

Downstairs, the wonderful family and friends we've collected over the years are here for me. They've been with us every step of the way. It's hard to imagine a brilliant mind like Roy's succumbing to Alzheimer's. Watching him disappear was brutal.

Roy's brother, Charlie, grabs me and gives me a bear hug. "So, Dot, what are your plans now?"

"I'm going to walk the Caminho," I tell him.

The room quiets.

Karl puts a hand on his sister's arm. "It's just the grief talking," he whispers to her.

I hear him. A mother always hears.

"No, really. I've given this a lot of thought, and I know I can do it. I'm going to walk to Santiago." I didn't know it until this moment, but I am serious.

Karen puts her arm around my shoulder as if she's the mom and I'm the daughter. She addresses the crowd.

"Thank you all for coming. It means so much to Mom and the family. You took care of us while Dad was sick. Let us take care of you today. After Father Francis gives the blessing, we'll have lunch. It's a buffet starting at this end of the table. We have tables and chairs set up on the lanai. Just find a place to sit. There's an open bar with both non-alcoholic and alcoholic beverages. Enjoy."

"Please bow your heads," Father says.

I'm ashamed to say that I don't even hear the blessing. My mind jumps back to the Caminho and that picture of Valerie in front of the Cathedral. Her joy transcends the space between us and settles in my soul.

• • •

I say goodbye to the last guest.

Karen and Karl collapse on the couch. I sit between them and put one hand on each of their thighs.

"Thank you, children, for being here."

"Of course, Mom," Karen says. "It's been a hard road, but we kept Dad at home where he wanted to be."

"I couldn't have done it without you both."

"Are you really going to walk the Caminho?" Karl asks.

"Yes." I nod as I say it. "I've been studying it while I sat with your dad. He didn't want me to sit around and grieve. We talked before Alzheimer's got his brain, and he encouraged me to live fully if he died first. I wanted the same thing for him if I went first. It's not like his passing is a surprise. I lost him eight years ago, when the doctor diagnosed him—and took away the car keys."

"Yes, that was a hard day," Karl replies. His eyes fill with tears.

Karl, my youngest, is so tender-hearted. I rest my head on his shoulder. He wraps his arm around me and hugs me tight.

Karen stands up. “It’s like we lost him twice. Once when the doctor told us he had Alzheimer’s, and now.”

“Mom,” Ashley calls from upstairs.

“I’ll go see what that daughter of mine wants,” Karen says as she heads for the stairs.

“So, about this Caminho thing. Are you really serious?” Karl asks. “I’m okay with it. But Karen, well, she’s taking this hard, and I don’t think she wants you to get that far away.”

“I know. I can’t sit in this house and wither. You both have your own lives to lead, and I’m grateful for the time you have given your Dad and me over the past eight years. But we have to move on.” A tear slips down my cheek.

“I get it, Mom. I really get it.

Karen, well, we’ll help her understand. And if she doesn’t, I’ll sneak you to the airport and put you on the plane, then tell her afterwards.”

I start laughing. My son is so like Roy.

“What are you two laughing about?” Karen says as she and Ashley come down the stairs.

“Oh, just memories, darling,” I say, and get up to meet them.

Ashley slips an arm around me.

“So, Gran, are you really going to walk the Caminho?”

“I’m thinking about it. But I have a few things to do first.”

"Well, I'd go with you, but I don't think I could get out of school that long."

"You are sweet." It's time to change the subject. "Now, I can't eat all this food, so help me package some of it up for you all to take home."

Once the food is packaged, I walk them to the door.

"Are you sure you don't want me to spend the night?" Karen asks me.

"No, darling, I'll be just fine." I have to restrain myself from pushing them out the door and on their way. I just want to be alone.

I wave politely as they get in their cars, then I go inside and collapse on the couch. I pull out my phone and send a message to Valerie.

Dot: *I am thinking about walking the Caminho.*

Valerie: *It would be really rad if you did. If you want to talk, I'm available.*

What a sweet child. I think I can call through Messenger. Well, why not? I'm not getting any younger. I push the button, and it rings.

"Hello... Dot?"

"Yes, it's me. Is this a good time to talk?"

"Yes, I'm just waiting to board for my plane home."

"Congratulations on completing your Caminho. It was so fun following you."

"Aw, thanks, Dot. It was so amazing."

"I would like to ask you about the Caminho."

"Have you thought about which route to walk?" Valerie asks.

"There's more than one route?"

"Oh yes, several. The northern route, which I did. The traditional route—the Francés—from southern France to Santiago de Compostela. And the Portuguese route. Any of the routes you can make shorter if you don't want to walk the complete route."

"Portuguese, as in Portugal?"

"Yes, it starts in Lisbon. But many people walk a shorter distance by starting in Porto."

"I've always wanted to go to Portugal. So many options."

"Yes, I was going to walk just the last one hundred kilometers from Sarria to Santiago, but I ended up walking the complete Norte—about 550 miles. How far do you want to walk?" Valerie asks.

"Wow. Hmm? I am guessing if you start the Portuguese in Lisbon, you walk all the way through Portugal?"

"Yes, and you finish up in Spain. I believe it is about 400 miles. When are you thinking about going?"

"I thought about September. That will give me time to get myself organized."

"September would be beautiful. Don't wait too long. Once the Caminho calls, you must go," she says.

I laugh. "Well, I have been called, and you are the voice I hear. I will plan on September."

"Dot, I know we really don't know each other, except on Facebook, but you know the scarf that I carried?"

"Yes, that beautiful multicolored scarf. I remember."

"Well, I have to pass it on to another pilgrim, and if you are really going to walk, I would like to give it to you."

"Oh, Valerie, how sweet. But you don't have to."

"Yes, I do. I must pass it on to another pilgrim. It got me safely to Santiago, and I wish that for you. I want you to have it. But there are strings attached, pun intended." She laughs.

It's a lovely laugh.

"And what would those strings be?"

"You must commit to starting the Caminho. You must post on Facebook so I can follow your journey. And when your Caminho is complete, you must pass it on."

"You're on. Send me the scarf."

• • •

The first Saturday hike is only five miles. Five miles used to be nothing to me. Now, halfway up a dusty incline behind the nature center, my lungs burn, and my calves tremble.

A woman named Denise walks beside me. She has silver hair braided down her back and carries her pack as if she were born with it.

"How long has it been since you've done distance?" she asks gently.

"Since before my husband got Alzheimer's."

She nods. No pity. Just understanding.

We crest the hill, and I feel the strange thrill of not quitting.

At mile four, a hot spot forms on my heel. I know enough to stop. I sit on a flat rock, remove my shoe, and press moleskin into place with steady fingers. I have learned many things in eight years of caregiving. Patience. Endurance. How to adjust before something breaks.

"This isn't about miles," Denise says when we start walking again. "It's about showing up."

We reach the parking lot, and sweat runs down my spine, and my shirt clings to me. My legs ache.

But I am upright.

Alive.

Moving forward.

CHAPTER 3

LISBON TO VILA FRANCA DE XIRA

I open my eyes to muffled giggles from the girls in my dorm at the albergue. I feel better. What a delightful way to wake.

I have breakfast, then don my pack and walk to the cathedral. When I toured it yesterday, the docent showed me the first arrow. It's faded into the granite of the bottom stone to the right of the front door. I follow the arrow around the corner. There is scaffolding on the cathedral and no follow-up arrow in sight, just more scaffolding—and businesses lining the other side of the street. Not the most auspicious start.

I pictured fanfare. I'm embarking on a journey of 626 kilometers. Shouldn't there be some kind of bon voyage?

Well, Scarf, it is just you and me. We'll have to make our own celebration—and find our own way.

Valerie, the young woman who gave me the scarf, did not know her way either, but she found it. I have many more years of experience to call on. And plenty of people have walked this way before. I should be able to do it too.

I stop long enough to take a picture of the faded arrow painted on the cathedral stone—my official beginning. Then I open Facebook.

> POST: Bom dia, Camigas. Day One. I found the very first arrow in Lisbon... and promptly lost the next one under scaffolding. Scarf and I are officially underway.

Last night, I spent some time with my guidebook. I wanted to confirm the route and book tonight's stay. I figure I can walk about twenty-four kilometers—about fifteen miles a day. I practiced at home with my full pack in the hills near my home in Southern California. And tonight I'm staying in a pension. I love this word—"pen-see-own." It sounds so continental. Not at all like a motel.

I know the Caminho follows the Tagus River, past the tile museum that I explored yesterday. I saw an arrow there. If I just walk as close to the river as possible, I'm sure to find my way. It's not the first time I've had to try to figure something out on my own, and it won't be the last. And I'm not afraid to ask for directions. Like taking care of Roy, I learned as I went along.

I walk along a row of commercial buildings and find a faded arrow on a pipe by what looks to be an abandoned business. It's pointing the direction I am going, so I must be okay. I thought this was supposed to be easy—follow the yellow-arrow road. That would make a great song. I laugh.

The river is blocked by buildings and a railroad. There must be a way to get over there. I'll just keep walking and see what happens.

I come to a roundabout, and there's a sign for a Unicorn Factory. Really? *A Unicorn Factory.* The sign points to the river, so I have to follow it. Maybe the unicorns will show me the way.

Oh, Scarf, I'm already losing it, and I haven't even started.

Maybe Karen was right. I've never traveled alone. Roy was always the planner and the navigator, and I was fine with that.

Oh, Scarf, what have I done?

But there's no turning back.

The road takes me to a pedestrian walk by the river with the Unicorn Factory on my left. It looks like a bunch of small businesses under one roof. On the riverside, there is a gondola with an aerial cable going over and along the river. This looks like a tourist spot. A couple sits on a bench beside the river. They're too busy kissing to notice. I remember being so busy kissing that I didn't notice my surroundings. It feels like another lifetime ago.

Past the factory, an area opens up with sculptures and water features. This must be the aquarium. At the end of the aquarium, there's a line of flags and a yellow arrow pointing me to turn right for the Caminho. The walk brings me closer to the water, and I leave the city behind as an airfield appears on my left and a city park on my right.

There is a sculpture of giant letters that spell LISBOA facing away from me. I stop to take a selfie. A family comes along the path behind me, and the wife asks in excellent English if she can take my picture. I hand her my phone and pose. Her daughter, who looks to be in her twenties—about the same age as my granddaughter, Ashley—asks if I am doing the Caminho. I smile and say yes. She tells me she walked from Porto to Santiago last summer and that it's beautiful.

Did I make a mistake starting where the guidebook says to start—in Lisbon, or Lisboa as they call it here? Why don't we call places by the names the locals use? Lisboa. Note to self: Start a trend.

Based on my research and conversations with other pilgrims at home, I've learned that many start in Porto if they don't have time to walk the entire way. I have plenty of time, so that's not an issue. I want to see all of Portugal, or at least most of it.

I ask if I'm going the right way. The woman's mother speaks up, points out a wooden pedestrian bridge, and tells me that's the way I must go. I wave goodbye, and they call "Bom Caminho" after me.

I cross the bridge to a boardwalk along the river. It's stunning. I stop at a sign stating that the boardwalk is six kilometers long, about four miles. Large, possibly pink birds are feeding in the shallows. I pause at a plaque. Yes, flamingos. They migrate here in October. They're right on schedule. Or maybe I am.

A little farther on, there's a shelter covering an observation bench. I take off my backpack and pull out a bottle of water. It feels good to pause and breathe. The air smells fresh with a hint of salt.

Lisboa is a port city on the Atlantic Ocean, and this part of the Tagus River is tidal. The boardwalk runs over a salt marsh, alive with birds. The ripples in the middle of the river are caused by larger fish chasing smaller ones toward the marsh, right into the beaks of the birds.

I take a photo of the birds in the marsh, then share it on Facebook.

> POST: Camigas, I'm walking on a boardwalk over a salt marsh along the Tagus. The air smells like the ocean, and yes, those are flamingos. Flamingos!
> I didn't even know Portugal had flamingos.
> Scarf is behaving. I am too. Mostly.

I could sit here in the cool breeze all day, but I need to reach Verdelha de Baxio today. The pedometer on my phone tells me I've walked six kilometers, and it's only ten a.m.—not bad for an old woman. Eighteen to go.

The boardwalk ends at a road, which leads to Main Street. The traffic noise is jarring after such a peaceful walk. I turn my GPS on again to find my hotel. After a few kilometers, the hotel's name is up ahead—but no visible door. There's a snack bar. The waiter points me to the side of a building.

Laundry? Heat and chemicals hit me as I step in. I walk back to the bar, thinking I've misunderstood.

The waiter takes me back to the laundry and calls out a name. A woman, red-faced, probably from the heat and chemicals, turns around. She comes to the table and sits on a folding chair, motioning for me to sit. She asks for my passport and my credencial. I pull both documents from my fanny pack.

As she works, another pilgrim plops down in the chair next to me and lets out a big sigh. I assume she is a pilgrim because she's carrying a backpack. A huge backpack. She has an arresting look—olive skin, dark hair, and startling grey eyes. Probably in her thirties or forties. She looks irritable and not too friendly.

I keep the peace. I'm tired too. The pedometer on my phone says I have walked almost twenty-six kilometers, two more than I expected. My feet are sore, but I don't think I have blisters.

The laundry woman completes the paperwork, stamps my credencial, and hands me a slip of paper with all manner of numbers and codes. She turns to the other lady, who gives her name and paperwork. I didn't catch it. Maybe we'll talk later.

"*Vamos*," the laundry woman says and leads us to a door on the other side of the snack bar. She shows us how to punch in the codes from the paper and then takes us up two flights of stairs. I can hardly lift my legs.

At my bedroom door, she shows me how to punch in the code to access my room. What a system. I'd better not lose that slip of paper. I'll never remember all these codes. It's a small room with a single bed. She then takes me down the hall to the bathroom, where she nods and leaves. I call out a thank you as she shows the other woman her room. That's it—my first night on the Caminho, alone.

I clean up, go downstairs to the snack bar, and ask for a menu. The waiter, who is also the chef, offers to make me a Caesar salad with chicken. Perfect.

While waiting for my meal, I notice two big, burly men at the table across from me. The chef comes out with a massive platter of meat and places it in front of them. A woman follows him with a large basket of bread. They exchange pleasantries. I had asked for a small salad, but I'm hungry enough to eat whatever animal that meat came from. What was I thinking?

The young woman brings me a huge salad with what looks like an entire chicken on top. She offers a yogurt dressing. It's delicious. So I don't feel so depraved, I order dessert too. Flan. I love flan. A favorite dessert of the Hispanic community back home, it tastes like home.

Now back in my room, I discover I missed a call from Karen. That daughter of mine, I should have known she would be checking up on me. I don't want her to worry.

I dial her number. She picks up on the first ring.

"Oh, thank God," she says when I speak her name. "I was so worried when I didn't hear from you. So many things can happen, and I don't want anything to happen to you."

"I know, darling. I'm so sorry. I got to my hotel, took a shower, and went out to eat. I needed to get the basics taken care of, and a hot shower felt so good after a long day of walking."

"You could have sent me a quick message that you arrived safely."

"Yes, I know. I will do this in the future."

"So, how was your first day?"

"It was an education. I passed the test. I'm safe, I didn't get lost, and there are no blisters on my feet."

"Did you meet anyone else?"

"Actually, no. Another pilgrim is staying at the hotel, and I hope to connect with her tomorrow. She looked worn out. In fact, she looks to be about your age."

"You know, Mom, I would have walked with you if I could have left the children and my work that long."

"I know. I didn't mean to imply that you should be here. In fact, I really want to do this by myself."

"Yes, you said something about needing alone time now that Dad is gone."

"Yes, and that doesn't mean I love you less. I'm just emotionally exhausted. In fact, today is the first time I believe the physical exhaustion is greater than the emotional exhaustion of the past few years."

"That's a good thing. You know, Mom," Karen's voice gets softer, "I could use that too."

Tears spring to my eyes. This controlling child of mine has learned a few things over the years. "Thank you for understanding, darling."

"I love you, Mom."

"I love you, too. And I will send a quick message when I arrive in Valda do Carregado, tomorrow evening."

POST: First night on the Caminho. I made it to Verdelha de Baxio, showered, ate, and my feet are still intact.

> I found my room through a laundry and somehow ended up with an actual bed. They gave a slip of paper with seventeen entry codes for the doors. If I lose this slip of paper, I may live here forever. I'm safe, Camigas. Scarf is on guard duty.

Smiling, I tuck myself in.

You know, Scarf, I'm the only parent she has left. I do need to be gentler with her fear. But I have to take care of myself, too.

• • •

Morning now. The young woman who waited tables last night makes me a fabulous omelet and serves it with toast, butter, jam, and *café con leche.* I have never tasted such nectar of the gods as café con leche.

She is working such long hours. I ask her about this. She gives me a weary smile and says she's a single mom and must pay the bills. My heart goes out to her.

I finish breakfast and leave her a generous tip. It's the best I can do. I head back upstairs, my thighs protesting with every step. I brush my teeth and get my pack, making sure I haven't left anything behind. I don't have much, and everything I have is essential. I was warned not to pack any 'just in case' items and to keep my pack as light as possible. The lighter the pack, the more successful the Caminho. After just one day, I can understand this reasoning.

I stop at the snack bar and ask where I can find the next yellow arrow. The woman points straight out to the street, indicating that I should keep walking in the same direction as yesterday. Cool. As tired as I was last night, I must have missed it. Shouldering my pack, I head out and start walking. I don't see an arrow, but it has to be around here somewhere.

I walk in the right direction along a busy four-lane highway. I need to see an arrow soon. I don't like this at all. Maybe that's why people start in Porto—wherever that is. But I keep going. I don't want to prove my children right. They think I'm too old to be galivanting off to Portugal alone with only a backpack. They'd rather see me on a guided tour.

Bingo—a yellow arrow painted on a lamp post, pointing me along the street in the direction I'm going.

I eventually run out of sidewalk, and the road shoulder disappears. I must have missed an arrow somewhere.

I was watching for them, Scarf. Really, I was.

An on-ramp to a freeway is in front of me. This is plainly dangerous. I scan the area.

There's a frontage road to my right. Looking back the way I came, I realize I passed a pedestrian bridge that crosses the railroad tracks between me and the frontage road. I start walking back, looking for a crosswalk to the bridge. No such luck. When I get even with the bridge on the other side of the four-lane highway, I wait for a break in traffic and jaywalk to get to it. I hope they don't arrest people for jaywalking in Portugal. I don't know where that bridge leads, but I'm going that way.

The steps down on the other side of the bridge lead me onto the frontage road, in front of an apartment building. A woman walking down the street with a bag of groceries smiles at me. She points to the corner of the apartment building and says '*Bom Caminho*'. I smile back in relief. Sure enough, I turn the corner, and there is a pedestrian path through a park by the river. I look back along the river. The pedestrian path has been following the river for a while. How did I miss it?

I turn left to continue the way I was going. I can tell because the river is on my right. I see a sign for the Caminho pointing in the direction I am heading. I love being validated. Why couldn't there have been an arrow showing me how to find this pathway back there on the highway? I might have missed it, but I was watching for it. I'm about over this guessing game.

A bell rings. There's a bike coming at me. I jump aside — as much as I can jump with a fifteen-pound pack on my back. I look down. There are little figures painted on the walk—pedestrians on the right, bikes on the left. My bad, as the kids say.

Oh, look, Scarf, a bench. Someone put it right there just for us.

I check to make sure no bikes are coming, then I cross the bike lane. I am trainable. I sigh as I take off my pack and set it down on the bench beside me.

I touch the scarf. Am I too old for this? Valerie made it look so easy, and she did one of the more challenging routes. I chose to walk the Portuguese route because it's known to be gentler.

"Also," I whisper to the scarf. "I had to come to Portugal to see if he is here."

But it's been almost fifty years. Another old lady's fancy, trying to relive her past.

Am I wasting my time? But what was I going to do? Sit around and disappear? Play it safe?

The tears stream down my cheeks, and I wipe them with the scarf. I have lost so much of my life. Roy lost so much of his life to that horrible disease, Alzheimer's. It's not fair. But I'm not going to waste any more of mine.

My phone vibrates in my pocket. I almost ignore it. I don't want advice, worry, or someone telling me what I should be doing.

A message from Karl.

Hey Mom. Just checking in. No pressure to reply. I just wanted you to know I'm thinking of you and cheering you on. Dad would have loved this adventure of yours.

I press the phone to my chest for a moment. That boy always did know when to show up and when to stay out of the way.

I type back: *Still upright. Still walking.*

I shoulder my pack and step back onto the path.

CHAPTER 4

VILA FRANCA DE XIRA TO VALADA

I'm not getting any younger sitting on this bench. I slowly stand, my legs protesting. Groaning, I shoulder my pack. Why did I think I needed all this stuff?

I start walking. It's a pleasure to be on this path. Families are out enjoying the day, and children are playing. I smile, thinking of my grandchildren when they were little. If only I could bottle that energy. I don't remember getting sore muscles as a child.

I finally come to the end of the path and follow the road to an old train station along the tracks. There's a sign on the door with a WhatsApp number for the proprietor. While I'm sending messages, I send Karen a quick one to let her know I've arrived safely. Promise fulfilled. Now it's time to take care of me.

The proprietor comes and lets me in. I'm the only guest in this small hotel. He gives me a key to my room and another to the hotel's front door. He explains how to unlock and lock the doors. What am I—the new manager?

The proprietor points across the street to a bar and tells me that I'd better go soon to get something to eat before they shut down. He also advises me to buy something for breakfast because nothing will be open on Sunday morning.

I shower and wash my clothes by hand, then cross the street to the bar. I take a seat at a small, empty table. The bar is filled with old men drinking beer and wine. A couple of them glance my way and then whisper something to each other that I can't understand. I bet they're wondering why I'm sitting here alone. I'm not sure what I would do if they approached me or followed me out of the bar. I have the key to the front door of the hotel. If necessary, I'd rush across and lock myself in.

The waiter comes over, and I order veggie soup and bread. I love veggie soup with a good whole-grain bread to dunk in it. Roy was always after me to eat more protein, but I love my veggies.

The men rise, pay the waiter, and leave. I breathe a quiet sigh of relief. Then the waiter brings my soup—hot and delicious. When I finish, I buy a can of iced tea for my morning caffeine fix and choose a pastry from the glass case on the counter. I reach my hotel, post on Facebook, and fall into bed, exhausted.

POST: Camigas, tonight's lodging is a tiny hotel by the train tracks. I have two keys, three instructions, and a sudden promotion to Night Manager. I'm safe, fed, and horizontal. So is the scarf

• • •

I get up with the dawn. It's more of the same—follow the arrows and lug this pack. I wonder what the kids are doing. Karen is probably cleaning the house. She's meticulous that way. I hope she doesn't start on ours—mine. I told her not to touch any of Roy's things. I want to take care of them when I get home. I just didn't have the time or the heart to do it before I left. He has some nice clothes, and someone will make good use of them. I have to get them cleaned and decide what I want to let go of. There's that soft flannel shirt of his, and Karen better not wash it. The flannel smells of him. After he died, I used to take it to bed and hug it. The smell would soothe me. If she washes it, there will be hell to pay.

Oh my, did I miss an arrow while my mind was off gathering wool? How can I miss an arrow? I've been following this gravel road beside the train tracks forever. I miss walking beside the river, but this is the way. There is nowhere else to go. Maybe that's why there's no arrow;

the way is obvious. Even so, a few more arrows would do wonders for my peace of mind. A validation arrow. That's what I need. I wonder who I should talk to about this?

I'm startled by a strange noise. It sounds like one of those noisemakers that carnival workers whirl over their heads at the state fair. Damn, I can't think of the name. Maybe a whirligig? I'll have to Google it just like the grandkids do. First, there's the high-pitched pulsing whir, whir, whir, and then the train speeds by. Interesting.

The train's speed makes me feel so slow. But, Scarf, isn't that the whole point? To slow down, really see the countryside, and reflect on life.

Oh, there's an arrow pointing underneath a railroad bridge and a town on the other side. This must be how you get safely across the tracks. When I pop up on the other side, there are two young men with bicycles. They point in the direction of the arrow. But there's a giant mud puddle right in the middle of the path with no way around it. Motioning to me, the bicyclists indicate I should follow them up the embankment to the side of the tracks. There is a small right-of-way across the top of the bridge, parallel to the track. We go across in single file. I sure hope we make it before a train comes. It's not very wide, and the wind of a passing train could knock me off balance, but at least the whirligig sound will give me advanced warning.

We cross safely and pass a small building, then take a gravel road that appears to lead to town. Well, that obstacle is done. I smile my thanks to the young men, and they give me the universal thumbs-up symbol. I can think of another universal symbol worthy of that mud puddle. What a wicked old broad I am.

The boys smile back and wish me a "Bom Caminho." I'm glad they can't read my mind. They jump on their bikes and take off.

> POST: Camigas, two cyclists just saved me from a mud lake that had "twist your ankle and ruin your life" written all over it. Kindness keeps showing up before I even ask.

Gratitude flows through me. It's amazing that they were there before I knew I even needed them. And that woman with her groceries. Right there when I needed her. It's as if I have a guardian angel.

I head into town to find something to eat. But it's Sunday, and I was told nothing is open. There's a truck stop just down the way, and an attached café filled with people. I go in and order a cup of coffee, but the only thing to eat is pastry. I'm really getting tired of pastry.

You didn't hear that, Scarf. No one would ever believe it. I'm the pastry queen at home. I guess one can have too much of a good thing.

I'm hoping this little walk helps me take a few pounds off the middle. As Roy got sicker, he just did not want to eat. I would make so many things to tempt him, and they would end up tempting me instead. My knees will be happier when some of this caregiver weight comes off.

I leave the truck stop and notice a grocery store across the street that's open. So much for things not being open on Sundays. I go in and browse the shelves. Everything looks so good and fresh, but I must remember that I have to carry anything I buy. I pick up some protein bars and tangerines. These will be delicious on the road. I slide them into the top compartment of my pack. Valerie said she called it the pantry. I like that. I don't have to open my pack to get my snacks.

I follow the arrows. There are yellow ones pointing toward Santiago and blue ones leading to Fátima. I was told to be careful and stick to the yellow ones, or I might end up walking to Fátima. I plan to take a bus from Tomar to Fátima since it's a bit out of the way. If I walked to Fátima first, my pilgrimage would be a few days longer. Decisions, decisions. But these are easier than some of the choices I had to make as a caregiver.

Fátima is famous for the Virgin Mary, who appeared to three young children in the fields tending their sheep in 1917. This apparition has been well documented. I appreciate that they believed the children. Too often, children are dismissed. There are stories of healing linked to this shrine. It sounds intriguing.

I make my way through the town of Azabuja. It was too far for me to walk to yesterday. It's so pretty. Families are out in the park, the flowers are still blooming, and it's October. I would have loved to stay here, but I can't see and do everything. I would never go home. Now that's a thought.

I walk into Valada, my stop for the night. I can't find a sign for the albergue, so I put the location into the map app. The directions lead me in circles around town. I end up by the river. There's a bar on the sandy bank, with jet skis pulled up to it. The bar is doing a fine business. I am taken back in time as I walk through these villages that have probably had the same stone walls for a millennium. The jet skis are a jarring juxtaposition.

A young woman walks up from the beach. I ask her about the albergue and show her the address, which turns out to be next to her vacation house. She comes here every year to swim in the river and enjoy the quiet town. She walks me to the door. I had only passed it twice. This doesn't seem like a vacation spot. I'd be at the beach by the ocean somewhere exotic. Oh, I am somewhere exotic. I smile. I crack myself up sometimes.

The owner opens the door and greets me. I ask her for a moment, then quickly text Karen.

I've arrived and am safe.

"I told my daughter I would text her the minute I arrive at my albergue each night," I tell the hospitalero. I feel like a bit of a child who is required to report to their mother.

"That's kind. It takes the worry away from those at home," she says.

"Yes." I smile, realizing I should not begrudge this small task.

I'm the only pilgrim in the albergue. The woman introduces herself as Luz, the owner of the albergue. Luz tells me she has walked on more than forty pilgrimages around the world and plans to undertake one in South Korea this spring. I look at the mementos on the walls, showcasing her adventures. She knows exactly what pilgrims need: encouragement, a bed, food, and clean clothes.

Pilgrimage is a way of life for her—an adventure, perhaps. What's the difference between a pilgrimage and an adventure? I'm too exhausted to ponder that now. All I want is to fulfill my pilgrim needs.

Luz takes me into the large bathroom, complete with a washing machine for my dirty clothes.

"It costs three euros to wash your clothes," she says.

"Bless you. I haven't washed clothes since I started walking."

I shower and throw my dirty clothes into the washer, then hang them on a rack to dry. Luz suggests I take the rack outside into the sun. She assures me no one will bother them.

"Who runs the place when you are out walking?" I'm always concerned about the practical matters.

"My family helps run the albergue when I'm walking. I text them regularly, so they know I'm safe." She smiles. "I own the albergue, but it's a family effort."

"And what drives you to walk twice a year? This one may be enough for me."

"I walk because it gives me time for introspection and connection. It takes both to keep me whole. The connection with others gives me insight into myself, and then I need time for introspection. This gives my life meaning and purpose. This is why I own an albergue."

"What do you mean by 'whole'?"

"Maybe that's not quite the right word in English. To me, it means staying in a state of love, and when I am in that state, I am whole. I don't mean sexual love, though that is nice, too." Luz winks. "I mean an energy of love. There are no false emotions of hate, fear, or anxiety. I just feel in a state of love, and when I am, things always work out perfectly. It's no effort to live. For example, if something goes wrong here, I can get angry, but if I shift to a state of love, a solution suddenly comes. If I stay angry, there is no solution, only anger. That is not a whole way of living."

"How do you stay in 'love'?"

"I have learned how it feels. I practice the feeling. Do you know how it feels to feel anger?"

I nod. Yes, that's easy. I think about Alzheimer's.

"Do you know the feeling of looking at your newborn child and the love flows through?"

"Oh, yes," I say.

"So create that feeling of love in your body."

I do the same. I imagine holding Ashley, my granddaughter, right after she was born. She instantly stole my heart.

"Now create the feeling of anger."

I can do this as well. Even when there's nothing to be angry about, I can manufacture it.

"Do you see how the feelings you stir within yourself shape your steps—and how the world answers them? So practice staying in love. Or when a situation creates another feeling inside you, be aware of it and bring it back to love. You will be amazed at the way things change for you in that moment."

"Ok, I'll try it."

"To quote Yoda in Star Wars, 'There is no try'." She smiles.

I laugh. "So true. I used to say this to my piano students: You can either try to play the piano, or you can play it."

Is that what I am doing out here? Trying to find meaning and purpose in my life? Or am I actually finding it?

I take a deep breath. I've been so busy—first as a music teacher, choir director, and church organist—and then, somehow, I fit Roy and the children into the equation. I never focused on what it all meant or why I was doing those things. It was just the way life unfolded for me. It's been a good life. Yes, I've made a few mistakes, but doesn't everyone?

Connection—well, it's just you and me, Scarf. And plenty of time for introspection.

I'm in a room that has space for at least six pilgrims, and there's another room with the same. But I'm the only one here. Is this really the Caminho? I thought it would be packed with pilgrims walking to Santiago. One of the people in my American Pilgrims Chapter back home said that the Caminho gives you exactly what you need. Maybe I need this alone time. Life has been overwhelming.

Luz gives me a key to the front door and tells me where I can find a restaurant for dinner. It's the busy one down by the beach. Seeing how much business they do, it must be good. Luz says she'll leave breakfast out for me in the morning and then tells me to please take something for the road. She also reminds me to fill up my water bottles. There are no services between here and Santarém. I tell her that I have some food in my pack too. I don't want her to think I am unprepared.

She has to go home to her family, but she gives me a phone number in case there are any issues. She asks me to check when I leave in the morning to make sure the door is locked behind me. It locks automatically, but I should try it and make sure it latches. I'm to leave the front door key on the table—such a level of trust. No one would do this back home.

> POST: Made it to Valada. Couldn't find the albergue, walked in circles, ended up by jet skis, and then, of course, it was the door I'd passed twice. Luz, the owner of the albergue, is wonderful. I'm here. I'm safe. Scarf is smug.

CHAPTER 5

VALADA TO SANTARÉM

I have a lovely breakfast, tidy up, and take an apple for the road. I walked twenty-nine kilometers yesterday—but not on purpose. There were places to stop, rest, and eat. I have twenty-five with no services today.

I can do this. Roy and I used to go backpacking in the mountains. We always made sure we were self-sufficient because one never knows what might happen. We lived by the Scout motto, "Be Prepared."

I make my way to the river and the first arrow. The river has become my constant companion. The breeze through the bamboo makes such a soothing sound. The birds flit in and out of the fields, picking up the harvest's leftovers. There must be enough tomatoes on the ground to make red sauce for all of Portugal! I have never seen such abundance. I never thought of Portugal as an agricultural country, but this fertile river basin is an Eden.

I think about what Luz said last night. Such wisdom in someone so young. It must be the pilgrimages. I deliberately run through several emotions, feeling each one in my body. I hadn't thought before that I could actually change what I feel. What an interesting idea. There isn't much out here to send me into fear, anxiety, or anger. In fact, it's a beautiful day. I will practice feeling joy today. It will give me something to do while I walk.

What is that? It looks like a swing on the embankment by the river. I get closer. Someone has built a frame out of telephone poles and hung a swing from the crossbar. It's huge. There's a sign burned into the top beam: *Baloiço do Peregrino.* Google Translate calls it "Pilgrim's Swing." This is amazing, and I wonder who built it.

I walk up the embankment to the swing, drop my pack, sit on the varnished wooden seat, and swing out over the field in front of me. I haven't done this in years. Honestly, I don't remember the last time I was on a swing, and this one is incredible. The breeze on my face gives me an extra push as I swing up, and rush back down.

When I was a child, we had a book of Robert Louis Stevenson's poetry, *A Child's Garden of Verses.*

How do you like to go up in a swing,
Up in the air so blue?
Oh, I do think it's the pleasantest thing
Ever a child can do.

Ever an old woman can do! I could swing up into the blue and fly over these fields all day. But nature is calling in another way.

I get off the swing, unzip the front pocket of my pack, and pull out my pee kit. I have a plastic bag with biodegradable doggy bags, toilet paper, and hand sanitizer. I look both ways down the path, and there's no one coming. There hasn't been anyone out here all day. It's been glorious to be alone. But it would be my luck for someone to come by while I'm squatting.

I step off the mound into a grassy area. There are no trees or bushes to hide behind. I take care of business and put the used toilet paper in a doggy bag for later disposal. "Leave no trace."

I clean my hands and grab my apple and a protein bar from the top compartment of my pack. Sitting on the swing, I eat my lunch and drink my water. Three men come speeding up the hill on bikes. Perfect timing. I get off the swing so they can take a turn.

We take turns capturing this reclaimed moment of childhood with photos. They rush away again, disappearing down the trail as fast as they appeared.

POST: Found a Pilgrim's Swing along the river today. Dropped my pack. Sat. Flew. And so did the scarf. Turns

> out joy doesn't require permission—or youth. Shared the Pilgrim's Swing with three cyclists who appeared out of nowhere. We laughed, took photos, and vanished from each other's lives. Caminho magic again.

It's time for me to hit the trail, too. I shoulder my pack and carefully make my way down the embankment to the gravel farm track. I think about the conversation last night—connection and introspection.

OK, Scarf, to be honest—and isn't that what introspection is about? Without honesty, it wouldn't be worth doing. I didn't come to walk the Portuguese Route because it's what people expect of someone grieving. It's about reclaiming a part of my youth.

Let me tell you about a certain man, Scarf. This is safe to share because you won't tell anyone. He had dark, wavy hair, which was always groomed. His eyes were pools of rich chocolate. They always reminded me of Omar Sharif's eyes when he looked at Lara in Doctor Zhivago. I could just melt into them. His features were ordinary yet pleasing. He was no Clark Gable, but he was still nice to look at. His lips were full, and when he talked, it was like resonant music. I could listen to him talk all day, and it didn't matter what he was saying.

The first time our eyes met, a jolt of electricity surged between us. I know, Scarf, this sounds like one of those cheesy romance novels, but I wouldn't have believed it was real until it happened to me. The connection was instant. It was love at first sight. I know he felt it too.

Roy introduced us, which was part of the tragedy. Peter (coincidentally Portuguese) was Roy's client, and he had come to L.A. to discuss hats and shoes with Roy. Roy was one of the producers on a new film. Apparently, Portugal has some of the world's best shoemakers and hatmakers. They would order shoes and hats custom-made for each film star.

We invited him to dinner, just like we often did for Roy's clients. Roy and I had been married for two years. I asked one of my single girlfriends to join us so it wouldn't be an awkward threesome. We had a lovely evening, but I could tell, even though they were friendly, that Shirl and Peter didn't quite click. And that was fine with me. Yes, Scarf, it was fine with me. I knew then that the electricity between us was special.

A couple of days later, Roy called me from his office. He asked if I had time to run down to the studio and take some paperwork to Peter at his hotel before he flew out. I did not hesitate. I called my afternoon piano student and rescheduled her. It was almost... well, to be honest, it was premeditated on my part. I could have told Roy that I couldn't reschedule my lessons. I could have encouraged him to hire a courier to deliver the papers. But I jumped at the chance.

Nine months later, Karen arrived. Roy and I had been trying to get pregnant, so he never suspected anything. But Karen has his eyes. Mine are blue, and Roy's are brown, but not the deep, rich brown of Peter's. The instant she opened her eyes, I knew.

Scarf, I knew I couldn't tell anyone, so I let Roy think he was the father. Good girls didn't cheat on their husbands, much less get pregnant. I was so wracked with guilt... I made a bargain with myself that it would never happen again.

Of course, the mind is a contrary thing. Tell it not to think of something, the more insistent it becomes. Peter became a ghost that refused to leave me—in the unanswered question of what might have been, and in the memory of wanting more.

In the overcharged world of the seventies film industry, desire seemed to hum in the air. Affairs were always rumored, names paired and traded like currency—whispered about loudly, as though secrecy itself were part of the spectacle. Against that backdrop, I found ways to excuse my own transgression.

We speak so little of women's desire, and when we do, it is often to restrain it. If a woman strays, she is marked and judged. If a man strays, he is admired. He earns applause for his appetite while she wears a scarlet letter. All I know is that the forbidden fruit was made all the sweeter by the thrill of the transgression.

I'm a widow now, yet the years of marriage have seeped into my bones. They shaped my reflexes, my loyalties, even my silences. What was once forbidden by vow now feels restrained by age.

Yes, I want to reclaim my sexuality. I want to feel that current again in my blood. It seems society is comfortable with widows in black, but not with widows who still feel the stir of desire. We are expected to fade gently, to become benign, to trade desire for dignity.

But here is what I have learned, Scarf: Dignity and desire are not at odds.

Who writes the rules for a woman who has outlived her marriage? And why should I still be bound by them?

The kilometers fly by. The scenery changes from flat farmland to hills. The muscles in my legs tense as I approach the first incline into Santarém. The path turns into a road, and the cars zooming by are disconcerting after walking quiet gravel farm roads. Safety becomes paramount.

I lean into the hill, and soon I'm at the top, following the arrows. I turn on the maps app to navigate to my albergue. I find it. Maybe I'm getting better at this. I wait in line to sign in. I booked a mixed-gender room with eight beds. A woman with a young man is in front of me. She is trying to find him a bed in the dorm. She apparently has a whole group of students here. I can just imagine the noise all night.

Now it's my turn. I tell them I've changed my mind and ask for a single room. Thank God one is available. The hostess gives me a ten percent off coupon for the attached restaurant and says it's good for either lunch or dinner. Lunch is only being served for another thirty minutes, then the restaurant will reopen at eight o'clock tonight for dinner. I drop my pack in my room and head down without showering. It feels strange to sit in a nice restaurant at a table for one, in grubby clothes and without a lunch date. Hunger wins out over discomfort.

As I wait for my meal, I text Karen a picture of me on the swing. This should ease her mind.

My phone dings.

Karen: *Mom, OMG—what are you doing? You could get injured.*

I text back, remembering to stay in love: *I am perfectly fine. Thank you for being so concerned. I love you.*

My phone dings again.

Karl: *Mom, just saw the swing picture. You look like yourself. Dad would have loved that grin. Keep going.*

I smile and shake my head. That boy always knows what to say.

I type back: *Still walking. Still smiling.*

The food comes. There must be a whole chicken on the plate. It smells so good. There is no way I can eat all this, but less than fifteen minutes later, it's gone, and I find myself wiping up the juices on the plate with a hunk of bread. Walking definitely stimulates appetite.

I go up to my room, shower, and wash out my walking clothes, then wander over to the church. The ornate stonework and beauty of the front door remind me of the decoration on a wedding cake. It draws me in with the promise of more wonders inside.

A young man is sitting behind a desk. He motions me over and asks for my pilgrim credencial. Am I that obvious? He can't be older than my grandson, who's in his twenties. He stamps my credencial and starts telling me about the church's history.

"The church was built on the foundation of a mosque after the Reconquista, in the thirteenth century. The Reconquista is when we took our country back from the Moors. Then, in the fifteenth century, it was refurbished in the Gothic Manueline style. Do you see some of the pointed arches in harmony with the rounded arches of the Romanesque style?"

"Yes, I see." I'm fascinated by his knowledge.

"The arch over the altar is of the Moorish style. The gold frame around the altar is in the Manueline style, with a rope motif. Do you know the Manueline style?"

"I heard the term in Lisboa."

"Manueline style incorporates maritime elements and shows the wealth Portugal acquired from its seagoing exploits. Is it not beautiful?"

I nod.

"The tiles came later in the eighteenth century, after the great earthquake of 1755 damaged this church."

"The earthquake of Lisboa reached this far?"

"Yes, it's not so far from Lisboa." He smiles at me. "It only seems so because you are walking. We have over 67,000 azulejos tiles here."

"Azulejos?" I slowly turn, my eyes registering the enormous amount of tiles on every wall.

"Yes, that is the name of the style of tile. We inherited the blue from the Moors."

I look up into the choir. "What a beautiful organ."

"Yes, it was also a new addition after the earthquake. Would you like to see it?"

"I would. I play the organ at my church and didn't even think about seeing such beautiful ones here when I made plans for my pilgrimage."

He takes me through a door of the nave and up a spiral staircase into the choir, which overlooks the church. The scale of the tiles and grandeur are even more apparent from this angle.

"Would you like to play it?" he asks.

"You would allow me to even touch it?"

"Of course. Beauty must be experienced, or it is worth nothing." He turns the organ on. "It's been upgraded since the 18th century, but the pipes are the original."

I slide over onto the bench, take off my shoes, and settle myself into position. I make sure the stops are set to play softly, then scoot to the edge of the bench so my feet can reach the pedals and test a note. The rich bass reverberates through the church. It must be the tiles. It's like singing in a bathroom.

My right hand tentatively touches the swell— the top keyboard, as I pick out the notes of the old hymn, *Holy, Holy, Holy.* My left hand automatically reaches for the great lower keyboard, and the sweet harmonies of the hymn fill the church. My feet find their notes, and the rich bass underscores the entire piece.

I finish a verse and start again as the young man's rich baritone seamlessly slides into the hymn, *Santo, Santo, Santo.* We go through a repertoire of familiar hymns, reveling in the sound and holiness of this place.

We finish to applause and look down into the nave. A girl about my guide's age has entered the church.

The young man looks at me and smiles. "My wife. Come meet her. Oh, my name is Jorge, and my wife is Maria."

"I'm Dot," I say when we join up with her.

She exclaims her praises in Portuguese. I have no need for an interpreter. She grabs me and kisses both of my cheeks, then turns to her husband with a flood of Portuguese.

"Maria insists that you join us for dinner tonight," he says.

"I would not want to impose," I say, hoping he will ignore my politeness and ask again.

"We insist. Dinner is at eight. I will meet you here and bring you to our home. It is close by."

I agree.

I ready myself to go and ask him about a grocery store so I can get some food for breakfast and my walk tomorrow. He points me in the right direction.

I walk to a market to pick up a few items for breakfast and a bottle of wine for my hosts. The street takes me past a huge, old stone wall. A plaque on the side states that the Romans built this wall in the third century. Well, that makes me feel like a youngster.

Maybe that's the appeal of the Caminho. Our lives are so brief compared to the permanence of these structures. They give us a sense of longevity, of making our mark. Leaving something for future generations. I hope I will leave a legacy for my children, but I'm not sure what that is.

Now back at the hotel, I head to the floor with a kitchen for pilgrims and put my supplies in the fridge. I hope no one takes my food. I go up to my room and post some pictures and observations on Facebook. Checking my watch, it's time to meet Jorge. I take a quick look at myself in the mirror. I hope that my hiking clothes are acceptable attire, as I have nothing else.

Jorge meets me at the church and guides me to their home. It's behind one of those mysterious doors that line the street. It opens to a courtyard lined with more doors. There is a second floor with balconies overlooking the courtyard. This is so pleasant. I hand them the bottle as they lead me to a small table by a fountain in the center of the courtyard. It is beautifully set for five.

"I hope you don't mind, but our children are joining us."

"Lovely. I have two grown children and four grandchildren."

I take a seat, and their daughters bring out bowls of soup for us to start the meal. They sit, and my guide says a blessing. The evening wraps me in the warmth of family, with an undertone of missing my own, as we make our way through each course.

We finish dinner, and Jorge walks me back to my hotel. I express my gratitude to him for such a lovely afternoon and evening.

•••

It's morning, and I head to the kitchen. A couple of men are packing panniers. We exchange greetings, and they tell me they are cycling the Caminho. So much for someone to walk with. I go to the fridge. My breakfast remains undisturbed. I love that people don't mess with things that aren't theirs.

I check out and ask the clerk where I might find the next yellow arrow. She motions vaguely down the street. This is starting to feel like a ritual — I ask, and they wave. According to my guidebook, I know it's close to the Portas do Sol. There are street signs pointing in that direction. So that's where I will go.

I am glad that I don't have to decide where to go anymore. I follow a set path. It wasn't like that when Roy got Alzheimer's. I felt lost. I didn't know what I was supposed to do. I wish I'd had some yellow arrows to follow. And a goal. With Alzheimer's, there is no getting better. Death becomes the goal. A tear slips down my cheek.

CHAPTER 6

SANTARÉM TO VILA NOVA DE BARQUINHA

I don't want to think about death or Alzheimer's. I want to find the next yellow arrow. I arrive at Portas do Sol, a beautiful park near a church, but I can't find any yellow arrows. There are usually arrows near churches. There's a woman jogging around the park. I walk over to where she'll pass. Likely noticing my confusion, she stops. I say "Caminho," and she immediately signals for me to follow her. She takes me to an alley beside the church. There's a construction barrier on one side. She points to the arrow, showing me that I should walk through a narrow arch. It's part of the city's ancient walls.

I thank her and walk off under the arch. The alleyway is narrow, with cobblestones underfoot. The cobblestones end with a quick right onto a steep, rocky, descending dirt path. Again, no arrows, but there are markings for the GR route, which stands for "*Grande Randonnée*," or in English "Great Hike." These are long-distance hiking trails across

Europe, named in French because many originated there. It's an international system. The GR routes are marked with yellow and red lines and take a different path from the Caminho, so I remind myself to look for arrows, not straight lines. Since there was no other way to go, I carefully make my way downhill. I don't want to have an accident this early in the journey.

The path leads me onto a busy street. Everyone seems to be heading to work. I do my best to find and follow the arrows as I wander around town. The guidebook says there is a bridge over the river, but the only bridge I see is crowded with cars and has no pedestrian lane. This can't be it.

I head back into the town center, retracing my steps and searching for the arrow I must have just passed. And then I see it—a half-faded yellow arrow on the side of a building. I change course, only to lose my way again. A man steps out of his house and gets into his car. I stop him and ask for directions. Graciously, he walks me to the next arrow, painted on a building just a few doors down.

When I mention villages and homes, one needs to understand that these are old stone houses fronted by narrow cobblestone streets that seem untouched for centuries. Maintaining places this old to modern standards must be challenging. The plumbing and electricity alone must be a nightmare. But the charm of these places is beyond words.

I reach the small stone bridge over the river. It's lovely. I can finally breathe. The arrows become more consistent as I walk on a farm track through fields preparing for harvest.

There is the crunch, crunch, crunch of boots on the gravel path behind me. I turn to see a tall, slender man with long legs and a backpack—a pilgrim—coming up quickly behind me. We stop for a moment to chat. His accent sounds Germanic, and he confirms this when I ask. I explain that I am having trouble finding the arrows. He pulls out his phone and shows me the Caminho map app he's using. He says it's fantastic. I promise to download it when I get to my albergue with Wi-Fi.

He wishes me "Bom Caminho" and walks away. These tall young men and their long strides. He'll be finished by the time I reach the halfway point. But it doesn't matter. I have time, but he needs to get back to work or school. I'm so happy those days when the work schedule controlled my life are behind me.

Now I have a secret weapon, an app to keep me on track. The day is warm, the sun is shining, and I am walking on gravel farm tracks, not on cobblestones. The tracks are so much easier on my feet. Life is good.

It's incredible how these routes were mapped out, connecting towns while mostly avoiding main roads and busy areas. The locals must have played a role in this. Still, someone had to put it all together. Pilgrims have been walking to Santiago for over fifteen hundred years. These are ancient trails, though they have likely been altered by highways and industrial development. I offer a prayer of gratitude and love. Yes, I need to remember to stay in a state of love.

Last night, I booked a place to stay tonight, about twenty-four kilometers away in Azinhaga. The guidebook helps with these decisions, but sometimes the distances aren't very accurate. I wonder how they calculate the distances.

I don't want to do the recommended thirty-kilometer stages. There's no way my body will walk over thirty kilometers a day, day after day. Anything over twenty-four and I start to ache all over. My body can tell.

As I walk into the town of Azinhaga, a couple of young men with backpacks signal to me to join them at a small building near a water treatment plant by the road. I cautiously walk over to them.

They're standing at an office door, and there's a man behind a desk. The pilgrims are gulping down glasses of water. There's a clear jug of ice water on the desk. The man at the desk sees me and motions for me to come in. He offers to stamp my credencial and pours me a glass of water. Heaven. This is definitely a trail angel. I've been reading about them, and now I get to experience another one.

The young men are Americans. They introduce themselves

and tell me they have been lifelong friends and just had to do this Caminho together. There are a few streaks of gray in their hair. Their tall, strong builds led me to believe they were younger. Finally, I'm meeting other pilgrims.

They say they're headed to the next town. I bid them a "Bom Caminho" and walk into the village to find my albergue. Well, that didn't last long. Alone again. Signs are pointing to the albergue. This makes it easy. The albergue stands at the far edge of the village. There is a wall around it and a locked iron gate. This seems to be the style here. I ring the bell, and while I'm waiting, I send Karen the obligatory text.

The gate to the side yard opens. "Welcome. Come through here."

The woman speaks English—what a relief. She asks for my passport, credencial, and twenty euros for the night. This includes dinner. She tells me she has vegetable soup for the first course and asks if I want chicken or beef for the second. I'm not terribly hungry, so I order only soup and bread. She mentions she has a lovely flan for dessert and asks if I would like that too.

"Yes," I say. Who can turn down flan?

"What time would you like to eat?"

"Anytime works perfectly." I smile at her, grateful for the hospitality.

She guides me to a comfortable room with six beds and an attached bathroom. No one else is there. I pick a bed near the bathroom, so I won't disturb anyone when I get up at night to pee. She encourages me to freshen up while she gets dinner ready. Perfect.

How do these people make any money? Maybe during the high season. I am a little late in the year.

I wander out to the dining room, and she has set a place for one. She has included a small carafe of wine and a pitcher of water. This is unusual. Most places don't serve water unless you ask for it. She must know that pilgrims need to hydrate. The proprietress brings me a lovely homemade vegetable soup and bread for dinner. There's something comforting about warm soup and delicious, hearty bread.

I finish eating, wash up my dishes, and put them in the drainer. There is a self-serve breakfast of yogurt, cereal, bread, jam, ham, cheese, and, of course, coffee. There is a price list on the refrigerator. On the counter sits a jar with a handwritten sign asking anyone who takes food to leave money there, another quiet act of trust along the Camino.

I connect to her Wi-Fi and download the recommended app. I hope this helps me.

•••

I'm up before dawn, so I will get an early start. I have about twenty-four kilometers to Vila Nova de Barquinha.

I want to get there early, Scarf, because I am going to visit a castle by boat.

The sun rising over the fields creates a golden glow. I smile, feeling the joy of walking inside. Well, that joy didn't last long. I reach my first arrow, and it points down another heavily traveled road with a minimal shoulder. It's scary sharing the road with vehicles. I can't let fear take over me. I just have to stay in "love." Maybe the drivers will feel it and avoid me. Maybe my children were right about the bright orange backpack.

I walk into the next town, Golegã. There's a small café in a park across the street. Perfect, I really need to use the restroom. I go inside and order a cup of café con leche and a couple of those *pastéis de nata*. It's becoming a habit.

"*Onde está a casa de banho*?" I ask in halting Portuguese.

She gives me a puzzled look.

"*Baño, aseo, servicio.* How do you say 'bathroom' in Portuguese?" I slip into English.

Her expression tells me she doesn't understand.

I resort to universal sign language. I cross my legs, point to my crotch, and bounce a little.

She starts laughing. "WC?" She points to the door of a small building next door.

I start to laugh and rush to the WC before I lose control all over her floor. Who knew? We use "WC" for water closet in English. Well, this definitely makes it easier.

Relieved, I return inside for my coffee and pastry. She offers to stamp my credencial, something I had entirely forgotten. I tuck it back into my fanny pack. She points me toward a table outside overlooking the park and follows with my snack in hand. Such kindness.

I finish and carry my cup and plate back into the café. She smiles and signals that I should leave them on the counter. I step outside and shoulder my pack. Consulting my new app, I see that the Caminho leads into town and then turns right. Arrows confirm the route.

The town is precious. Another one I could have enjoyed spending some time exploring. As I leave town, the cobblestone lanes turn into a narrow blacktop road, running between cornfields.

"Hey," someone behind me yells.

It's the two Americans, and they've teamed up with the young man who showed me the app. I'll get to walk with them.

"Tell me your name so I can properly thank you."

"I'm Jacques from Germany." He extends his hand.

"And we're Dave and Chris," Dave says. "It's good to see you."

I introduce myself and let Jacques know I downloaded the app last night, and so far, it has been working great for me.

They adjust their pace so I can keep up. I ask them about all the horse motifs in Golegã since they spent the night there. Chris confirms that this town is very serious about its horses. He says that when they went out for dinner last night, they walked past a garage under a house and, instead of cars, there were seven horses. Then, in the bar where they were eating dinner al fresco, a man was sitting on his horse, smoking a cigar and drinking whiskey. I'm wondering how much whiskey they had.

I giggle. "So, Chris, who was drinking the whiskey and smoking the cigar, the man or the horse?"

Dave hoots. "Probably both."

As we get closer to Vila Nova de Barquinha, I turn off toward my hotel. The boys say goodbye as they head to Tomar, twenty-one more kilometers down the road. I doubt I'll see them again. I'm starting to understand the rhythm of companionship along the Caminho.

There's a castle in the middle of the Tagus River near this little town. It's a Templar stronghold. I want to see it. At my age, I may never pass this way again, and I'm going to do all those things I want to do. I'm sorry to have missed the guy on the horse with his cigar and whiskey.

I drop off my pack at the hotel and walk the three

kilometers down a busy road to the boat ramp. It doesn't look like any dock we have in California. This one is a long, steep stone ramp leading to the water, with a small floating platform tied to it. A man arrives in a van and goes down to the boat. I follow him and ask if he is the person I am supposed to meet for the tour. He blows me off. I've traveled a long way to see this castle, and I don't want to miss it. But how do I say this to him? He clearly doesn't speak English. He gets in the boat, starts it up, and drives across to the other side of the river.

What did the Luz in Valada say? "Change your emotions."

He docks the boat. Maybe he picks up passengers there first, then comes back for us? I keep watching and try to feel that love inside me. It's almost time to leave, and he's making no move to come back across the river. There are three other couples waiting with me now. They seem relaxed. Stay in love.

Another boat arrives at the dock. The captain steps out and warmly welcomes us to the tour. What a relief. I'm so glad to get a nice boat captain. There are seven of us, three couples and me. One of the couples is holding hands, and my heart lurches.

We start up the river, and the captain asks where we are from. I tell him, and he adjusts by sharing the history of

Almourol Castle in both Portuguese and English. What a blessing to be able to speak multiple languages fluently, and to be so kind as to include me. Staying in a state of love works.

A fortification built by the Moors has stood on this site since the eighth century. The Moors called it Al-moralan, meaning "high rock." When the Portuguese reclaimed the land during the Reconquista in 1129, the then seventeen-year-old King Dom Afonso Henriques, Portugal's first king, gave the castle to the Templars to protect Portuguese territory and trade. They adapted the original name into Portuguese, and it is now known as Almourol. Between 1160 and 1171, the original fortress was transformed into a military castle. This river serves as a key boundary and trade route, and the Portuguese were determined not to lose it again.

The Templars held the castle, and in 1311, they were disbanded by the pope in Rome. Those clever Portuguese renamed the Templars the Order of Christ. They continued to guard the border. Eventually, when the Moors were evicted from Spain and Portugal, the castle was abandoned.

The 1755 earthquake damaged the castle. It was the same quake that leveled Lisboa. That was one huge earthquake. I remind myself of what Jorge in Santarém had said about Lisboa not being far away.

The boat drops us off at a dock. We walk along a path to the castle's gate. Inside the castle, there is an ancient stone staircase that ascends to the top of the walls. I take a deep breath. I've always been nervous about heights, and this staircase looks like it has been here since the twelfth century. My rational mind tells me it would be blocked off if it were unsafe. There's no railing. I hug the stone wall as I climb the staircase, the other side dropping to the stone courtyard below. If I slip, I will plunge to my death.

At the top, I walk close to the protection of the crenelated walls. The view over the river is breathtaking. The defending knights could see their enemies approaching from a great distance. The walk along the top of the wall takes me to a tower. I enter a room with plaques explaining the history and lore of the fortress.

One plaque inside tells the story of D. Ramiro. He was a brutal knight who fought the Moors. According to the story, he was returning to Almourol after chasing the Moors when he encountered a mother and daughter carrying a jug of water. He asked for some, and the daughter, flustered, dropped the jug. Ramiro took personal offense and killed them both. Soon after, he encountered a young Moorish boy and took him prisoner. It turned out it was his mother and sister Ramiro had killed. He kept the boy in the castle and put him to work as a slave. The boy gained favor and eventually poisoned Ramiro's wife for revenge and successfully seduced his daughter, who had fallen in love with the young man. When Ramiro discovered this, he had both of them killed. It is said that on the night of St. John, the ghosts of the young lovers can be seen embracing at the top of the tower.

Such a sad story. The innocent always seem to suffer the most, not just from war itself, but from the ruthless revenge that fuels it.

A metal staircase attached to the stone leads to the top of the tower, where the lovers' ghosts appear. I take a deep breath. There's no way I'm going to let a silly fear stop me.

Right, Scarf?

I head to the top as my mind fills with silly worries about impending earthquakes. I gaze out over the land. The view is breathtaking. I understand why this was such a strategic spot for defense. While holding onto the railing, I carefully descend the metal staircase.

Not so bad, huh, Scarf?

There are displays in the tower room featuring various legends and pictures of knights from medieval times. I take pictures of them so I can read about them later. It is about time to head back to the boat.

I walk back along the top to the wall and then to the stone staircase. My heart leaps into my throat. I'm not sure I can walk back down this thing. The stones are smooth, uneven, and probably slippery from centuries of knights and tourists going up and down. I can't believe there's no railing. Going up is always easier for me than going down. When I go down, I feel like I'm going to fall.

The young couple from the boat comes up behind me, and I move aside so they can descend. The wife looks at me and asks if she can help. I nod. Her husband goes first, and I follow. She comes down behind me. He goes very slowly and tells me I can put my hand on his shoulder. I decline. I don't want to be responsible if I fall or if he falls. I feel ridiculous, so I just focus on his back and the next step down as I hold onto the wall. We get to the bottom safely. I'm so grateful. They must wonder what an old woman is doing out here in the middle of Portugal by herself.

We wander back to the boat, and the nice young man helps me aboard. When we reach the dock, they offer to give me a ride back to my hotel. I accept, grateful.

I go back to my room, send Karen my nightly message, and let her know I am headed to Tomar tomorrow.

> POST: Camigas, today the Caminho delivered helpers just when I needed them—kind strangers, good timing, and steady feet. Then I crossed the Tagus by boat and stood inside a Templar castle rising straight out of the river, Almourol. Stone walls, legends, and a view that made my heart race. Scarf is clearly enjoying her medieval era. Boa noite

CHAPTER 7

VILA NOVA DE BARQUINHA TO FÁTIMA

I leave after a hearty breakfast and start looking for the yellow arrows to Tomar. They are on the same posts as the blue arrows for Fátima. The two routes share the same path through town. At the edge of town, both arrows point to a gravel forest track leading into the hills and a eucalyptus forest. The fresh, clean smell of eucalyptus blows the remaining L.A. smog out of my lungs. It feels so good. I love being back in the woods. It's been my special place since I was a child.

I start to think about Fátima and the documentaries about this special place. I'm excited about visiting it after I reach Tomar.

The trail ends at a T-junction. A yellow arrow points right to Tomar, and a blue arrow points left to Fátima. I'd planned to take the bus between Tomar and Fátima, but why bother with a round trip? Why wait? Fátima is on my mind. There must be a reason it's calling me. Yes, it's longer, and I don't have a guidebook, but I can just follow the arrows. There will be accommodations along the way. Have faith, I remind myself, just as the children did.

It's almost noon when I reach a town. I go to the local café, where there are a couple of old men drinking beer. I ask about food, and the owner points to a case of candy bars and a few tired-looking pastries. This is not what I had in mind. I order a soda and a candy bar. I try to ask about places to stay closer to Fátima. I know I can't walk the additional twenty-four kilometers that Google says I have today. I've already done twelve.

Another man walks into the bar, and the owner brings him to me. This man speaks excellent English. He helps me find a place to stay for the night with food. It's only twelve more kilometers. I make a reservation.

What have I done, Scarf? Roy always said I was impulsive. I have rushed across Portugal with no safety net. Maybe my children were right. I'm not fit to be out here alone. Well, I can't turn back now. I have to keep going. And no one knows that I'm heading to Fátima. They think I'm going to Tomar. If something happens, they would never trace me to this small town.

I follow the blue arrows to a turnoff up a gravel mountain track. The arrows disappear, and I turn on my road map app. The Caminho app will not help me here. At least, I know how to do this. I use the GPS. I put it in

Walk mode. Yes, I'm on the right road to get to the town of Fungalvaz.

The track deteriorates to a path through the eucalyptus forest. I can just make out the highway below through the trees. I don't know how I would get down that hill if I had to. I must have missed a turn somewhere.

Trying to avoid panic, I touch the scarf, remind myself to breathe, and try to put myself into a state of love. I think about Ashley, my granddaughter, and when she was born. Love flows through me. I recheck the map. I'm on the right track. My battery is getting low, so to conserve it, I will only turn it on if I come to a crossroad.

Along the path, there are signs of wild boar rooting. We have them in California, and they can be pretty fierce. I'd rather not meet one up here. There are birds singing, so that's probably a good sign.

The path eventually opens up into a narrow road at the edge of the town. The road leads to an intersection, and there's a sharp descent if I turn toward town. There's a grocery store on the map at the bottom of the hill. The map tells me to stay high at the intersection, and the pension should be just ahead. All I see are houses surrounded by stone walls with closed metal gates. I stay high.

The map shows that the pension is just a few meters ahead. There's a blue sign with a "P" on the wall beside a wrought iron gate. I check the address. This might be it. I find a bell and ring it. A woman comes out with several dogs and a young boy. She smiles at me.

"You are our guest tonight? I'm Ana," she says in English. I could just kiss her.

She takes me to a door beside the garage, and it opens onto a lovely, small apartment with a bathroom, bedroom, and kitchen. She tells me about the washing machine in the bathroom. Then she tells me that I have a choice: walk the one-half kilometer downhill to the grocery store to buy food for dinner, or they will figure something out. She says they usually have a couple of days to plan for a guest, and they have nothing prepared for a last-minute guest.

I don't know. But she makes the decision for me.

"My husband, João, is a sushi chef, but we don't have supplies. I will call him, and he'll pick up pizza for dinner. What do you like on your pizza?"

"Veggies," I say, letting out a sigh.

She leaves me to take a shower and wash my clothes. The washing machine stops, so I take the clothes out, put them in the basket provided, then head to the back door to find the clothesline. I step outside and feel like I've stepped into paradise. The back deck surrounds a beautiful pool with clear, inviting blue water. I spot the clothesline and hang my clothes. A fresh breeze from the mountain blows through, and I know they'll dry quickly.

Now finished hanging up my clothes, I go to the pool and stick my hand in. Too cold for my blood. I'll not be swimming tonight, but it sure is relaxing to look at. And the view looks across the forested mountains. I breathe in the fragrant fresh air, allowing the unimpeded view of the forest to wash over me.

There really isn't much to do. I love this. All I have to do is care for myself.

OMG, I forgot to text Karen. I rush in, grab my phone, and send the message. I don't want her reaching out to the local authorities about her missing mom.

João returns with the pizza, which he clearly dressed up with goat cheese and spinach. They set up a table for me on the pool deck. I wasn't sure if I would eat with the family, but this is okay. They need to keep their family life and business separate.

I wish my family were around the dinner table. I always insisted that we eat dinner together at six p.m. No matter what anyone was doing, the world stopped for family time. It's a good rule. After dinner, the kids would wash the dishes. Roy and I would go sit in the living room under the guise of catching up on the day. What we were really doing was listening to the kids talk. We learned so much about their lives this way. As they became teenagers, it helped us keep a handle on them. They rarely caused trouble, but I knew what some other families were going through with their teens, and I wanted to nip everything in the bud.

I can't eat the entire pizza, so I save half to take with me the next day. There won't be many services. João comes and takes my dishes. He talks with me for a while and tells me how blessed he feels to have made a home here for his family. He works in a restaurant in a larger nearby town, but this is his retreat.

He asks what I want for breakfast, and I choose the omelet. We agree that he will bring my breakfast before driving the children to school so I can get an early start. It's twenty-two kilometers to Fátima and only ten to Tomar. How did I get so off track?

> POST: Camigas, I'm tucked in for the night at a small pension, clean clothes, feet resting, heart full. Pizza, laundry, and kindness—everything a pilgrim needs. Tomorrow, I walk to Fátima. For now, boa noite

•••

It's morning, and João brings me the best omelet I have ever eaten. I could take him home with me. He gives me his phone number and clear directions. Then he cautions me that there aren't many pilgrims walking to Fátima, so I might find myself alone in the woods. He says the only danger is the wild boar, but if I need help, he will come. His kindness reminds me of Roy.

My clean clothes carefully stowed, I shoulder my pack with trepidation and follow his directions along with the blue arrows out of town. Just as he said, after a few kilometers, an arrow points me up a gravel farm track. But I'm not alone at all. It's the olive harvest. Many workers are in the trees on ladders, stripping olives from the limbs and pruning branches. They have blue net-like tarps under the trees to catch the falling olives. Someone on the ground is shaking and knocking olives off the cut branches, while the person in the tree is also stripping olives and letting them fall into the nets. It looks like they've been using this technique for millennia, not a machine in sight. We call "Bom dia" to each other as I pass. I take comfort in their presence. All is right with the world.

I pass a grove of olive trees where no one is harvesting. There is a branch full of small, black, ripe olives hanging over the farm track. I really want to pick and taste one fresh off the tree. I love olives, and I can't even imagine what a ripe, fresh one would be like. My mouth waters. Everything tastes better fresh off the tree. But if I pick it, I'm stealing. This is their livelihood. I have so much respect for our food producers. I see what they go through in the valley outside of LA.

But, Scarf, I may never get another chance to taste an olive right off the tree.

I touch one of the olives. It's soft, so it must be ripe. It easily falls off and into my hand. Well, I can't put it back on the tree or waste it either. I take a nibble, careful of the pit. A horrible, bitter, dusty taste floods my mouth. Yuck. I throw the rest of it into the grove. What kind of olives are these? No wonder no one is pilfering them as they walk by.

The trail leads into a small town. There's a church in the square with a bench outside. This is the perfect place to sit and eat my leftover pizza. It's not quite as good as last night, but it will give me the energy I need to reach Fátima. Still, how can I be hungry after that omelet for breakfast? A pilgrim's need for fuel.

I throw my trash into a bin at the edge of the village. It's so interesting that these small villages have trash and recycling bins at the start and the finish. It must keep things much cleaner.

The blue arrows lead me to a crossroads. A sign points up another hill. I've been told multiple times that Fátima is at the top of a long, steep hill. The sign says ten kilometers remain. How can that be? I've already walked fifteen. I'm fed up with these conflicting distances. I'm eager to arrive. I check the map. Taking the road is closer than the farm track. I'll take the road, even though it's riskier with the traffic.

They were not kidding about the hill. The road steadily climbs until I get to the outskirts of Fátima. At the top, there is a broad yellow sidewalk with beautiful landscaping and prominent blue arrows. I giggle and sing to the Scarf, "Follow the yellow brick road."

The map tells me I still have several kilometers to go before reaching my hotel, so I keep walking. I encounter a detour through the outskirts of town due to construction. Really? I'm so tired.

The road takes me past a large church. A sign next to it says *Mosteiro do Rosário Perpétuo,* but it doesn't look like what I'm searching for, though I don't really know what a shrine looks like. I consult the map again. I still have over a kilometer left to walk. I'll go to my hotel first, then figure it out.

The street widens into a four-lane road through the commercial area of town, lined with shops and cafés. Finally, my hotel is up ahead. I check in and drop off my pack at the reception. My room isn't ready yet. According to my map, the shrine is less than two blocks away. I'll go there now, and when I return, my room should be ready.

I send Karen a quick text that I am safe in Fátima.

When I turn the corner, the basilica greets me. I walk into its quiet interior. The graves of the children who saw the Virgin Mary are in the side chapels. This cathedral seems to be of the neoclassical style, one of the least ornate cathedrals I have seen. I like that it is not all covered in gold. It matches the children's simple shepherd lifestyle and innocence.

I sit quietly in a pew and let the peace of this place wash over me. After offering a prayer of thanksgiving, I walk out through a different door into the shrine area. It's huge. I stop in wonder at the sacredness and vastness of the space.

Then it strikes me. I walked here. I actually walked here. I want everyone in the shrine to stop and applaud. I giggle.

I hear singing, and it's beautiful. It seems to fill the entire shrine. I look around the shrine and see a shelter where many people are sitting. The singing is coming from there. I walk down to it. It's a roofed area that protects a small, dollhouse-like white chapel behind two waist-high white walls. The first wall surrounds the small chapel, and a statue of the Lady of Fátima is in a glass case next to the white chapel. Also within this wall is a pulpit, some seating, and the organ. I don't see a choir, but all the participants are singing. The second wall also surrounds the chapel area, with benches backing onto the wall. There are people on their knees, making their way between the two walls. The devotion is evident on their faces. I sit on a back pew and let the sacred energy of the place wash over me.

The service ends, and I ask the person sitting next to me about the chapel. He tells me it is the Chapel of the Apparitions, built on the exact spot where the Virgin Mary appeared to the children. He points to the statue of the Virgin and says that one of the bullets used in the attempt to assassinate Pope John Paul II was placed by the Pope himself in her crown. The man tells me that the Pope credited his survival to Our Lady of Fátima. The assassination attempt occurred on May 13, 1981, the anniversary of the first apparition, and reinforced the Third Secret of Fátima, which said a pope would be struck down. Chills run up my spine.

I thank him, then rise to continue exploring the shrine area and look for a place to get my pilgrim's credencial stamped. People are on their knees coming down a hill from another church in the shrine area. They are following pavers clearly set to mark their path, which ends by circling the area between the chapel walls. To endure such pain by kneeling through this distance in search of an answer to your problems is truly an act of faith. I hope they find what they are seeking.

I ask a woman wearing a habit who is walking by if there is a place where I can get my credencial stamped. She points me toward the office. I walk into the office and pull out my credencials. The young man at the desk asks me about the group I came in with. I tell him I walked here alone.

"You walked here alone, from where?"

I proudly say, "Lisboa."

His eyes widen in astonishment. "You are amazing."

I feel the blush rising on my face. Yes, I do feel amazing. I wallow in his words. My heart sings. I am not too old. I am still capable.

He stamps my credencial and tells me about the pilgrim house outside the sanctuary. This house allows pilgrims to stay in the dorms for only ten euros a night. I wish I had known this before I made hotel reservations. But I did come here kind of half-cocked. He invites me back to the nine-thirty p.m. service and tells me where I can get a candle for a one-euro donation. I'm usually asleep in bed by nine-thirty, but I don't tell him that. I want to keep him amazed by me.

I leave the sanctuary and check in to get my room and take a shower. Then I give myself a stern talk. I've come this far, so I can stay up late and attend the service.

I leave the hotel with plenty of time before the service. I head to the gift shop just outside the shrine, which has many souvenirs. A thought of a friend who is Catholic and coping with stage four cancer enters my mind. I should get her something blessed. But I need to be able to carry it. I see a pretty handkerchief embroidered with pink thread, featuring the Virgin and the three children. I go up to the cash register and ask if a priest has blessed this. She says no, but tells me that I can ask a priest to bless it. I pay and go in search of a priest to bless this handkerchief.

I walk back onto the shrine area. I'm glad they keep the area sacred by keeping the gift shops out of the shrine itself. I start looking around for a priest, but there's none in sight. I do a bit more sightseeing around the shrine, then find something to eat for dinner. I put my headlamp in my pocket because I'm a bit nervous walking the streets of Fátima after dark. These eyes aren't what they used to be.

I enjoy a lovely dinner of veggie soup and bread, then head back to the shrine to buy a candle. There is a huge crowd of people buying candles. A woman takes a candle and a plastic cup. She inserts the candle's end into the cup, then drops her donation into a box. I follow suit.

I arrive early and find a seat in the front row of the Chapel of the Apparitions. There are people, mostly women, on their knees, making their way around the altar area. I watch with fascination. Soon, fifteen priests arrive, along with one who appears to be officiating. A young boy dressed like a priest is sitting with them in the altar area. Since I am not Catholic, all of this is new to me. It makes me very curious, but this isn't the time to ask questions. I grew up in the Episcopal Church, and as long as I treat their beliefs with respect, I don't think they'll ask me to leave.

The officiating priest speaks some words in Portuguese and lights a candle. Then he continues the service. Not long into the ceremony, he asks the other priests to come and light their candles from the central candle. A priest brings his lit candle to me and helps me light mine. He gestures for me to light the candles of the people behind me. Soon, several thousand candles are glowing in the dark. The service continues. Now I understand why the candles are so large.

People from different countries are invited to take turns saying prayers at the pulpit and participating in the service. The priest then speaks about the importance of peace and hope. He says this is the message of the Virgin of Fátima.

There is a soft exclamation from the congregants when a priest carrying a white cross, glowing with light, appears from behind a curtain behind the altar. He starts a procession around the altar area and through the congregation. The people part to make way for him and the priests behind him. Next, six men carrying a platform bearing the Fátima Virgin, standing on top in all her glory, come out from behind a curtain in the back of the altar area. They follow the cross out into the sanctuary. Each of us, with our glowing candles, follows in an orderly, respectful manner. It is a procession of peace, with people from all over the world. It gives me goosebumps to be part of such a movement. After we circle the sanctuary with our candles, people begin to disperse.

I go back to my hotel. My body is overflowing with love. I have not felt this in so long. Tears roll down my face. There is something much larger than me that is right with the world.

> POST: Camigas, today I walked somewhere I didn't plan to go. I followed blue arrows, trusted my feet, and arrived in Fátima on my own two legs.
> Candles. Silence. Song.
> I don't have words yet. Only gratitude. Boa noite

• • •

I wake and discover I missed a text from Karen last night. She's asking what I am doing in Fátima. What can I tell her? How do I explain being guided here by something I don't yet understand? I text back.

I decided to come here first, and I'll take a bus to Tomar this afternoon. I'll let you know when I arrive.

My first task this morning is to find breakfast, then locate a priest. The first is easy to do. I walk to a small café near the hotel I saw yesterday, offering pastéis de nata and, of course, café con leche. I find a seat and order. Then I text Karl.

Detoured to Fátima. Walked in alone. Candlelight service. It got under my skin.

His reply takes a few minutes. My, he's up early.

That makes perfect sense, Mom. You said you wanted to see it. Sounds like you found what you needed.

The proprietor comes to my table with the café and the nata. The nata is piping hot, and she holds a shaker filled with spice. "Would you like cinnamon on your nata?"

"Oh, yes, please. I love cinnamon."

She shakes out some cinnamon onto the hot pastry, and I take a bite. It melts in my mouth, and the cinnamon explodes the flavor. "How do you make these?"

"The original recipe was created by monks at St. Jerome's

Monastery in Belem in the eighteenth century. They used egg whites to starch their clothes. They didn't want the yolks to go to waste, so they made this egg yolk custard and filled their tart shells with it," she explains.

"How clever. Waste not, want not. Though I believe the pastry has outlived the starching of clothes. What do they do with the egg whites now that clothes aren't starched anymore?"

"Make meringue, of course. We are too conservative to allow food to go to waste. Would you like one of our cakes with meringue frosting?"

I laugh. "The pastry will fill me up just fine. Obrigada."

"Nada," she says, taking the cinnamon back to the counter and greeting her next customer.

I review maps on my phone while sipping my coffee. My bus to Tomar doesn't leave until late this afternoon. I probably have time to walk to the village where the children lived, and along the way, stop at the shrine to find a priest. It has to be crawling with them.

I walk back to the hotel and pack. I take my backpack downstairs, but I really don't want to carry it around with me all day. The girl at the desk is scrolling through her phone when I approach.

I clear my throat to get her attention.

She finishes doing whatever she is doing on her phone,

slowly puts it down, and looks up at me with an attitude. Her hair is dyed jet black, flat, not even shiny, and her eyes are heavily made up. Long black fingernails drum on the counter.

"May I leave my backpack here while I go sightseeing? I'll be back to get it in a couple of hours."

"We don't hold people's luggage."

"But you all held it yesterday afternoon when I was checking in."

"That's because you were checking in. You can leave it in the lobby, but it's not our responsibility if someone takes it."

Leave it in the lobby? You've got to be kidding. This is all I have. My irritation rises. I throw the room key on the desk, shoulder my pack, and walk out towards the shrine to seek a priest.

Then it hits me. My behavior didn't show much love. She was just doing her job, following her superior's rules. Yeah, she could have been a little more polite, but I don't know what her life looks like outside the reception desk.

Does staying in a state of love mean I let people walk all over me? If so, I don't love myself. I'm allowing myself to be a doormat. How can I stand up for myself while remaining in a state of love?

The first time I heard about the Caminho was when I read *The Camino: A Journey of the Spirit* by Shirley MacLaine.

She wrote about encountering a pack of wild dogs on her Caminho. That's certainly worse than a surly receptionist. She stood her ground, sent them love, and they backed off. What self-control it must have taken to stand there and not let fear be the emotion you radiate, but love.

I took my frustration out on this receptionist, thinking I could make her change her mind. Maybe even get special treatment. Maybe she doesn't have much control either. Maybe she's just defending her job, which she needs to survive. Those feral dogs had no control. They were just trying to survive.

Instead of throwing my keys and giving the receptionist a sharp look, I could have offered her kindness. Perhaps her tone would have softened if mine had. Perhaps not. The ending might have been the same. I would still be walking the streets of Fátima with my backpack. It was her snobbish reply that stirred my anger. But I have lived long enough to know that anger rarely arrives alone. Maybe she stands behind that desk all day absorbing impatience and complaints, until courtesy feels like a luxury she can no longer afford. And perhaps I added my own small weight to hers.

Jesus said to forgive. The words are easy. The living of them is not.

The crowd in the sanctuary is much larger than yesterday. It dawns on me that it's Saturday, the weekend, so many people are probably spending their days off here. I walk to the Chapel of the Apparitions, drawn like a moth to a flame. I sit on the back pew and breathe deeply. My mind relaxes as a feeling of love washes over me. I soak it in. Then, thinking of the receptionist, I send some to her. It's definitely easier after the incident. I remind myself that it's a practice.

I move through the crowd. A young priest approaches me. I believe he is a priest because he's wearing black and has a clerical collar. I ask if he can bless the handkerchief. "It's for a sick friend."

He smiles and, with an American accent, says, "Sure."

He takes the handkerchief from me and gently holds it. Inhaling deeply, he closes his eyes and prays. He smiles and offers the handkerchief to me. When I reach for it, he cups my hands. A warmth and stillness pass through me.

Not wanting to disturb the moment, I whisper a thank you as he lets go of my hands.

"You're welcome," he says, and continues walking in the direction of whatever is calling him next.

I find a place to sit, open my pack, and carefully place the handkerchief in a baggie inside an inner pocket where it will be safe. It has a long way to go.

I pull up my map app and enter the name of the village where the children lived. I'm guided down a four-lane urban road, lined with stores and restaurants. Many of the stores sell Fátima souvenirs. The shrine area has successfully kept the commercialism out, but the rest of the town is doing its best to capitalize on it.

A row of tour buses is ahead, waiting to turn at the next light. I glance at my map and realize they are heading in the same direction as I am. When I turn the corner, I see the buses unloading hordes of tourists. I quicken my steps and follow them into the old part of the village. It has been preserved, and no cars are allowed. I get into a short line in front of a house, which is the home of one of the children. I follow the line from room to room. It mostly consists of places to sleep and places to cook and eat. There is a loom room and a workshop. It is not a place of leisure. This makes sense to me. These were hard-working folk, doing subsistence farming and raising sheep.

I walk through the rest of the village but don't line up to see another house. Besides the children's houses and a few statues in gardens and groves, there are many souvenir shops and restaurants. This place doesn't seem to have the same restrictions as the sanctuary.

I walk back toward the sanctuary and the bus station, about two miles away. What were those children's mothers thinking, letting them be so far from home alone? I laugh at myself. It was a different time. Those children were working to support their families. Everyone worked just to survive. I am so blessed.

I will find the right bus. I have never even ridden buses before; we always drove. This is a new experience. But judging from the number of people at the station, it's typical in Portugal. And everything is in Portuguese. But I have a voice, and I use it. People are so kind and help me find the right bus.

CHAPTER 8

TOMAR

I really needed a day off from walking—a recovery day. Yeah, right. I check my pedometer. Over eight kilometers today with my backpack. Well, there's always tomorrow.

I leave the bus station in Tomar, and music fills the air. On the way to my pension, I come upon a stage and a spread of vendor tents around the corner. I'll go to my pension first, drop off my backpack, then come back and explore.

People are everywhere—children playing, balloons bobbing in the breeze, and adults laughing. Joy is in the air. The main street narrows into cobblestone lanes lined with old stone-faced stores and restaurants. A group of young people in black robes clusters at the next corner with instruments—playing, singing, and laughing. I stop to soak in the energy and am transported back to medieval times.

The musicians move on, and so do I. It's time to drop this pack and join the fun. The cobblestone lane opens into a plaza with black-and-white stone tiles in a checkerboard underfoot. A statue of a knight sits on a pedestal right in the center. I'm drawn to get a closer look. He looks like a knight from *Indiana Jones and the Last Crusade*, but this isn't a movie. It's real. I step closer and read the inscription: *D. Gvaldim Pais, Fvndador de Tomar 1160–1162–1938*. They look like dates. Below it are the dates 1162–1962: 800 years.

I turn to look for clues and see a church to the east. A plaque on the facade indicates that this church is dedicated to John the Baptist. But it's closed. My cue to find my pension.

Just past the church, I turn down a wider cobblestone street lined with pensions and restaurants spilling out into the street. Mine is only a few doors down. I open the door and am confronted with a metal staircase. My day wouldn't be complete without stairs.

The hospitaleiro steps out of a door connected to the first-floor lobby, wiping his mouth with a napkin. I must have interrupted his evening meal. In Europe, the ground floor is where you enter, and the first floor is one flight up.

"Do you need help with the stairs?" he asks in perfect English.

What a relief. English.

"No, thank you." I grab the railing and pull myself up the ten steep stairs to where he is standing. From behind a lectern, he pulls out a spiral notebook. He leafs through it and finds today's date at the top of the page.

"Ah, you must be Dorothy Wilson," he says, consulting the pencil marks on the page. He apologizes that the only room he can give me is up another flight of stairs.

I ask him about the statue in the plaza. This sparks a lecture on Tomar's history. He pulls out a map of the town, shows me where the tourist information, the Convent of Christ, the Templar castle, the Church of St. John the Baptist (which I saw in the square), and a synagogue are located. He tells me these are the most important sites to visit and shares their hours, noting they're not open now.

I ask him about doing laundry, and he takes me to a rooftop sitting area with a hose. He finds a bucket for me and shows me a small sink where I can pour out the used water. There's a clothesline strung between the buildings over an alleyway. It's a bit rustic, but so are my clothes.

I go up to my room. It has a small twin bed with just enough space for a dresser and a bedside table. I open the closet door and see that it's a bathroom. The toilet faces the room, and when I sit on it, my feet hang into the room. There is barely enough room to stand in front of the sink or squeeze through to the shower. But it is all mine. I don't have to share it with anyone.

I call Karen, and she answers on the first ring.

"Mom, what are you doing? First, you are going to Tomar, then you end up in Fátima."

"I decided to go to Fátima first. It was lovely. Now, I'm in Tomar."

"I know. I can follow you on the map."

Of course you can.

"That's wonderful," I say, remembering to send love with my words. "It's comforting to know you're keeping tabs on me. But truly, I'm fine. I'm loving this journey."

"Now what are you going to do?"

"I'll be here for a couple of days. There's plenty to see."

"You'll let me know when you decide to leave—and where you're going next."

"Yes, darling, I will."

Though she will know regardless. The small blue dot that is me moves obediently across her screen. It is meant as care, I remind myself. Still, I feel the faint tug of a short rein.

Once upon a time, I was the one asking where she was going. Now I report my movements like an adolescent with a curfew. I smile at the irony.

When we hang up, I slip the phone into my pocket and take a long breath. I am walking across a country. I am not lost. I am not fragile. I am a grown woman with sturdy shoes and a map of my own choosing.

I will start at the festival, then go see the sights in the morning. I walk back downstairs, and the proprietor is standing at the lectern. I ask him about D. Gvaldim Pais, the founder of Tomar.

He tells me that D. Gvaldim Pais was a Knight Templar who fought alongside King Afonso Henriques to retake Portugal from the Moors. The king was so impressed with him that he was granted knighthood. He also served in Jerusalem with the original Knights Templar. When he returned to Portugal, he rebuilt Almourol Castle and constructed Tomar Castle, which he says I will see tomorrow.

"I saw Almourol Castle. It was amazing."

"If you were amazed by Almourol, just wait until you see the Tomar castle and the Convent of Christ."

I can see how proud he is of his heritage.

"What is the Convent of Christ, and how is it different from the Templars? The tour guide at Almourol Castle said something about it, but I didn't quite understand."

"The Templars were extremely wealthy. They lent and managed money for some of the most powerful individuals of their time. Unfortunately, they had lent a fortune to King Philip IV of France. Good old Philip had neither the intention nor the means to pay them back. Pope Clement V was concerned about the Templars' growing power and wealth, so he and Philip conspired to dismantle the order.

On Friday the 13th, 1307, they arrested the Templar Grand Master Jacques de Molay, who was living in France, along with as many other Templars as they could find. The king imprisoned them, seized their assets, tortured them into confessing heresy, and then burned them at the stake. Some say this is why Friday the 13th became unlucky.

But we offered the survivors clemency—sanctuary. This was quite shrewd of us. The name Templar was changed to the Order of Christ, and they somehow managed to keep most of their assets in our fair country. You will see how significant and wealthy they were when you visit the Convent and Castle tomorrow."

"Tell me about this event you all have going on?" I ask. "I thought I would check it out."

"It is in honor of St. Iris, or Irene in English. She is our patron saint, and her day is October 20th. We celebrate for a week."

"Oh, so that's what the young people in the black robes with musical instruments were celebrating."

"Well, no, those are students celebrating the end of classes. We like to celebrate here." He winks. "Go, enjoy, and try some of our local food and drink."

"Thank you, I will. And thank you for the history lesson. You're amazing."

"No, Tomar is amazing." he smiles.

I walk by the river to the festival grounds and come upon a row of tents with all sorts of goodies. Stopping in front of a stall of walnuts, I buy a pound. I nibble a few as I make my way to a stall selling local liquors. I have to have a taste. The proprietor pours me a shot glass of *Ginjinha*. He says that it is made of cherries and pairs well with chocolate. The first sip slides smoothly across my tongue. He offers me a small square of chocolate as a chaser. It reminds me of the chocolate-covered cherries that Peter would bring when he visited us from Portugal. I have to be careful. This will go straight to my head.

I pay for a small airplane-sized bottle of Ginjinha and a chocolate bar. It will be a treat for later. I take a seat in front of the stage where a play for children is going on, and I just enjoy sitting. There are families milling around, and a group of old men are sitting at a table, sipping beer from a tent nearby.

The scents of aftershave, soap, and cigarette smoke waft past my nose, taking me back to the hotel room at the airport where I first met Peter. Wouldn't it be something, running into him after all these years? I wonder if there is anything left of that old spark.

It's strange. It only happened once, but the memory is so powerful. I shiver thinking of that afternoon, how carefully he brought me to a climax before surrendering to his own pleasure. Exquisite sex. I felt so alive.

Really, Scarf, I must be fair. Sex with Roy was good—more than good. It was steady, affectionate, and rooted in the kind of trust that only years can build. As time passed, we had to be more intentional, to surprise each other, to keep the familiar from becoming merely habitual.

But when Roy died, I didn't just lose a husband. I lost the easy reach across the bed. The warmth of another body in the night. The quiet language of touch that needs no words. Widowhood is not just the absence of a person. It is the sudden emptiness where affection once lived.

If by chance I ever meet Peter again, it will be on my terms—not as the younger woman who responded to a man's desire before she understood her own.

I nibble a piece of chocolate and follow it with a small sip of the Ginjinha. I sigh as I put the top back on the bottle.

"Good, eh?" a man says from behind me.

I turn. It's Sean, and Sydney is with him. I jump up and hug them both like long-lost friends, careful not to spill my precious treats.

"Where's Ian?" I ask.

"He's back at the hostel, grabbing a wee nap. We'll meet up later on for dinner. Any chance you'd like to join us?" Sean says.

"You bet."

"We're heading back now. Meet us down at the Curry Indian House at eight, will ya?" Sydney says.

"You're starting to sound Irish."

She laughs, and we hug again. I promise to meet them. What a wonderful treat. I won't be dining alone tonight.

• • •

I reach the restaurant first and get a table for four. The three straggle in, with Ian looking like death warmed over. I jump up and fuss over them. They bring out the grandmother in me.

"So why are you here? You left a couple of days ahead of me, and I have been taking my sweet time."

"Well," Sydney says and looks at the boys. "First, I came down with a nasty bug, then it spread through the pilgrims like wildfire. I must have caught it on the plane."

Heat rises in my face. "Maybe it's my fault. I had a touch of something in Lisboa, but I had had my flu vaccine, and it only had me down for about twenty-four hours."

"Well, none of us are vaccinated. I thought that was only for old people, but it sure has put a crimp in our Caminho," Sydney confesses.

"I'm so sorry," I say.

"I'm on the far side of it now," Ian says. "I thought I might dodge the whole thing, but two days back, on the road out of Santarém, I started feeling a bit off. Still and all, I'm grand enough—just starving, is all."

"Well, you must be on the mend. Let's get you something to eat. A good curry will cure you," I say, trying to lift his spirits.

"We're that far behind now, I might have to get the bus on a bit," Seán adds. "Otherwise, I'll never make it home in time for work."

"Can you call your boss and see if they will cut you some slack?" I ask.

"Me boss is me dad. He's fierce about the work—no slack at all."

"Yes, family can be hard. I have been trying a new technique I learned at an albergue in Vilada. It seems to be working well for me. Spend a few moments and let a feeling of love flow through your body." I turn to Ian with a smile. "Not that kind of love."

He groans and then laughs at me.

"Send a beam of love to your dad. Then call him and ask, and see what happens. It all may work out," I suggest.

"Sounds like pure Irish hocus-pocus. Still, I've nothing to lose. I'll give it a lash and let you know if there's any magic in it."

The waiter appears with our food, and we tuck into a delicious meal.

"When will you all start walking again?" I ask, wondering if I will be on their schedule now. I'm not sure I want to give up my independence.

"We'll start again tomorrow," Sydney says. "Do you want to come with us?"

"No, tomorrow I will go see the Convent of Christ and explore the town. I only arrived this afternoon."

"See you in Santiago for the birthday party then. I haven't forgotten," she says with a smile and gives me a farewell hug.

> POST: I arrived in Tomar thinking I'd be on my own tonight. Instead, I found music in the streets, generosity at every turn, and dear Caminho friends to share dinner with. This road keeps reminding me: I may walk alone, but I am not alone.

• • •

Awake early, I go find an open café. I have my breakfast of champions—café con leche and pastéis de nata.

The castle and the convent don't open until nine a.m., but I walk over there anyway. There is an open gate leading to a garden and a statue out front of the Infante D. Henrique. It says he was the governor of the Order of Christ in 1420. My head is spinning from all these names and titles. I walk into the garden instead. Even though it's autumn, I can see the promise of beauty.

I check the time, then follow a path from the garden

up a hill to the castle. I reach a round tower and an open gateway. There's no place to pay, so I go inside. There's no way to enter the tower. Through the gate, the inner courtyard of the castle unfolds before me. The exterior crenelated walls attract me, and I climb a stone staircase. The view from the top of the wall, overlooking the city of Tomar below, is breathtaking.

I wander around the top of the wall, searching for an easier way down. How do I get myself into these situations? I'm kind of like the cat that gets stuck in the tree; it's fun climbing up, but coming back down is terrifying. I understand how my phobia works, and here I am again. Well, there's no one to rescue me now, so I have to figure it out. Isn't one of the reasons I'm on this pilgrimage to push my own boundaries? To fully experience life before I die. I keep reminding myself that if it were truly dangerous, there wouldn't be a way to access it, just like the tower.

I see and hear a tour group through a stone lattice in a wall above me. I yell to them, but they ignore me. I want to join them, but how did they get up there? I make my way along the wall. There is a set of stairs with a railing. I slowly make my way down, one step at a time. It leads me into an orchard, with a path that goes to a medieval gate. The massive wooden doors are open to me, but I can see how impenetrable this castle would be to an enemy.

Out through the gate, there are signs to the tourist entryway. Tour buses are parked along the roadway. There's a road up here? I consult my map, and sure enough, there is a road. Well, the garden was prettier.

I pay at the entrance and am given a set of headphones with English audio.

I step into the *Charola*—round, twelfth century, and unlike any chapel I have seen before. And it was inspired by the temple in Jerusalem.

I head to the living quarters. The hallways are so long, lined with small monk cells with stone floors that have just enough room for a bed. Winters must have been freezing cold. I can't even imagine living here.

The dining room has huge, long stone tables and a display case with monogrammed pottery. I walk down some stone steps to reach the underground cistern, which is more like a cavern, and it's fed by an aqueduct. They even have a laundry. This was the perfect place to be when the Moors tried to invade, as they could survive inside these walls for years. I understand why it's a UNESCO World Heritage Site.

I walk back down to Tomar through the garden and find a place for lunch. Then it's off to the Church of St. John the Baptist and a Jewish synagogue. I hadn't thought about Jews being in a town so centered on Christ. I learned that there was a large Jewish population in this town in the fifteenth century, and that they coexisted with the Christians. What a history! I love that they coexisted, but it didn't last. Eventually, the Jews were expelled from both Spain and Portugal. But now they have acknowledged the history of the Jews in Tomar and refurbished the synagogue. There is hope for a peaceful world, just like Our Lady of Fátima advocates.

I finish visiting the must-see places, then head back to the festival area and buy some more snacks for dinner and the road. There's a children's play on the main stage, and I watch it for a while, enjoying the children's reactions in the audience. I wish my family were here to enjoy this festival. Feeling a bit homesick, I walk back to my hotel and text Karen to let her know I'll be leaving Tomar in the morning.

I'm a stranger here—a pilgrim. I truly don't belong, but I am welcome.

What is a pilgrim? Anyone can put on a backpack and go on a tour. But I get special prices to stay at albergues and for 'pilgrim's meals', yet that is just the surface. I know I don't want to stay here in Tomar and be a tourist. I want to walk. Maybe that's what a pilgrim is. Someone who walks and gets a small taste of the world, which opens their eyes and broadens their minds to many possibilities. I was thinking of staying another day, but I don't want to. I want to walk.

I remember and text Karen: *I'm leaving Tomar tomorrow and will go to Cortiça.*

She texts back a heart.

My heart leaps with joy. It's the weirdest feeling. Actually, I can only compare it to how a puppy acts when you say, "Do you want to go for a walk?" The tail starts wagging, the mouth opens slightly, and the entire body shakes with excitement. The happiness and excitement are clear. That's how I feel.

I wanna go for a walk, Scarf.

CHAPTER 9

TOMAR TO ANSIÃO

I wake before sunrise, shoulder my pack, and head out to find an open café. The only other people awake are the street cleaners. They'll know where I can get breakfast. I ask one, and he points to the end of the street, then gestures for me to turn right. I love that we can communicate this way.

As I turn the corner, there is a pool of light down the block on the right. Walking into the café, I can smell the coffee. My mouth starts to water.

There are a few other early birds in the café. The display cases are full of lovely pastries. I order a café con leche and pastéis de nata for breakfast. The creamy filling oozes into my mouth, and the protein gives me the energy to walk all day. Or maybe it's the sugar. I laugh at myself and my dietary justifications.

I look at my guidebook. I will walk to Cortiça—twenty-six kilometers. There's no way I'm walking the recommended thirty-two kilometers to the next albergue, especially since it's all uphill. The flat land is behind me.

I make reservations at the *quinta's* dorm. A quinta is an old estate with a manor house, outbuildings—often including a chapel and a stable—and surrounding farmland. I'll see when I get there.

I leave Tomar, and the arrows guide me onto a dirt trail. It feels wonderful to hike through the woods. I enjoyed the farmland scenery, but this feels more like wilderness hiking. The sound of lumberjacks harvesting eucalyptus trees in the background reminds me that I'm not far from civilization. After a short climb, the path drops down toward the river and passes under a huge highway bridge. Once I'm under the bridge, my mind goes where it always goes—desperate people sleep under bridges.

The hairs on the back of my neck stand up. I've heard stories—rare but real—of men exposing themselves to female pilgrims. There's no one else out here but me. I couldn't get help if I screamed. The loggers wouldn't hear me.

Okay, Scarf, I am getting myself all worked up over nothing. I'm ruining the beauty of the woods, the river path, with fear.

Thinking about Luz and her advice to stay in a state of love. I consider my advice to Sean. I must practice what I preach. I work on replacing feelings of fear with love. Yes,

I should heed my intuition, and while fear can be a warning, I don't want to panic unnecessarily.

I make sure my phone is easily accessible, ready to dial 112, the emergency number in Europe. I breathe through the fear; I refuse to let it control me. I remind myself that for the best outcome, I need to stay in love. I picture Ashley again and smile—staying in love while remaining aware of my surroundings. This elevates my practice to a whole new level. I pass under the highway, and the path begins to rise again. The birds are singing in the trees, and I start to relax. As they say on Star Trek: "Stand down from Red Alert."

I plant my poles to help me tackle the incline. I love these poles. They are saving my knees.

The path ends at a paved road leading into a small village named Cálvanos. Two pilgrims are sitting at a bar having coffee. I join them. It's so good to finally be in the presence of other pilgrims. This is my tribe.

The man introduces himself as Luc from Belgium, and the woman as Kate from the Netherlands.

"Are you the woman I saw at the hotel just outside Lisbon?"

She looks at me closely. "Yes, I am."

"You sure look better today than you did at the hotel."

She smiles. "I'm not going to walk that far in one day again. I will only walk a short distance today, and I must go.

I have to get to my albergue." She stands up and leaves. Not so friendly, this tribe member.

"I'm headed to Cortiça," Luc says. "These old bones don't do thirty-kilometer days."

"So am I." We're going to the same town, and there is only one place to stay. He picks up my empty coffee cup and takes it into the bar. What a lovely gentleman. When he comes back, I thank him.

"See you tonight," he says, then shoulders his pack.

I go into the bar and use the bathroom. I shoulder my pack, grab my poles, and step out onto the road.

What am I thinking, Scarf? I just talked myself through a potential scare, and now I'm telling a complete stranger where I'll be staying tonight. It's like if someone has a backpack and claims to be a pilgrim, they're trustworthy—or so we like to believe. Well, not entirely. There was nothing about him that raised suspicion. He's older, from Belgium, speaks great English, and he sounds educated. I don't pick up anything to fear from him. At least I won't be alone at the Quinta. The owners will be there. It's not like I've agreed to go to a deserted place.

I quickly catch up to Luc. I try to slow my pace, but it doesn't feel comfortable. Why shouldn't I walk at my own pace?

He comments that I'm a fast walker. This surprises me, since he's much taller than I. We talk about pilgrimage, and

I learn that he has walked through France. That sounds wonderful. I'll add it to my bucket list.

"One of the things I've learned when doing long-distance pilgrimages is to walk at your own pace," he says. "I'll see you at the quinta."

I smile and say, "Bom Caminho," as I pick up my pace. My instincts are right. This man doesn't want to hurt me.

I spot a small bench a few kilometers later and sit down to enjoy the apple and nuts I bought in Tomar.

Luc comes along. "May I join you?"

My mouth is full of apple, I nod. He pulls a sandwich and a banana from his backpack. We chat a little about our lives, and I learn he's married. No wonder he's so considerate.

"How about your wife? Does she not like to go on pilgrimage?"

"My wife likes to walk, but she's still working and cannot get away." He winks at me. "Someone in the family has to pay the bills."

I laugh and tell him that I'm a merry widow, spending all of my children's inheritance. I don't want to talk about Roy—not to a stranger anyway. I don't want to bring down the mood. It's wonderful to have a pleasant discourse with a gentleman. I miss that.

I shoulder my pack and start heading downhill. He yells that I am going the wrong way. I turn around and walk back up the hill to the crossroads where I sat for lunch. He points out a yellow arrow I had missed around the corner. There's a blue arrow pointing down the hill toward Fátima. I've been there, done that. I laugh at myself and thank him.

He smiles. "Bom Caminho. See you tonight."

I arrive at the quinta just as the rain begins. The iron gate is open, leading into a courtyard with a buggy on display and a covered veranda attached to the main house on the left. On the right, there's a separate building with empty horse stalls and some farm equipment. It feels like I'm walking onto a hacienda straight out of a movie set in the Old West.

A friendly woman welcomes me into the main house. She introduces herself as Maria and offers me a glass of wine. I decline, wanting to clean up before I get too comfortable.

I look around the room. To my left, there's a spacious living area with leather couches, overstuffed chairs, and a grand fireplace. Beyond an open archway are tables and chairs. Maria walks toward a desk at the back of the living room. I follow, and she offers me a chair beside the desk. She takes a seat behind the desk and logs into her computer. Through the open door behind her, there's another room—a large formal dining room, decorated in keeping with the hacienda style.

Beyond the formal dining room, glass doors open onto a pool deck and a vegetable garden. She checks me in and asks if I want dinner. I say yes and place my order. She adds it to the bill and tells me breakfast is included with the bunk.

On the way to the bunk room, Maria points out the small breakfast room off the living room, which I noticed when I entered. She mentions that fresh bread will be delivered by seven a.m., and that breakfast will be self-serve. She shows me the refrigerator stocked with milk, butter, jam, cheese, ham, and yogurt. There is a bowl of fruit and a canister of muesli on the sideboard. She says the coffee will be ready in the urn and shows me where the cups, plates, and utensils are stored. Then she takes me outside to another building set up as a dorm room with four sets of bunk beds and a bathroom. She points out the laundry next door, which has a sink and a drying rack.

I'm the only one there and have my choice. I pick the bottom bunk, closest to the bathroom. After showering, I look at my basic clothes. What do I wear to dinner at a hacienda, or rather, a Quinta? I don't have many options. I wear my skirt and shirt for walking and keep a pair of old hiking pants and a few heavier shirts as backups for warmth. I select a long-sleeved merino wool shirt and pull on my old hiking pants. It's good enough. They have to be used to pilgrims and what we carry. I hand-wash my clothes and hang them up to dry in the laundry room.

I walk back into the main house. Luc has arrived and is sitting in the living room drinking a beer. He must have a private room because no one else has entered the bunk room. I have a private room by default, too.

Busy on a phone call, he gestures for me to come over. I remember to text Karen to let her know I'm safe, so I take care of that quick task, then post on Facebook.

> POST: Today the Caminho asked me to trust—my instincts, the road, and the quiet kindness of a fellow pilgrim. Fear showed up, but it didn't get the final word. I walked on.

Maria comes in and asks if we'd like anything to drink. Luc asks if I would like a glass of wine and what I prefer. I tell him that I would be pleased to have a glass, and I like white.

Maria goes over to a wine rack, and Luc follows her. They begin a discussion about the merits of Portuguese wine versus wine from other countries. Luc chooses a local wine and buys a bottle for us.

We sip wine and get to know each other. His work as a doctor was in research, particularly in the pharmaceutical industry, specializing in vaccine research. I find it fascinating, especially with the vaccine controversy back home.

Luc is straightforward. He believes Americans are naive, allowing diseases once eliminated by vaccines to return. I completely agree. All my kids and grandkids have been vaccinated. I remember my mother, who had a permanent limp and many health issues later in life because she had polio as a child. She was firm about us getting our vaccines.

What a lovely evening. I had forgotten how it feels to sip wine and converse with an intelligent man.

Roy was sharp—before Alzheimer's took him. We used to have the liveliest conversations. Luc's wife is a lucky woman, and I think it's probably mutual.

Luc pulls out his guidebook. "How far are you walking tomorrow?"

I consult my guidebook. "I'm thinking about Ansião."

"Yes, that seems like a reasonable distance. The hotel looks nice, and it says they have an excellent restaurant. I'll call them. May I book you a room?"

"Yes, please," I say, relieved that I don't have to struggle with the language barrier.

He says something into the phone, then covers the mouthpiece with his hand. "It costs thirty-five euros for a single room with a bathroom, including breakfast, and they offer a pilgrim's dinner for an extra fifteen euros. Is that all right?"

"That's perfect," I say, and he makes the arrangements.

"I like to know where I am spending the night after a long day of walking," Luc says.

"I agree. I usually book the next night, too."

Dinner is announced. Luc picks up his glass of wine and the bottle, and I carry my glass into the formal dining room.

Dinner is a delicious lamb curry. I just won't think about the poor lamb that gave its life for us. The vegetables are fresh from the garden behind the main house. The dinner conversation is excellent.

Dinner now finished, we retreat to our respective rooms. I reflect on the dinners Roy and I used to have. I recall when we went to Italy and sat at a small café by the water. The meal was relaxed, the food was delicious, and the wine, of course, was local and excellent. We talked and held hands for hours. No one hurried us. Tears start running down my cheeks, and I let them. I miss him so much.

CHAPTER 10

ANSIÃO TO COIMBRA

I wake early. With the rain, a cold front moves in. I shiver as I pull on my still-damp clothes. My body heat will dry them as I walk. I am alone for breakfast. I don't know whether Luc has already left.

Thinking about Luc, I wonder if I am ready for a relationship or a fling. Could I even kiss him, knowing he is married?

No, Scarf, I don't think so.

Luc hasn't made any romantic moves toward me at all. I'm unsure whether I should feel relieved or crushed by this. Maybe I'm too old to attract a man. Maybe he's just very married, and he's a lonely pilgrim like me, enjoying the company of another.

It is about feeling attractive again—not for approval, but for myself. It's about recognizing that I am still desirable, still alive in my body, still capable of wanting and being wanted.

What age has given me is choice. I no longer stand at the mercy of biology or reputation. There is no fear of pregnancy, no small life depending on a single decision. That freedom alters everything. Desire is no longer tangled with dread.

I spent enough years in Hollywood to understand the subtle transactions, the way stardom was promised with expectations tucked quietly beneath it. Relationships, now, can exist along the whole spectrum—from conversation and shared laughter to touch and intimacy—and I am the one who decides how far it goes. Not from hunger. Not from flattery. Not from the old script of possession. But from strength, from my own clear choosing.

Before I know it, I have summited the hill. I stop at a picnic table strategically placed under a beautiful oak tree and pull out the cheese sandwich and apple I pilfered from breakfast. Maybe that's the key to walking up and down hills—distraction.

Dark clouds are rolling in across the fields below. I pull out my rain gear. After lunch, I gear up and start walking downhill towards Ansião, about nine kilometers away. The rain starts in big fat drops that bring more and more with them. The dirt path becomes slick as the water turns it into a small stream. I slow my pace and, using my poles, carefully place each foot. I don't lift one foot until I am secure on the other. It is a slow process, but safety first.

As I approach the town, the path turns to cobblestones, and I deliberately step through a puddle to rinse the mud from my shoes. They're wet anyway—might as well make them cleaner. The yellow arrows guide me through town. The hotel is on a block with several other stores and faces a bar and restaurant. I try to shake off most of the water before I go inside. The owner is busy serving other customers while I stand there shivering and dripping onto his floor.

He finally turns to me, and I explain that I have a reservation. He checks me in, takes my dinner order, and tells me dinner is at eight. I go up to my room and take a hot shower. There is a drying rack in the bathroom, so I rinse the worst of the road dirt from my clothes and hang them on it. I love these heated drying racks. There are definite advantages to hotel rooms over dorm rooms.

Checking the time, I know that Karen is still at work. I text her to let her know I am safe. I then take advantage of the rainy afternoon and open a novel set in Portugal on my phone. I have been too tired to read much at night.

I wake to a knock on my door.

"Just a minute," I say. I pull on my clothes and check my phone. I have been sleeping for over two hours. So much for reading.

"Just meet me in the dining room for dinner," Luc calls through the door.

"Okay," I call back. Yes, his wife is a lucky woman.

In the dining room, I take a seat at the table across from Luc. He points to the carafe of wine. I nod, and he pours me a glass. We keep discussing world problems and pilgrimage, agreeing that if more world leaders took pilgrimages, the world would be a much more peaceful place.

The woman serving dinner looks remarkably like a portrait on the wall. Luc asks her about this in Portuguese since she doesn't speak any English. He translates. The portrait is of her mother. The hotel, bar, and restaurant have been family-owned for five generations.

I value the continuity of history, but I wonder whether this woman ever had the chance to pursue her dreams. Or maybe this is her dream, too. Still, she looks worn out.

After dinner, we review our options and decide to walk past Rabaçal and book a place in Zambujal. We enjoy walking the same distances, although I'm faster than he is. I suspect it's because he likes to stop at bars for a beer. How judgmental of me. This is a different culture. They find beer refreshing. I find a beer so relaxing that I don't want to move, and that becomes a problem.

Heading to Zambujal will mean a shorter walk to Coimbra the next day. Luc tells me when he gets to Coimbra, he's going home. This makes me sad. I've really enjoyed this time with him. But we still have another night in Zambujal.

• • •

The rain is pelting down when I rise for breakfast. I eat slowly, waiting for Luc to emerge. By the time I finish, he still has not shown himself, and the rain has slacked off. Time to walk.

The path mainly consists of rock and mud. Blue arrows point south toward Fátima, while some yellow arrows point north to Santiago. A man with a backpack approaches me. He looks gaunt and seems to have been walking for a long time.

"Bom Caminho," he says in greeting. "Where are you headed?"

"I'm going to Santiago."

"I came from there," he says. "I'm headed south."

"You have walked to Santiago and now are walking back south?" It's incredible. I have about 400 more kilometers to go to Santiago, and he has come from there.

"Yes, I am thinking of going to Fátima. There are a couple more pilgrims coming up behind me who are going that way."

So many questions are swirling through my brain, but I don't want to impose.

"It's all downhill until Coimbra. Enjoy," he says.

"Thank you, Bom Caminho."

We both start walking in opposite directions. I hadn't thought about this before, but I had heard some people leave their homes and walk to Santiago, and I just assumed they would take a plane, bus, or train home. But maybe not. They must have walked from home before we had motorized transportation. What an endeavor to start walking, knowing you have to walk back.

The muddy path descends from the rocky, barren hills to lush groves of olive trees on sunlit slopes. The harvest is in full swing, but workers take a moment to call out "Bom Caminho." Music plays from the radios in their vehicles, and I even see a few camper vans parked in the groves. They must rely on migrant workers just as we do back home.

The farm track leads to a paved road, and my albergue is at the edge of town. A sign on the gate makes it clear that pilgrims are welcome. A young man answers the bell and introduces himself. He guides me to a cabin on a hill behind the house. It has a bedroom and a bathroom, and it's quite cozy. On the wall, there is a fully stamped credencial in a frame and a Compostela.

"Are these yours, Miguel?" I ask.

"Yes, we walk part of the Caminho every year. This one is from the year I met my wife, Sophia," he says.

"You met your wife on the Caminho?"

"Yes, I'm originally from Africa and came to Portugal to walk. I met her on the second day at an albergue. She's Portuguese. We talked all night. I knew she was the one. We walked and planned our lives. We love living off the land and hosting pilgrims. I built this cabin myself."

"Africa. That's interesting."

"Yes, Portugal used to have colonies in Africa. Portugal is a seafaring nation, and it's a short sail to Africa, so it's easy for us to move between the two countries."

"That's so amazing. And you are quite a carpenter."

"That was my job back in Africa, and it's an easily transferable skill. You will enjoy dinner. All the ingredients are from our garden or locally sourced. Sophia is an excellent cook." He pats his tummy, but I don't see any extra rolls there.

"I'm looking forward to it," I reply.

"Now, I'll let you get cleaned up. I'll send my daughter up to knock on your door when dinner is ready." He steps off the porch and heads down the hill.

I thank him and head into the cabin to clean up. I shiver and turn on the space heater.

POST: Winter is beginning to whisper in Portugal. Harvested fields, shorter days, cooler nights—and a pilgrim grateful for warmth, shelter, and this road.

It's dark and raining when his daughter comes to get me for dinner. She skips back to the house. I put on my poncho and carefully make the short walk across the yard. I knock on the door and am let into a warm home. Leaving my shoes at the front door, I follow Sophia into the kitchen. She offers me a glass of wine, some cheese, and olives to enjoy while she cooks dinner. Luc comes in from another door. There must be a whole other wing of rooms for pilgrims.

Sophia calls for the rest of the family. The older girl I met when she came up to get me for dinner and her younger brother appear and take their seats. Miguel follows behind.

"Would you like olive oil for your bread?" Sophia asks.

"Yes, please. I am going to start doing this at home. It has to be healthier than butter. I saw the harvest as I walked through the groves today. How many olives does it take to make oil?"

"One tree, if it's healthy and producing well, will yield about fifteen kilograms of olives, which can make roughly two liters of oil."

"That's all? I go through that at home in a couple of months. Do you press your own olives?"

"No, we belong to a co-op where there are facilities to press the olives."

"And are these your olives?" I take another one of the delicious black olives and pop it into my mouth.

"Yes, they are."

"I'll have to confess, I pulled one off a tree on my way to Fátima, and it was terrible. Are there different kinds?"

Sophia laughs. "They all taste terrible off the tree. They have to be cured. Once harvested, we wash them thoroughly, then soak them in a cask of brine and spices. We usually let ours cure for at least a year, but the best ones are cured for five years or more."

"These are really tasty."

"Obrigada," Sophia says.

With everyone at the table, our host says the blessing, and we eat a vegetarian dinner of spaghetti, beans, and tons of vegetables. I'm loving the vegetables here in Portugal. I'm so blessed to be walking at harvest time.

Turning to the children when they finish eating, Sophia speaks to them in Portuguese.

Luc laughs. "This is universal, always asking the children if they have done their homework." The children laugh too.

"What are your favorite subjects?" Luc asks in English.

The boy appears to be around twelve or thirteen, and without hesitation, he says, "I want to be a doctor."

"Did you know that I'm a doctor? You have chosen a tough profession."

"My teachers say I am good at science. I really like biology. We get to dissect a frog next week at school."

"Good on you," says Luc. He turns to the girl. She is a little older, probably fifteen or sixteen.

"I want to be a chef and only use organic ingredients. We must take care of our bodies." She sounds older than her years, grounded and certain.

They switch to Portuguese as Luc talks with the children about their lives. As he interacts with them, he lights up. We had discussed our grandchildren one night over dinner. It's so wonderful to see him engaging with these children.

Before Alzheimer's took hold, Roy and our grandchildren shared a special bond. He would take them hiking in the hills and teach them all about the movie industry. They still recall their adventures with him. They were so caring toward him when he was sick. Ashley would sit with him and sing his favorite songs. Sometimes he would join in. He had a lovely voice. It stayed true almost to the very end.

That's how we met. He was in the church choir that hired me to replace their retiring director. He could hit those high notes, would always clown around at the right times, and would work hard when he needed to. His singing cast a spell over me. We were meant for each other.

"I'm so sorry," Sophia says. "We're speaking Portuguese and leaving you out. We must speak English."

"No, this is your country. I wish I knew your language, but I've never been very good at languages. I was enjoying the family harmony. You have a lovely family."

"Thank you," Sophia says, then chases the children off to do their homework.

"What do you want for breakfast? We have fresh eggs and, of course, bread, jams, and jelly. I make my own."

"All of the above," Luc and I say simultaneously. Walking works up an appetite.

Sophia offers to have it ready for us at seven-thirty a.m.

I go back to my cabin, log on to the Wi-Fi, and book a hostel for two nights in Coimbra. I'm not sure how long my money will last, and I can't keep spending it on hotels and pricey dinners.

I call Karen. "Darling, it is so good to hear your voice."

"It's a relief to hear you, too, Mom. Where are you?"

"I'm staying with a family at an albergue in an olive grove. It's lovely. They have two young teens, and I thought of the grandchildren. How are they?"

"Well, you know, being teenagers. How did you and Dad survive those years?"

I laugh. "You and Karl were good kids. We were lucky. And so are you."

"Yes, they don't cause me the trouble that some others get into."

"Well, darling. I just wanted to check in. I need to get some sleep. I have a long walk tomorrow."

"Goodnight, Mom. And thanks for checking in."

• • •

While eating breakfast, I tell Luc that I have booked an albergue in Coimbra. He says he hasn't made plans for the night yet. He will go to Coimbra first, spend the night, and then take a train to Porto and fly home. I feel a pit forming in my stomach. I'll be alone again.

I go back to my cabin, take care of my morning toilet, then pack and walk down to the main house. I don't see anyone, and I don't want to disturb them, so I start walking.

The road transforms into a forest footpath covered with gold and brown leaves. There's a river that the path follows, but it runs far below me in a gorge. The scenery is breathtaking. There are more arrows for Fátima pointing back the way I came and more marks for the GR trails than yellow arrows, but my app confirms I am on the right track.

I reach the outskirts of Conimbriga and find Luc sitting outside a café, drinking coffee. I drop my pack at his table and go inside to order one for myself. I join Luc, and we pick up our conversation as easily as an old married couple, not two people who met days ago.

He finishes and announces that he's going to get a head start because he knows I will catch up with him. I laugh, lean back, and sip my coffee.

He shoulders his pack and says, "Bom Caminho."

I've heard there are some well-preserved Roman ruins here, but given the threatening weather and the time, I'm not going to stay and sightsee. I shoulder my pack and follow the arrows through the city. One city begins to blend into another. I turn onto a side road where tourist buses are parked, and an overlook offers a view. Urban sprawl is alive and well here. I wonder where Coimbra begins. There is a line of black clouds coming in from the east. As I walk back to the Caminho, there's a shout, and I look toward the sound. A couple is running toward the buses, which are surrounded by tourists.

There seems to be an ongoing debate about the difference between tourists and pilgrims. There was a sign in an albergue that said, 'Tourists demand, pilgrims are grateful.' I definitely feel grateful not to be on someone else's schedule. I can take my time, explore, and enjoy experiences as they come. I don't have to rush to catch a tour bus. But if that rain comes in faster than I can reach my albergue, I'd rather be on a tour bus.

But maybe that's part of the difference. With a pilgrimage, there are hardships and obstacles to overcome. On a tour, you have paid someone to pave the way for you and make it easy. Maybe I would rather not be on a tour bus, even if it rains. After living with death for so long, it's the challenges that are bringing me back to life.

CHAPTER 11

COIMBRA

I cross the river into Coimbra just as the rain begins. The riverfront is stunning, with parks on both sides and walking paths threading along the water. A tall bronze statue of a man greets me, welcoming me into the city's commercial district. The cobblestone streets are lined with restaurants and shops. Shielding my phone from the rain, I follow the map up a narrow, steep side street through a medieval-looking gate. This city knew how to defend itself.

There's a coffee shop with beautiful pastries just inside the gate. People are lined up to get theirs, even in the rain. I know where I'll be having breakfast tomorrow. I follow the narrow cobblestone lane up the hill to my albergue.

Inside, there's the reception and a large common room with a small kitchen. When I check in, I am given the code to the front door. A room on the second floor, two flights up. No wonder people here can eat all the pastries they want and stay slim. All I've been doing since I arrived in town is climbing hills or stairs.

I have two roommates for tonight: a young woman, Maura, a pilgrim from New Zealand who looks young (she must be in her twenties), and a woman about Karen's age, Zoe, from Ireland.

Maura is sharing a story about when she walked out of Tomar into a lonely part of the forest. She noticed the arrows seemed vandalized, and some pointed in the wrong direction on her map. She said she heard a sound on the other side as she approached the river. She looked across the river, and there was a man masturbating. She said she froze, then, realizing there was a river between them, she yelled, blew her whistle on the chest strap of her backpack, and took off running as fast as she could.

She said she had to stop running at the top of the next hill, totally out of breath. She turned and looked, but there was no sign of anyone. For a moment, she wondered if it had been real but then trusted that it was. She had cell service at the top of the hill and called the police. They said that since she was not in immediate danger, they would meet her at the next town. If the circumstances changed, she should call and they would be standing by. She said she talked to them in the next town, and as she made her report, she remembered that there was an old ruin behind the man. The police said they would investigate, but she has not heard of any follow-up yet.

"I am so glad you are safe and reported it to the police," I say.

"Me too," Zoe says. "He needs to be castrated."

"Agreed," Maura and I say in unison.

"You two hold him down," Maura says. "I'll use my pocketknife. It should make a fine mess of the job."

"Thank you for sharing," I say. "I'll be more cautious when I walk. It never even occurred to me. I thought it was safe for women here."

"It is safer here than in many other countries, but there are idiots everywhere. The police take it seriously, too," Maura adds. "But let's not give him any more power over our Caminhos. I want to tell you about the coolest tour I took, for just a donation. I simply booked it online." She pulls up the website and shows us how.

"Yes, you're right," I tell her. "We will not let the perverts ruin our experience. So, tell me about this tour."

"I was in Lisboa, and a pilgrim staying at the same hostel invited me to join her on a free walking tour. We met the tour guide at a central location, and he took us around explaining the sites. We didn't go inside any place that would have required paying an entrance fee. I then went back later to the places I was particularly interested in," Maura says. "When we were finished, we tipped him according to what we thought the tour was worth. He worked hard and was so knowledgeable."

Zoe pulls up the website and asks if I want to book one with her for tomorrow afternoon. I agree. It would be fun to spend the afternoon touring the town with someone.

Maura also shares information about a free Fado show at a local café and another restaurant that offers affordable pilgrim meals. This woman is a wealth of information.

"What's Fado?" I ask.

"It's the region's music, kind of like folk music, and quite sad. Mostly about broken hearts. It is beautiful and definitely worth experiencing. The show starts at six p.m."

"I heard back from the tour guide, and we are scheduled for a two-hour tour at four p.m. tomorrow," Zoe tells me.

"I wonder if we can end at the Fado café? Do you want to join us, Maura?" I ask.

"No, I'll start walking tomorrow. I'm a bit pressed for time and need to get to Santiago in time to catch my plane home."

"I'll ask if he can end at the café." Zoe messages him back, and he replies affirmatively.

"That's perfect. I have a ticket to the Joanina Library at the University in the morning. Well, I'd better get cleaned up and then find something to eat. I need to do laundry, too," I say.

"There's an inexpensive laundromat close by," Maura says. "I did mine today."

I open my pack and take out my clean clothes. I'm not sure how clean they are since all I have been able to do is rinse them in a sink. Smelling the target zones, I don't find any offensive odors, but I could be used to my own odors.

I head to the shower, thinking about Maura's experience with the man by the river. That could have been me. She is young and seems resilient. I have tried to downplay the dangers to my daughter. I don't want her worrying about me or even trying to stop me.

Life is dangerous. How trite. I think about my first pregnancy with Karen. It was touch-and-go there at the end, with my blood pressure skyrocketing. Choosing to do it again with the knowledge that I could die was a risk I was willing to take to bring a second child into the world. I have been taking risks my entire life, and I am not going to stop now. Even breathing is a risk. We learned that in the pandemic. But like during the pandemic, we mitigated our risk by wearing masks, keeping our distance, and washing our hands frequently. I mitigated the risks for this pilgrimage by training, educating myself on what to pack, and learning the route. And Valerie sent me this lovely scarf, connecting me to all the women who have done this before me.

I text Karen, letting her know I'm safe and telling her what I plan to do on my zero day tomorrow. Backpackers call it a zero day when you are not walking the trail. From the way things are shaping up, I will be walking a lot tomorrow, but at least I won't have to carry my pack.

Karen responds: *Oh, Mom, that sounds wonderful. I wish I could be with you.*

I text back: *Wish you could be here too, darling. I'll post pictures.*

•••

Awake now, I get the laundromat's address from the hospitaleiro and add it to my map app. I can go start the laundry, then find a place close by for breakfast. The map leads me back down to the commercial area and up another side street. Then it points me left up a narrow, steep stone staircase that looks to go on forever. The laundromat is at the top of the staircase. I start up. The stones are polished and uneven from years of use. Stopping on a small landing, I venture a look behind me. The view over the river is spectacular, but looking down makes me dizzy. I quickly look back up, but I can't see the top. There's nothing to do but keep going up. I grab the scarf and invoke Valerie's courage. I lose count of the steps as my pace slows, and gravity tugs me out into space. I start to sweat.

A couple of young boys with school-size backpacks come rocketing down towards me. I hug the wall and let them pass. I start climbing again. The steps end at a narrow archway. The laundromat is across the road.

We did it, Scarf. There's no way I'm going back down there to find breakfast. My stomach can wait.

I put my clothes in the washer, sit for a minute, and Google that staircase. It has a name and is marked as a tourist attraction, Escadas do Quebra-Costas. Good thing I'm not a tourist. I don't want to do that again. I'll look for an alternative route back to the hostel, and the map shows it on the same road as the laundromat. Wait a minute. There are cars on the road in front of the laundromat. They didn't use that wicked staircase. Enlarging the map, I realize my program sent me the long way around, instead of walking a few doors up the street. I'll have to remember that maps are not infallible.

I get my laundry back to the hostel before the rains start. I find the Joanina Library on the map and carefully plan my route, including a stop at a café for the breakfast I missed.

I get to the library and see that it's attached to the University. The person at the door tells me that she can't let me in before the time on my ticket. She gives me a campus map and tells me the palace will close at noon for a special ceremony, and if I want to see it, I should go now. Taking her advice, I head across the Paço das Escolas, the plaza in the middle of the University, to the palace.

I get in the short line and join the next tour group. The guide first takes us to the rooms on the ground floor. He shows us the dungeons where they locked up bad students. Karl would have had his name on one of those cells. Karen was the good child. Karl was the handful. But I could never stay mad at him. It was his brilliance, energy, and curiosity that got him into trouble. It still rules his life, but he has learned to channel it into his scientific work and now holds several patents. I'm so proud of him.

We climb more stairs to see the receiving rooms, classrooms, and an ornate room with chairs set up for the afternoon's ceremony. Imagine being part of something that goes back so many generations.

After visiting the palace, I check the time. Another half hour to spare. My map tells me St. Michael's Chapel is on the way back to the library. I walk through the plaza and turn right into the building that houses the chapel, the university bookstore, and the cafeteria. Inside the small chapel, Manueline gold ropes frame the altar. The walls are covered with azulejos tiles. There are also tiles with yellow and green, but I don't know all the terms. A tourist brochure says the chapel was built for King Alfonso Henriques, the first king of Portugal, in the twelfth century. He definitely gets around.

I ask about getting my credencial stamped. I need to get at least one stamp each day. The docent in the chapel directs me to the gift shop. I get my stamp and make it to the library just in time for my tour.

The library is held in more sacred accord than the chapel. I join my eleven a.m. tour group. We are warned not to take pictures, touch anything, or talk. We will have twenty minutes in the library to look around. I follow the group, and we enter the sacred space. It's magnificent. The ornate architecture and the two-story bookshelves reflect the importance these people place on education. Several large tables are set up for reading. To even touch one of these tomes, you would need impeccable credentials. The twenty minutes are too short, and we are ushered out a door that opens onto the Paço das Escolas.

I head for an archway across the plaza, leading to the rest of the campus. My ticket enables me to visit the science museums on campus. This university is well known for its explorers and scientists. Karl would love this.

I text him: *Just toured the old university. They used to lock misbehaving students in dungeon cells. Saw them and thought of you.*

I walk back down the hill toward the albergue. Someone calls my name. It's Luc, and he's having lunch. I'm so happy to see him and congratulate him on completing this part of his Caminho. I was worried I had missed my chance and would never see him again. Serendipity. What are the odds? I just happened to be walking past the café in this large town at the same time he was there eating lunch. I sit, and we exchange contact information, then take a few photos to mark the moment. I blink back the tears as I hug him goodbye.

I hardly know this man. Yes, we've only been walking companions for the past three days, but I will miss him. I'll miss the conversation and companionship. He touched me in that tender place.

Ok, Scarf, it's not the time or place to break down. I head back to the albergue to meet Zoe for our tour.

Zoe guides us to the tour meeting point. As we walk down the street, I feel a sense of déjà vu.

She stops. "The map says to turn here, but it's a staircase."

"I know, I did the same thing this morning. I really don't want to tackle that staircase again. I just didn't put it together when we started walking this way."

"Well, I don't know of an alternative." She hesitates a minute, then mounts the stairs.

I feel her hesitation. "Well, I survived it this morning, I can do it again," I say and follow her up. "This staircase better not be on the tour."

She laughs.

We meet our tour guide at a park overlooking the botanical gardens, next to the aqueduct. Layers upon layers of history unfold before us. We don't go into any buildings, but he shares the history of the major spots. He takes us to the plaza in front of the Machado de Castro National Museum. We stop at the edge of the plaza overlooking the town. He describes the scene as it was in Roman times when this site held the forum, a meeting place for government and merchants. The Roman catacombs are built into the rock cliff below us. I shiver thinking about all the death this site has seen.

The guide jumps to the thirteenth century during the reign of King Denis and Queen Elizabeth, also known as Isabel of Aragon, a Spanish princess. She was married to the king at the age of twelve to serve as a peacemaker between Spain and Portugal. He tells us that she was canonized for her charitable works. She would hide bread from the royal kitchen in her skirts and walk among the poor, distributing the loaves. The king reprimanded her for this and forbade her, saying it wasn't fitting for royalty. She ignored his command and continued her practice. She wasn't going to let her people starve when she had so much.

One day, the king followed her to see if she was obeying his orders. As she approached a poor person, he tapped her on the shoulder from behind. She turned around, knowing she had been caught red-handed. When he had her open her skirt, there were red roses instead of loaves of bread.

He apologized and let her go. She continued living a devout life and entered a convent after the king's death.

The tour guide recommends we go back to visit the museum, not just to see the catacombs but also to view the royal jewels. He explains that the queen would lend her jewelry to women getting married who couldn't afford to dress up on their wedding day. When the jewels were returned, there was often a small precious stone or gold link missing. She accepted this because she understood they needed the items to survive.

I love that she chose what was right over obeying her king and husband. Because of her, peace and compassion flourished. I let those feelings flow through my body. These feelings, along with love, give me strength. Like the queen, if I keep connecting with the world on this level, maybe I can also become an instrument of peace.

We continue our walk down to the lower levels of the town. Our guide points out where the old walls once stood for fortification and the ancient churches. We stop in front of a restaurant. Our guide says this is where we can get the best *cabrito assado* in town.

"What's that?" I ask.

"Roast goat. When the town was attacked by the Moors in the Middle Ages, the citizens closed all the gates, and the city was besieged. Remember, I showed you where the old walls used to be. They couldn't continue feeding the animals or they would starve, so they slaughtered the goats and put the meat in casks of wine to preserve it. They had plenty of wine.

When they ran low on fresh food, they would pull the meat from the casks and cook it. This allowed them to survive. I recommend that you come here and have some. It's delicious."

We finish our tour in front of the Santa Cruz bar, with one last story. He tells us the tale of Pedro and Ines. Pedro was the son of King Alfonso IV and next in line for the throne. The king told him that he had to marry a woman who would make his country richer and stronger. It was arranged that he marry Constance, a noble woman from Spain. This was to be her second marriage. Constance had brought her own lady-in-waiting, Inês de Castro, to Portugal. Pedro and Constance did their duty and produced heirs. Constance later died in childbirth.

But in the background, Pedro had fallen in love with Ines, and she loved him back. They had a secret affair. After Constance died, Pedro was free to marry Ines. However, Pedro's father was not happy because, politically, this was not a good decision for Pedro. Pedro told his father to take a leap. He had done his duty to the kingdom, and now it was time for his happiness. So he married Ines anyway, and they had a very happy life ruling together.

His father held a grudge, and he plotted to keep them apart. There was an uprising elsewhere in the kingdom, so his father took the opportunity to send Pedro there to handle it. While Pedro was gone, his father had his henchmen kill Ines. Pedro found out when he returned, and his anger and grief knew no bounds. He built a grave where they would both lie upright so that, when they were resurrected, the first thing they would see would be each other. When he died thirteen years later, he was buried beside her.

Tears spring to my eyes. A love so committed, destroyed by a power-hungry, jealous old man, is a travesty.

The guide leaves us in the right mood for the lost love expressed in fado music. He tells us one last story about the history of fado. He says that if we like the song, we should rub our throats and make a purr. This tradition of showing appreciation began when young women, serenaded beneath their windows, dared not applaud for fear their fathers would discover the courtship.

Our guide earns his keep, and we are generous with our tip.

Zoe and I go into the bar and find two empty seats up front. I order a sparkling water with black currant juice, and she orders a hot chocolate. We both order pastries.

Three men take the stage: a six-string guitarist, a Portuguese guitarra with twelve strings, and a singer. Fado is traditionally performed by men in Coimbra. In Lisboa, both men and women perform.

The songs touch my soul, even though I don't understand the words. My eyes fill with tears all over again. After the show, we walk back to the albergue in silence. I am pensive and cannot put my feelings into words.

> POST: Coimbra wrapped itself around me today—history stacked on history, sacred libraries, legends of love and loss... and music that made me cry even without understanding the words. Some places don't just teach you things. They move you.

•••

I wake to thunder and lightning. It's pouring rain outside. My phone says it's six degrees Celsius, which is forty-three degrees Fahrenheit. Karl has responded to my text about the dungeons: *LOL*

I smile and go back to bed. I don't want to walk in this. I want to stay right here in bed. I bet the hospitaleiros would let me keep it another night.

Zoe stirs and asks if I'm leaving this morning.

"I was going to, but I don't want to walk in these storms. Maybe they will clear, and I can get a few kilometers in."

"That's wishful thinking. My weather app says we're in for it all day."

"I hope Maura is in a safe place," I say.

"So do I. How about you stay another day, and we go up to the museum and see the Roman ruins and catacombs? I want to see Queen Elizabeth's jewels too."

"I love that idea. I'll check with reception and see if I can keep the bed for the night. But first, breakfast. We can go to the little café next door."

I get a bed for another night, and Zoe and I spend the afternoon at the museum. We stop at the little restaurant where I saw Luc and where our guide said they had the best cabrito assado—goat. We have to try it, along with the recommended paired wine. I can now say I ate goat.

Scarf, I'll leave it there.

Back in my room, I get into bed, and my phone dings. It's a text from Karen.

Are you all right? I usually hear from you by now. Worried in California.

Oh dear. I forgot to text her. This is getting annoying.

I'm sorry, darling, all is well. It rained all day, so I stayed put. Instead, I had a lovely day sightseeing and a delightful dinner with a new friend. I'll start walking again tomorrow.

I plug the phone into the charger, turn off notifications, and close my eyes.

CHAPTER 12

COIMBRA TO ESCUSA

I wake to overcast skies but no rain. Yes, it's time to walk. My happy puppy body trembles with excitement. I walk out of Coimbra in the pre-dawn. I'm a bit nervous walking through the streets alone, thinking about Maura and her experience.

Around the corner, there are four young men talking and laughing. They're dressed in white shirts, black ties, black trousers, and black capes. Their ties are askew. One has his shirt unbuttoned; the tie is loose and looped around his neck. There's a heart with initials drawn on his chest in magic marker.

Young love, I think with a sigh.

I keep quiet and move into the shadows of the buildings. I'm careful not to stare, but I watch them in my periphery. Their gait is unsteady, and as I walk by, a cloud of alcohol envelops me. It's Sunday morning, so this must be leftovers from last night. I pass them silently. They pay no attention to me.

Dawn breaks when I exit the city beside the river. Early morning joggers and cyclists are already out. The crunch of gravel under my feet keeps time with the song of the birds. The way diverts from the river to a road beside a cornfield as I make my way along to Mealhada.

Twenty-six kilometers later, I stop for the night at my albergue. I've been sleeping alone in hotels and albergues. This will probably be no different. The owner shows me to a room with twelve beds. I have my pick. I choose one near the bathroom, which is easier for nighttime trips. I avoid the two sets of bunk beds at the end of the room, grateful for a single bed.

There's a restaurant nearby. After showering and washing my clothes in the outside sink, I hang them in the weak sun to dry and head out for my first good meal of the day. I had my favorite breakfast of café con leche and pastéis de nata in Coimbra, but that feels like a long time ago.

The restaurant is packed, but I'm just happy it's open on a Sunday. I keep forgetting that the streets roll up in Portugal on Sundays. The patrons are in their Sunday best, and I'm in my about-town pilgrim clothes: old black hiking pants and my wool tunic. I'm not up to their caliber. I'm also alone. Many families are eating and laughing together—young children fussing over their food, seniors smiling and tolerating the noise. It's the noise of loving families.

Scarf, I really don't mean to put Karen down all the time. I love her. She has been my rock, but sometimes she annoys me. And I would give anything for her to be here now, annoying me.

I check my phone. I wonder if she responded to my cryptic text from last night. Oh yeah, here it is.

I'm glad you are all right. I'm sorry to intrude on your fun evening, but it's important that you let the family know where you are and that you are safe.

Time for me to text back. I'll beat her to the punch today. Why does she get under my skin?

Hi, darling. Thank you for your concern. I walked again today and am in Mealhada. I'll stay the night and walk to Águeda tomorrow. Love you.

Lunch finished, I walk back to the albergue. There's a man sitting on the bench by the front door, pulling off his boots. I nod a greeting and go into the room. On the opposite side of the room, there's a backpack by a bed.

So I won't be alone tonight. I wonder what language he speaks. I wonder if he snores. I wonder if he'll stay in his own bed.

I set up my bed with my sleeping bag, put my toiletries on the nightstand, and go out to see if my clothes are dry. No chance. I move the drying rack into the sun and wind, hoping it will help.

At the sound of laughter, I make my way back to the dorm. A couple of women close to my age have arrived. We exchange names and places of origin. One is Fiona from England, the other Sally from Australia. We then share where we started our Caminho. We all began in Lisboa, but this is the first time we've seen each other.

More pilgrims arrive, and the room begins to fill. One of the men announces he's going out for a drink and asks who wants to join him. A couple of the men go with him. I lock eyes with the other two women, and we silently agree that this will be a noisy night of light sleep. I search for my earplugs.

Soon, a woman comes in. It's the same woman I saw at the pension just outside of Lisboa and at the café in Cálvanos, just outside of Tomar. She introduces herself as Kate from the Netherlands. She chooses the single bed next to mine, sets up her belongings, and pulls out a laptop. She explains that she's a digital nomad, working on the road. I can't believe she's carrying a laptop across Portugal.

Next, a young man limps in. He's from France. The women gather around him at once, asking how he is. Apparently, he's been struggling with his leg for days. I notice he already has more than enough mothers tending to him, so I stay where I am. I have done my duty before—gladly—but I do not have to claim every wounded pilgrim as my own. Is that cold? No one is looking to me for help. There is plenty of it.

Still, Scarf, why does a small thread of guilt tug at me for not rising to the call?

People start to settle down, and the young man has been pacified. It's lights out and earplugs in.

•••

After a night filled with people snoring, I rise early with the older ladies. We want to get a start on the twenty-four-kilometer day. I go out to the clothes rack. My clothes are still damp. I don't have a choice. I head to the bathroom to put them on. They'll dry eventually.

We older ladies head out, focused on our own Caminhos and unwilling to walk with anyone else. This suits me just fine. My goal is Águeda, and I have made arrangements to stay at the Albergue San António. It has a very high rating and was recommended by my local chapter of American Pilgrims. They were so helpful in coaching me about my Caminho.

I'm feeling grouchy today and find it hard to stay in a state of love. I finally met pilgrims last night, but I've really enjoyed walking and being alone, so I'm not sure I want to connect with anyone. Sharing the bathroom and a bedroom full of people who snore is not restful.

And I'm hungry. I haven't seen a café this morning. I should have gone to the grocery store like some of the others did yesterday. But no, I was too lazy. I noticed on the map last night that there's a small town with a café about five kilometers up the road, but it's off the Caminho. I'm a little nervous to leave the Caminho in case I can't find it again. I can just hear Karen now, bringing out the Portuguese police in a search party for her addled-brain old mother.

The road turns into a trail through the woods. Clearly, there are no cafés around, but I won't die of hunger.

I focus on the birds' songs and the scent of eucalyptus in the air. The rain has made everything so lush and clean. I inhale deeply. The gentle ups and downs are no match for my trail-hardened legs. There are men's voices in the distance, as well as the sound of chainsaws. There is quite an industry with these trees. I'm glad they're good for something.

The path ends at a road on the edge of a small village. A yellow arrow points toward a square. A group of teenagers is gathered there, waiting for the school bus—backpacks, teasing antics, and cell phones. Teenagers are pretty much the same everywhere. I bet they know where to find the closest open café. I walk up to them and ask in a mix of English and Spanish, with a few Portuguese words thrown in for good measure. One of the young women tells me in perfect English to walk to the next street. It's about a block down on the right. She tells me that it's open, and they have fantastic coffee and pastries. Jackpot.

I follow her directions, veering away from the Caminho. Just around the corner, there are people entering a shop empty-handed and coming out with bags full of bread. Bless that young lady.

The owner welcomes me, and I order my café con leche and my nata—my naughty nata. It's so delicious, it must be naughty. He asks for my credencial, and I give it to him for a stamp. It's so fun collecting these stamps. They'll be wonderful reminders of my pilgrimage.

Retracing my steps is easy, and I'm back on my way, energized by caffeine and a full stomach. Going off the path and then returning to the arrows wasn't so hard. The silly things I worry about. My mind must be bored. It has to find something to fret over.

Scarf, I wonder if that's where Karen gets her worrywart tendencies. Oh my God, did I teach her that unintentionally? I was a bit of a helicopter mom with her. Karma sucks. Now I'm stuck accounting for my every move. Karl didn't get those tendencies. He's much more laid-back, like his father.

As I walk into Águeda, I'm struck by all the buildings and cafés along the river. Colorful umbrellas adorn every balcony. So welcoming. This will be a great place to have dinner. I'm hungry, but I want to find my albergue first.

The map shows I have another kilometer to go, and it looks like it's all uphill, of course. The cafés by the river are probably really expensive and full of tourists. I bet there will be a place closer to where I'm staying that serves pilgrims.

I finally get to my albergue and claim my bed in the dorm. This room has only four beds, and I request women only, if possible. I want to mitigate the snoring and actually get some sleep. The earplugs help, but they're not the whole answer.

Roy used to snore and sometimes stopped breathing. He'd wake himself up with a snort. I finally convinced him to see a doctor for a sleep test, and he was diagnosed with sleep apnea. They prescribed a CPAP machine to help him breathe. It was not only good for him, but also for our marriage. I could finally get a good night's sleep. I wish I could strap CPAPs on all the snorers in the albergue. We would be better-rested, happier pilgrims.

The albergue owner tells me there are no restaurants nearby, but there's a grocery store just 300 meters down the road. She says I can use the kitchen to heat anything up.

No restaurant? I have to buy groceries and heat up food.

Really, Scarf, I did not come on this pilgrimage to cook. I'd had enough of this at home. This is my time. Now I have to walk three hundred meters—that's a third of a kilometer—and go grocery shopping. I don't even know what I want to eat.

And on top of that, shower and wash my clothes out. At least it is sunny and windy, so they'll have a chance to dry.

I walk along the shoulder of the busy road to the grocery store. It is full of patrons, and I just wander around. It's interesting to see what they carry versus what our U.S. stores carry. I stop at the bread case. It's full of beautiful breads, rolls, and croissants—some sweet, some not. A croissant with sesame seeds is calling my name. Now what to get with it? In the next case, there are premade single-serving refrigerated lasagnas. The veggie one looks fresh and amazing, and there's just enough for me. Sold. Now I need dessert. I see apples in the produce section that look good, and I put one in my cart. Next to that are yogurt drinks. I see one that says it's high in protein and chocolate. That one's for me.

I place my bag at the end of the counter and pack it as the cashier scans my food. The grand total is six euros and fifty cents. That's less than seven dollars. I couldn't get a meal like this at that price in a restaurant. Maybe I should start buying groceries more often.

You know, Scarf, I was a bit grumpy back there. Sorry. Staying in a space of love isn't easy.

Back at the kitchen in the albergue, I heat up the lasagna. While it's warming in the oven, I check the laundry. It's drying nicely. Back in the kitchen, I pull the bubbling, savory lasagna out of the oven, still in its container, and put it on a hot pad at my seat. I set the table with silverware and a napkin and put my protein drink beside a small plate holding my croissant and apple. Sniffing the aroma, I salivate as I sit down to the first meal I've made for myself in weeks.

A couple of pilgrims come into the kitchen and stop to stare. Walking all day, every day, definitely stimulates the appetite, and food becomes a necessary source of fuel. Like a car that starts to run low on gas, it sputters. These pilgrims are beginning to sputter. I direct them, as I was, to the grocery store down the road. They can walk just as well as I can. It's so nice not to have to jump up and take care of everyone else.

Oh yeah, I'd better text Karen.

I am safe and with other pilgrims in a hostel. I will be walking to Escusa tomorrow. I bought food at the grocery store this evening and prepared it in the kitchen in the albergue. So much more cost-effective—and delicious.

That should keep her from dinging my phone.

I finish eating and go out to the patio to sit with the other pilgrims. One young woman approaches me.

"You look wise," she says.

It's a trap, Scarf. 'Wise' is a euphemism for old.

"I ripped my pants," she continues, "and I don't know how to sew. I have this needle and thread. Can you show me?"

"Well, sewing isn't one of my stronger skills, but I'll see what I can do." It's a ninety-degree corner rip, between the crotch and the back pocket. I can see the frayed edges of the fabric. I know enough to realize this won't be an easy fix.

"Great, you've threaded the needle. That part is hard for these old eyes," I say.

"You're not old." She gives the standard answer.

I smile and take the threaded needle from her. "You need to double the thread and then tie the two ends together in a knot like this. That way, the stitch is stronger, and the knot keeps the thread from slipping through the hole you make in the fabric. Now turn your pants inside out."

She follows my directions and finds the rip. I hand her the threaded, knotted needle, take the pants from her, and show her how to put the edges together so good cloth meets good cloth. "You can't sew through the frayed edge. The stitches won't hold."

"Oh, I see."

I hand the pants back to her and encourage her to start sewing. She takes tiny stitches, which will be just fine. I sit and soak up the last of the warm sun while she concentrates on her task.

"How do I finish it?" she asks.

"Make a knot using the needle and thread." I show her how. She makes the knot and cuts off the excess.

"Now turn the pants right side out."

We look at the repair. It's serviceable.

"At least your panties won't show," I say.

"Thank you so much." She smiles, proud of her handiwork.

"You did the work," I say. I'm proud of her—and of myself. "Where are you from?"

"Germany," she says.

"Your English is excellent."

"I took it in school. I studied international business."

"Are you on school break?" I want to know more about her.

"Well, I finished in the summer and will start my first job in January. I decided to walk part of the Caminho in between. It's given me the break I needed."

"What will you be doing in your job?"

"I'm not quite sure, but I'll be working for a company that deals in agricultural exports. It's a start. You see, I'd like to help eradicate hunger."

"That's fantastic. You give me hope."

"I give you hope?"

"Yes, it warms my heart to see the younger generation working to make a positive difference in the world and in themselves. Thank you for showing me a bright future."

She blushes. "Thank you for teaching me to sew."

I smile and pick up my phone.

> POST: Tonight on the Camino, I helped a young pilgrim sew her ripped pants. Nothing fancy—just thread, patience, and making good cloth meet good cloth. Funny how a small ordinary skill can turn into a quiet moment of connection. This road keeps reminding me that we all carry what someone else needs.

A man stumbles out onto the patio with the proprietor of the albergue. He quickly regains his balance and asks where he can get some cash. She tells him where the nearest ATM is. He says his card won't work.

Another pilgrim—a good Samaritan—walks up. "May I assist?"

I'm glad to see someone stepping up.

"I don't have any cash," the man says, slurring his words.

I believe he's inebriated.

"Do you have enough to spend the night?" the good Samaritan asks.

"Yes, I gave her my credit card, and it works. I just don't have enough cash for the bar."

The Samaritan's expression changes. "I can't give you cash for the bar."

"I'll pay you back when I can get more cash. A lot of cash. But I need some now," the pilgrim says.

"No, sorry," the Samaritan says.

"Where's my bed?" the man asks the proprietor.

She leads him upstairs to another room. I'm so relieved he's not in ours.

"I was willing to pay for his night," the Samaritan says. "I wouldn't leave anyone on the streets. But I will not pay for alcohol."

Those of us on the patio who saw the interaction nod in agreement.

"Let him sleep it off. He's not a bad sort. He just likes to drink. I've seen him at several bars the last few days. I'm amazed he made it this far today," one of the men sitting on the patio with us says.

I go check my laundry. It's dry—a miracle—and I take it off the line.

Back in my dorm room, I see that two of the other three beds are occupied. They are ladies, and for that I am grateful.

One of them is the Samaritan. I remember seeing her at the albergue in Mealhada—Fiona from England.

"Thank you for offering to pay for his room. That was kind," I tell her.

"I've seen too much of that sort to be suckered in. Didn't we meet down the road a bit?"

"Yes, we met in Mealhada. I'm Dot. I had the bed across from you."

"Oh yes, my name is Fiona."

We sit and have a quick get-to-know-you chat. It's nice to know who you're sleeping with.

"Well, I'm off to the grocery store. I love the premade Caesar salads. May I get you something?"

"No, thank you. I've already eaten." What a kind soul.

• • •

Today it's all uphill to Escusa. At least I have a head start since I walked to the far side of town yesterday. I like uphill better than downhill. Downhill is tough on these old bones. Going downhill, I'm a bit unsteady on cobblestones and rocky trails, though the hiking sticks help a lot. I don't know how I'd manage without them.

Fiona and I looked at our guidebooks in the room last night when she returned from dinner. We booked a donativo albergue in the town of Escusa that provides both dinner and breakfast. Sounds perfect.

CHAPTER 13

ESCUSA TO SÃO JOÃO DE MADEIRA

I arrive at the albergue. I'm the only pilgrim and am given a nice room with two beds. It's been raining again, and my clothes are wet. The poncho helps, but nothing seems to keep out this rain.

The hospitaleiro tells me there is a laundry sink and drying rack in a shed by the orange grove. I shower and then head out to the sink. There's a break in the rain and a rainbow on the horizon. The hospitaleiro comes up to me, and I point out the rainbow. We pause a moment and take in the beauty in silence.

We move the drying rack into the weak sun beside the orange grove. He tells me he will bring the rack in if it starts to rain. How kind.

Humming "Somewhere Over the Rainbow", I do my laundry and hang it out. I get back into the albergue, and Fiona has arrived with another pilgrim.

"This is Sally from Australia," Fiona says. "She was in Mealhada with us, too."

"Nice to meet you officially," I say, covering up for my lack of memory of her. Fiona has been given her own room, and Sally is in the other bed in mine.

Sally and I head to our room, and Fiona heads to the shower.

"I'm glad I'm bunking with you," Sally says. "Fiona snores."

I laugh. "Oh yes, I remember from last night. But it's not awful."

"Yeah, not like the drunk guy. I heard he was at your albergue last night."

"Yes, but in a different room."

"He's harmless; he just likes to see the bottom of a bottle. We never know what sorrows people are drowning—or walking away from—on the Caminho."

"What brings you to the Caminho?" I ask.

"I love to travel. I worked to travel my whole life. I did settle for a while, when I had children and owned a shop, but once they were out on their own, I sold the shop and got on the road."

"Sounds wonderful," I reply, not wanting to push her about other family relationships or commitments.

"How about you?"

"My husband died this past year, and it seemed like the right thing to do."

We are called to dinner before I have to say anything more.

It's the three of us, a volunteer at the albergue who made

dinner, and the hospitaleiro. The volunteer brings in bowls of vegetable soup for the first course. There are carafes of olive oil, wine, and water.

"I was told that one tree makes about two liters of olive oil. Is this oil local?" I ask.

"Yes, this oil comes from my family's trees," the hospitaleiro replies.

"Do you press it yourself?" Sally asks.

"No, there's a coop with the local growers. We take our olives there to be pressed, and then the oil is distributed. We usually have only enough for our own needs. If there is any left over, it's sold in specialty shops. The big producers are trying to buy us out, but we don't want to lose our heritage or our quality. It's a problem."

"I'm sorry to hear this, but I see it happening all over the world. The big guys tried to run my wee shop into the ground, stealing all my customers with their lower prices," Sally says. "I finally got too old to keep fighting them, and I had enough with my pension to retire and travel. So here I am, with fewer headaches and a lot more freedom."

We all nod in agreement.

The volunteer rises and collects our empty soup bowls. We jump up to help. We're so used to being the ones who take care of others at meals. The hospitaleiro asks us to sit. "This is our pleasure," he says. "Do not take it from us."

They return from the kitchen with platters of baked chicken, potatoes, and cabbage. We serve ourselves family-style, filling our plates.

"What brings you to volunteer here?" I ask.

"I walked the Portuguese last year, and I was so well taken care of here that I want to give back."

"Where are you from?"

"I'm from Morocco. It's easy to get here," she replies.

"Well, you're an awesome cook."

She blushes. "Thank you. Where are you from?" This starts a round robin of the usual Caminho questions.

The conversation turns to reasons for walking, and Fiona shares her pilgrimage history.

"How can you get away for all that time?" I ask.

"I'm a free woman. I brought up children and a husband. I no longer have that responsibility, and now it's time to reclaim myself," Fiona says.

"Reclaim yourself?"

"Yes, I had lost who I was and what I loved amid the demands of others. Walking and exploring the world bring me joy. I now have the time to do it."

"I feel joy in walking too," I tell her. "I thought it was kind of strange."

"Oh, not at all," Sally says. "I've loved being a nomad in the world as long as I can remember. I've learned how to travel cheaply so I can travel often. It's my lifeblood.

Fiona, I liked what you said about reclaiming yourself. That's how I feel. I, too, had lost myself, my joys. I was dutifully acting out the life that was expected of me. Yes, we do have to make a living and raise our children, but we also have to do what makes our hearts sing, and pilgrimage does. It's all the sweeter because of the sacrifices I make to do it."

The hospitaleiro comes out with an ice cream cake and a bottle of liquor. He cuts the cake and pours five shots. "This is a liquor I make out of our oranges. It's bittersweet, like most of our pilgrimages. Would everyone like some?"

We all nod.

"Sip slowly and savor it. It's very potent."

Sally takes a sip. "I have to tell you what happened to me walking out of Coimbra on Sunday morning. I heard some rifle shots."

"I walked out that morning too and heard the shots," I tell her.

"Yes, there is hunting on Sundays, and please do not be disturbed by it. The hunters know the difference between pilgrims and wild game," the hospitaleiro says.

We all laugh.

"Well, I heard the shot and then felt something hit my water bottle on my backpack. It about knocked me over," Sally says. She's a tiny lady, but fearless.

"I stopped, in shock. Was I going to fall over? I had never been shot before, so I didn't know what it would feel like. But nothing happened. Then I felt a wetness trickling down the back of my leg. All I could think of was blood."

She sure has my undivided attention.

"I stood for a minute, holding my breath, hoping there wouldn't be a follow-up shot. But all was quiet, and the birds started singing again. Still on my feet, I decided to take off my pack and survey the damage. I noticed a wet spot below the left pocket of my pack, and I could feel it down my left leg. My water bottle is in that pack pocket, and the top of the bottle was gone. Touching the wet spot, I found that it was orange and sticky." Then she laughs. "I had opened an orange soda and poured it into my water bottle to keep it cold. The steady motion and heat of my walking must have built the pressure until the carbonation blew the top clean off. What a mess."

We dissolve into laughter. The hospitaleiro pours us another round. That orange liquor goes down easily.

"I searched for the top and finally found it in the bushes about five feet away. It wouldn't seal, so in the next town I stopped at a hardware store and bought some plumber's tape. It's now as good as new."

I'm in awe of this woman.

"To blowing your top," I say, and raise my shot glass.

Everyone chimes in with a "chin-chin" and drinks. We say our good nights and head to bed.

> POST: Tonight, I saw a rainbow over an olive grove, shared a table with women reclaiming themselves, and felt the Caminho do what it does best—turn strangers into companions. Grateful for shelter, food, and the steady lesson: Keep walking.

There's a text from Karen.

Shit, Scarf. I forgot to message her again. I picture her at her desk in California, checking the clock, checking her phone, trying not to spiral. It's not fair to make her sit in that.

I'd better call.

I pull on my jacket and step out onto the porch. The temperature has dropped sharply since sundown. The night smells like wet earth and woodsmoke, and somewhere nearby an orange tree gives off a clean, sharp perfume. It's nine p.m. here—one p.m. there. The end of her lunch hour.

I dial.

She picks up on the first ring. "Mom? Is that you?"

"Yes, darling." I keep my voice soft, one hand on the railing to steady myself. "I'm sorry. I forgot to message. It rained most of the day, and I wanted to put on dry clothes, rinse the wet ones, and hang them up. Then they served dinner. It just... got away from me."

A pause. A pause. I can hear her breathing—controlled and tight.

"You couldn't find ten seconds to text me that you're safe?"

I close my eyes. Here it is—the same knot, tied again.

"Karen," I say, keeping my tone level. "I'm your mother, not your child."

"Well, it's common courtesy."

"It's also common courtesy to trust the woman who raised you." The words come out calm, but they land with the edge I've been swallowing for days.

She exhales sharply. "That's not fair. I worry."

"And I'm choosing not to worry," I say. "I'm choosing to live."

"You're alone in another country, Mom. Anything could happen."

"Anything can happen in my driveway," I say. "Yet you don't ask me to text you every time I take out the trash."

"That's not the same, and you know it."

I watch my breath turn faintly white in the cold. My heart is beating harder now—not anger, resolve.

"No," I say, firmer. "What's not the same is that you think your fear outranks my judgment."

Silence.

Then, smaller: "I just want to know you're safe."

"And I want to know you believe I'm capable."

Her voice tightens. "Don't turn this around on me."

"I'm not turning anything. I'm finishing it." I lean into the quiet, the damp night, the scarf warm at my throat. "I walked all day in the rain. I navigated new streets and new languages. I got here safely. It's what I've been doing every day. And frankly"—I let myself say it—"I'm getting fed up with having to report in like I'm on parole."

"A text takes ten seconds," she says, clipped.

"So does a deep breath," I say. "And I took one instead."

"You could be kinder."

"I am being kind," I say. "I called. I'm talking to you. But I won't carry your panic for you."

Another pause. I can hear it—the shift. Her retreat, masked as offense.

"So what am I supposed to do?" she questions. "Am I just supposed to sit here and not worry?"

"You're supposed to live your life." My voice softens despite myself. "The way I raised you."

She is quiet for a long time. When she speaks again, it's different—less sharp, more exposed.

"You were always worried about me."

I stare out into the dark. Somewhere in the olive grove, the wind moves through the leaves like a sigh.

"Yes, I was," I say. "And if I taught you that... I'm sorry." I swallow. "But we can start a new page, Karen. We can learn how to live without worry running the show."

She lets out a breath that sounds like defeat—or surrender. Or maybe both. "Okay. But if I don't hear from you in three days, I'm calling the police."

I almost laugh, but it comes out as something softer. "I don't think that's necessary. And you know you can see my little blue dot marching along the map." I pause. "That's enough."

On the other end, she's silent—listening.

"I love you," I say. "And I'm not in any danger of dying."

"Mom..."

"I love you," I repeat, gentler now. I end the call before she can pull us back into the same argument. I slip the phone into my pocket and stand there a moment longer, letting the quiet win.

•••

It's morning, and it's raining again. But my clothes are dry. The owner had brought them in and set them under the dining room heater. It's such a delight to put on warm, dry clothes. And two days in a row. I must be living right. I know it won't last long, but what a luxury. I defined luxury differently in my world at home; dry clothes were an expectation.

The albergue owner has left us a do-it-yourself breakfast. I didn't sleep last night, tossing and turning after that call with Karen. I think I blew my top. But I'm tired of being treated like a feeble old lady. I'm a crone—an independent, wise woman who happens to have a child brought up to be a worrywart.

I shoulder my pack, don my poncho, and walk. The happy puppy is a bit subdued. Arriving in the next town, I stop at a café for a coffee and a break from the rain. At least it's a gentle, steady rain.

"Dot, we missed you this morning."

I stop drowning my guilt in my coffee cup and look up. Sally is shaking the rain off her poncho at the door to the café.

"Sally, welcome. Grab a cup and join me. It's nice and hot."

"I'm going to use the facilities first."

"I'll grab you a coffee then. What do you like?

"Americana is fine. I like my coffee strong, bold, and unapologetic."

When she returns, I ask about Fiona.

"She decided to take the bus to São João de Madeira. She'd had enough of walking in the rain. I understand—it can wear on you."

"Thanks for letting me know." Maybe we, as humans, want to make sure those we care about are safe. "Do you check in with your children every day?"

She laughs. "That would send them into a tizzy. They are so used to me going off on my own that if I checked in, they'd think I was sick."

"Well, my daughter wants me to check in every day, and I'm fed up with it. I know it eases her mind to know I'm safe, but..."

"I get it. But you need your space to remember who you are without children and a spouse. Both of these have defined us for so many years that we forget who we are apart from them. I find that pilgrimage allows me that space."

"Thank you. I was beginning to think I was being very selfish about not wanting to text her daily."

"You are being selfish, and that's just fine. Maybe you need some selfish time. I know I did after the divorce. I had to get away and clear my mind with no interference. It was the best thing I did for myself and my children. They were only teenagers at the time. My mum took care of them while I was gone. Your children are grown. They can take care of themselves."

"Thank you," I say quietly, and swallow the last sip of coffee.

She glances at her watch. "You'll have to excuse me for a moment. I have to call the realtor. I have an offer on my house, and we have to discuss it."

"No problem, I need some alone time. Bom Caminho."

She smiles. "Bom Caminho."

I finish up and begin my journey again. The route winds through small towns and into narrow streets where ancient stone walls press close on either side, holding the day's coolness within them. Every so often, I pass a portal — heavy wooden doors set deep into the stone, carved and weathered by centuries. I'm drawn to them. They feel like thresholds to another world, as if they might slide open like something from Star Trek, revealing lives hidden from the pilgrim's path. I think of the cozy courtyard in Santarém and how, for a brief evening, I was invited inside.

But like many wonderful things, there's a dark side. This dark side involves big vans, trucks, and cars that try to navigate these streets as if they were a four-lane highway. I lean against the stone wall, and with my backpack, I almost stick out too far for a vehicle to pass. It terrifies me.

I go uphill again into Bemposta, a town along an old Royal Road. I can tell that at one time this was a very high-rent neighborhood. But now the old buildings, too expensive to maintain, are deteriorating. All that's left are a few plaques to keep the history from fading away.

CHAPTER 14

SÃO JOÃO DE MADEIRA

I enter the city of São João de Madeira in the early afternoon. It's one of the most modern cities I've been in so far. I walk past a skyscraper with business logos on the front. I see an escalator through the modern glass front. It's a bit of culture shock.

My guidebook says this is an industrial town known for manufacturing shoes and hats. There's a museum displaying its history. Peter was in the shoe business. I wonder if he was from this town. The shoes his company provided to the film industry were top-notch. This will be a walk down memory lane.

I find my hostel and am ushered up a flight of stairs to a dorm room sectioned off by curtains—some semblance of privacy. And who should be in the room next to me but Kate from the Netherlands. Life on the Caminho is so interesting. It's like you bump into the same people over and over—Caminho karma. I didn't have a good initial impression of her. She was a bit curt, not too friendly. Now she's warming up a bit, but we are coming from two different worlds.

I stake out a bottom bunk and head to the shower. There is no place to do laundry. I wash my clothes in the bathroom sink and hang them from every horizontal surface I can find. They really need more hooks in these places.

I start to text Karen that I arrived safely, then stop. Yes, I have time, but just yesterday I told her I wouldn't text every day. I don't want her to think I'm complying with her wishes. And if I miss a day in the future, I don't want her to worry.

I am strong, bold, and unapologetic, Scarf. I am reclaiming myself.

With that, I head out to the hat and shoe museum. It's not far down the street. There are a few yellow arrows. This must be the way I'll walk tomorrow. It's nice to figure out where I'm going the next day. I see a little café and go in. I ask when they open in the morning, and the proprietor says seven a.m. This will be the perfect breakfast stop.

I go into the museum, and there's a man at the desk. He has wavy iron-gray hair and a pleasant, familiar face. I stop to buy a ticket. We pause and look at each other. I take a deep breath, and a familiar scent hits me.

No, Scarf, it can't be.

I hand him my credit card and purchase my ticket. There is puzzlement on his face. I snatch my card and ticket from him and follow the sign reading "Start Here."

Is it really Peter? Or maybe it's just my imagination. Entering this town made me think of him, and now I'm imagining him. I don't want to make a fool of myself by asking. Or be disappointed if it's not.

I focus on the first display. It shows how shoemaking started in the area in the fifteenth century. It's quite a skill. An apprentice would have to master each step in the process and, before becoming a master cobbler, pass an exam. The exhibits take me through how shoemaking went from a cobbler producing a shoe for a single customer to an industrial mass-production process. And it all started in this small town.

They would begin around age ten or twelve and go through the learning process, passing tests and demonstrating competency until they finally graduated as full-fledged shoemakers. A skilled shoemaker could make a pair of shoes in one day.

The next case shows a shoe salesman with a case of shoes he's taking to stores. Then there is a case of shoes made for the film and theater industry.

There's a reflection in the glass of the display—not just of myself, but of the man from the front desk behind me. I didn't hear him approach. I turn, and he smiles at me.

My stomach gives a little lurch—or is it my heart?

"Pardon. I'm wondering if you are Dorothy Wilson, married to Roy from California. I believe I knew you as Dot."

He sounds so proper. I'm trying to reconcile this man with the man I met so long ago.

"Yes, I'm Dot. Are...are you Peter?" His name rolls easily off my tongue. I've said it a thousand times in the past fifty years.

He smiles again, and I melt. Those liquid brown eyes have not lost their effect on me. Tears cloud my vision.

"Yes. It's been a long time. You haven't changed at all. Come sit with me. I know this is a shock." He takes me to a private room behind the ticket counter, reserved for employees. "Would you like a coffee?"

"Yes, please."

He goes to the counter, where a coffee machine stands. I look him over. There are silver streaks in his dark hair, giving him a look of sophistication and assurance. The years have been kind to him.

"I'm so pleased to see you." He turns that thousand-watt smile on me. "It's been...well, a long time. You look wonderful. What are you doing in Portugal?"

"Thank you, and so do you. I'm on pilgrimage."

"Que bom. Please sit," he says. "Are you going to start walking in Porto?"

"It is wonderful. I'm already walking. I started in Lisboa."

"You walked here? From Lisboa?" His tone is incredulous.

"Every step of the way."

"Where will you finish?"

"In Santiago," I reply, pride in my voice.

"Amazing, but I'm not surprised. Roy told me of the hiking you did in California. It sounded wonderful. Our family hikes too. In fact, we made a pilgrimage to Fátima last year."

Your family? Of course he has a family.

"I loved Fátima. I walked there from Lisboa and then went to Tomar to continue my way up the Caminho."

"You walked to Fátima when?"

"Oh, just about a week ago. I really wanted to see it, and I may never come to Portugal again, so I must do and see everything on this trip." I don't think he can wrap his head around the fact that I'm walking—that I'm a strong, independent woman, not the naïve young girl I used to be.

"Are you here with a tour group?"

"No, I came by myself."

He smiles. "I wish I could take you on a tour of the museum, but I have a private tour group coming in soon. Our families have been in the business for years, and we preserve our culture's history. We take turns educating the public on the glory of Portugal's industrial age. We are still a major exporter of specialty goods worldwide. Our artisans are second to none."

"I knew your products must be special for them to be imported for the films."

"Yes, they are. I'm so glad you came to see us. Roy must have suggested it." He turns and brings two cups of coffee to the table. "How are you? How is Roy?"

Once again, the tears threaten. "I'm fine. But I'm sorry to tell you... Roy died last spring."

"Oh, Dot, I'm so sorry. It must be so difficult."

"Yes, it is. He was sick for a long time, so it was expected. I was able to ease into widowhood."

He smiles again, his words polite. "I know you took wonderful care of him. I so enjoyed visiting your home. The meals were first class, and you made me feel like part of the family."

Yeah. And more, Scarf. Does he even remember we had an affair? Well, not really an affair. It only happened once, but it sure was memorable to me. Did he sleep with all the wives on his sales route?

"Thank you." I will be polite too.

"Forgive me. I'm just astounded to find you here...and then to learn that Roy has died and you're walking a pilgrimage. I mean, it's not unusual for women to come here and walk a pilgrimage, but you must be..."

About as old as you are, buddy.

I smile. "Yes, I'm seventy-nine years old and hope to celebrate my eightieth in Santiago."

"I forget myself. How long are you here in São João? You must come and have dinner with my family."

That's twice he's said "family". Well, I'd better ask.

"Are you married?"

"Yes, we've been married over fifty years, and we have six children and twelve grandchildren."

"How wonderful."

Well, Scarf—and perhaps at least one more child he never knew about. But who's counting? The scoundrel. Though I'm not entirely innocent myself. I decide not to tell him about Karen. That truth belongs to me. What good would it do after all these years but wound the innocent? I have carried it this long. I can still carry it.

"I wish I could, but I have to walk tomorrow," I say. "I've met some lovely people, and we're walking together."

"I'm sorry you have to leave so soon. It would have been wonderful to relive old memories." He reaches for my hand, and when he touches my skin, I feel the old electricity jolt through me. I jerk my hand away and stumble to my feet, looking for a quick exit.

He grabs my arm, turns me to face him, and looks deeply into my eyes.

Here it comes, Scarf...Will I kiss him back?

"I know seeing me must bring back the grief of losing Roy. I'm so sorry you've had to endure this alone. What can I do to help?"

"What you can do is enjoy every moment you have with your family, your wife. It goes by quicker than you can even imagine."

I step back and offer my hand. "Goodbye, Peter." Head high, I walk to the door.

A door chime rings in the distance. He escorts me back into the museum and greets a small group of women. The last thing I see is his 1,000-watt smile demanding their attention.

Well, Scarf, so much for exquisite sex.

I pretend to look at the museum displays and move quickly from the shoes to the hats.

What a fool I am to still be carrying the torch for him. I thought I would find the passion of my youth, that he would sweep me off my feet again and validate the feelings from long ago. Well, at least now I know I can still have those feelings. That's worth something.

I leave the museum and walk to a grocery store and wander the aisles. I choose a premade Caesar salad with chicken and my favorite sesame-seed croissants. I also pick up a single serving of rice pudding for dessert.

I go back to the albergue, take the elevator to the top-floor kitchen, and set out my lonely dinner. Kate comes in, says hi, gets her meal together, and joins me.

She points to my meal. "That looks good."

"Actually, it's much better than I expected. It's really fresh, and they're not stingy on the chicken. What have you been up to?"

"I've been working. I had to take a break. What have you been doing?"

"I went to the hat and shoe museum. It was fascinating. I had no idea that Portugal was such a leader in these industries. I learned where the saying 'mad as a hatter' came from. The material they used to soak the hats in contained nitric acid and mercury. The workers had their hands in it all day. Their hands would turn black, and the chemicals affected their minds as well, leaving many mentally ill. There were no labor laws back then, and people needed to work," I explain, not wanting to share any personal information.

"How sad," Kate says. "I feel blessed that I can work in a healthy environment. Though we don't really know what the side effects of too much screen time do to our bodies. I'm hoping my lifestyle offsets any negative effects."

"You know, I wore those fashionable hats and shoes, unaware of how it affected those who produced them. I never gave it a second thought. Now I better understand labor laws and why companies have to let their consumers know how they're impacting the environment. I must be more thoughtful in my purchases."

"That sounds fascinating. I would have loved to join you."

"I'm so sorry. I should have invited you to go along." Now I'm really feeling bad. Jilted by my long-ago lover, ignoring my daughter and Kate—am I taking this reclaiming myself too far?

"No problem. I love history. It's the best part of the Caminho for me. But I have to work, too."

"What kind of work do you do?"

"I'm a digital nomad. I have a small accounting business."

"That sounds fascinating."

"It pays the bills and allows me to travel. However, carrying my office in my backpack is tough. That's why I can't walk long distances. I'm only going as far as Grijó tomorrow."

"So am I. I don't want to walk the thirty-three kilometers to Porto in one day."

We finish our dinner and go back down to the bunk room.

POST: Sometimes the Caminho brings ghosts instead of miracles. Today I met a memory I carried longer than I realized — and I finally set it down. Walking on, lighter.

CHAPTER 15

SÃO JOÃO DE MADEIRA TO GRIJÓ

I wake and it's still dark. I try to fall back asleep, but no luck, so I prepare for the day. I quietly walk down the hall. Kate has already left. She said she liked walking early in the mornings. She wasn't kidding.

I stop at the café I saw yesterday and get my café con leche and pastéis de nata for breakfast. I finish as the early-morning sun illuminates the city. The happy puppy inside of me is anticipating the day.

The arrows point me up the hill through town to a residential area. This must be a bedroom community for Porto. It feels so far away, but if I were driving, it would be a very short commute.

It's not worth the risk of getting too tired and injuring myself, so I'm not going to walk all the way to Porto today. I've learned that when I get tired, I get clumsy. I don't always notice at first—I just push through—until I start tripping over my own feet or dropping things. My brain seems to shut down. I need to listen to those signals.

As a woman, I was taught to push through pain. It sure helped when I had my children. I couldn't just say, "Let's stop the contractions and come back tomorrow when I've rested." We have to keep going. I still tend to do that to myself. Talk about 'mad as a hatter.'

The sign tells me I'm entering the city of Concorde. Clouds are moving in, so I stop and put on my rain gear. Checking my guidebook, I see I have about fourteen more kilometers to go, but the elevation map shows it's all downhill.

The rain stays with me—a light drizzle all the way to Grijó. The town greets me with a high stone wall on the right, storefronts on the left, and a cobblestone road in between. It looks like every other Portuguese town I've walked into.

Just past a market on the left, there's an open wooden portal leading into a courtyard. That portal would make any feudal family feel safe behind it. On the ceiling of the portal, there are holes where they used to dump boiling oil on unwelcome visitors. But instead of boiling oil, there's a welcome sign on the wall, indicating this is where I'm sleeping tonight. I walk into the courtyard, and Kate is mounting the stairs to an upper room. Once again, there is no handrail on these ancient stone steps. I gently call out to her, not wanting to disturb her concentration. She turns agilely and waves me in.

"The hospitaleiro left me in charge." she laughs as I mount the stairs behind her. "Pick a room, any room. You're welcome to bunk in with me. There are three rooms on this floor, each with just one set of bunk beds."

One of the young men who stayed with us in Mealhada comes in. Kate repeats her spiel. He looks in each doorway and picks an empty room.

I remember that he snores. I sure don't want to be in his room. It's still early, and who knows who else will come in? I hem and haw. Why is it so hard to make a decision? This is not life and death. But it is sleep, and that is a precious commodity.

I decide to bunk in with Kate and avoid the snoring. She doesn't offer me the bottom bunk, even though she must be at least forty years younger than me. But I can handle the top bunk. All pilgrims are equal. I hang my wet gear on the bedposts. My shirt and skirt aren't too soaked, and I don't want to shower or change clothes.

There's a commotion in the reception area as a large group of pilgrims enters. A man takes charge and directs them back downstairs to a door on the ground floor. He must be the hospitaleiro. He greets me in Portuguese and asks for my passport. I provide this and my credencial. He lets me know that he only speaks Portuguese. I pull up my translation app and type in questions about food and things to do in the village. He points me to the little store next door for food. Then he pulls out a brochure in English describing the monastery, the town's centerpiece. He points to a crypt listed inside the brochure. The caption says it is the tomb of D. Rodrigo Sanches and is classified as a National Monument. He makes sure I see the scallop shell and the relief of St. James carved into the side of the crypt. He tells me it is currently closed but will reopen at five p.m.

Another pilgrim comes in asking about a bed. I recognize this young man as well, and I remember he snores a bit, too. I made the right decision to bunk in with Kate. The walls of the reception area I'm standing in have posters explaining the origins of the albergue. The Confraternity of Santiago runs it. It is a parochial albergue, connected to a church. It's comfortable but bare bones.

I walk down the hall to the kitchen and find the necessities to fix a meal. Maybe I can get something to cook at the small market next door. As I exit the kitchen, the bathroom is on the right. The cleaning supplies are in the corner, and the showers don't look very inviting.

But first, food. As it's gotten colder, I've noticed that I start to shiver if I don't eat enough. It's like fuel on a fire when it starts to burn down—no fuel, no fire. And it doesn't seem to matter that I have some reserve around my waist and hips.

I go back to the reception area.

"I'm starving," Kate says as she joins me.

"The hospitaleiro told me there's food next door. Let's go."

We grab our rain gear and head out. Inside the small store is a glass cabinet with the regular pastries and sandwiches on the top shelf. There is quite a variety of candy on the second shelf. One short set of shelves on my right completes the grocery offering. I don't see anything that looks appetizing, and I'm starving. Through an open door, there's a bar with a couple of empty tables. No hot food in sight. I ask the bartender about food. He motions for us to wait a minute.

While we wait, in walks the French boy with the hurt leg and the drunk we met a few days ago. Kate asks the boy how he's doing, and he tells her his leg pain is gone, and they're going to walk on to Porto after they get a drink.

A woman approaches us. We explain that we're looking for more than a chocolate bar off the shelf. She smiles and nods. She tells us they have a pilgrim's menu for ten euros. We look at each other and say, "Yes, please."

She leads us into a dining room adjacent to the bar, a room full of tables we somehow missed before. She seats us. Next, she offers beef or chicken, and soup or salad. We both choose soup and beef.

With the soup, she brings a basket of bread and a container of olive oil. I love bread soaked in olive oil. I know it takes a whole tree to make two liters, but I love it. My indulgence. Maybe I'm like the drunk, but only with olive oil.

We finish our soup, and the woman whisks the bowls away, then replaces them with two huge platters of beef and French fries—one platter for each of us. Calling it a plate does a disservice to the crockery. The beef is cooked to perfection—melt-in-your-mouth flavorful.

I'm not going to make the same mistake twice. I ask Kate if she would like to visit the monastery with me.

"Let's go," she says. "I love the old churches. I find them so peaceful. I love to sit and soak up the ambiance."

Replete, we pay our bill, don our rain gear, and walk out onto the busy cobblestone road. Treading carefully, we follow the road down a few blocks, looking for a way into the monastery. It's supposed to be on our right.

A graveyard sits to our left. We stop at a wrought-iron gate and peer in. There are men, women, and children polishing the granite headstones until they shine. They are also placing flowers on the graves. Little mausoleums with candles burning inside are interspersed between the headstones. Along the wall are discreet racks holding brooms and buckets for cleaning. It's a beautiful place, and the care it receives puts our graveyards to shame. We look at each other in amazement and agree to walk through on our way back from the monastery.

The high wall ends about a block further down on our right, opening onto a vast iron gate and a long, tree-lined driveway, with the Monastery of São Salvador's cathedral facing us. We walk up the drive to the church, where a plaque says it was built in Muraceses in 922 and later moved to its current location in 1112. It's amazing to build something this huge and then move it without modern technology. I think of those times as backwards and primitive, but in reality, they really had it going on.

We find the tomb and the symbolic carvings, then tour the church. It's beautiful, but not as opulent as some of the others I've seen. I prefer the simplicity. Kate and I each find a place to sit in a pew and enjoy several moments of silence.

We finish our tour of the monastery and return to the albergue via the cemetery. The people cleaning the tombs ignore us.

More pilgrims have arrived at the albergue. Some are headed to Santiago. The large group I saw earlier is headed to Fátima. They are in the kitchen cooking. They offer us food, but I decline. I'm still full from lunch. Presently, they join us in the sitting room. There is a curly-headed guy from Ireland and the Portuguese guy I saw in Mealhada who snores like crazy.

The curly-headed guy is complaining of shin splints. I go get my first-aid kit and show him how to use tape to ease the pain in his legs. And I wasn't going to get sucked into taking care of people. Well, I can't let people suffer, and it's not a long-term proposition.

I ask the Portuguese guy about the cleaning of the graveyard. He reminds us that tomorrow is October thirty-first, and the next day is All Saints' Day.

"This is the time we honor our ancestors, and it is very important to make sure the graves are clean and decorated with flowers. If a villager neglects a grave, they are subjected to community pressure and given a bad name. My sister takes care of organizing the cleaning for our family."

Imagine that, Scarf, the woman in the family getting saddled with the responsibilities.

Karen and I mainly took care of Roy. When I attended Alzheimer's support groups, they were filled with exhausted female caregivers. Karl was supportive, but his job got in the way of taking a more active role. Karen works too, but she somehow managed to fit it in. We women have the caregiving gene. I kind of miss our daily texts. But in texting her, I'm encouraging dependence, and this is not a role I'm ready to take on.

A couple sitting on the couch says they started their Caminho at the southernmost tip of the Iberian Peninsula and are making their way up through Portugal to Santiago.

The husband asks, "What is a pilgrim?"

There are so many answers to this question.

"A pilgrim is not a tourist," the curly-headed Irishman suggests. "A tourist seems to imply someone who takes from the country they are visiting and gives only their money. Money does not buy everything. The tourist packs against fear, not need. They tend to stay in places that are more like their own country. A bit of an oxymoron."

Kate chimes in. "Yes, pilgrims are walking through the country on a journey of seeking, both within and outside of themselves. They are open and aware of experiences, moving slowly and respectfully. They are grateful for things like a clean, comfortable bed, a hot meal, and a shower. Pilgrims give not only their money, but also themselves. Through supporting others' journeys, they find their way."

I like Kate. She was a bit hard to get to know, but it was worth pursuing the friendship.

• • •

A clap of thunder wakes me, and I become aware of flashes of lightning. The weather app had predicted this. I try to go back to sleep, but every time I'm about to drop off, there's a rumble. I grow more restless, anticipating the walk in these conditions, and sleep eludes me. Finally, Kate is stirring, and I know it's time to get ready to leave. A flash goes by the window, and it takes me a minute to realize we are next to a road and some of the flashes are car lights.

"You can turn on the light. I've been awake for hours," I tell Kate.

"Thanks. And happy Halloween."

What an auspicious start to Halloween—rain, thunder, and flashes of light. We carefully put our gear into our packs, mindful of the risk of it getting wet, and then put on our rain gear.

"Is my poncho over my pack?" she asks, turning around.

I check. Everything looks secure.

We quietly walk into the reception area, then through the door leading down the steps into the courtyard.

A woman from the group looks out from her dorm room door. "Where are you headed?"

"Porto today, but eventually Santiago," Kate replies as I slowly and carefully negotiate the stairs in the pre-dawn. "Where are you headed?"

"I'm with the tour group. We're headed to Fátima."

"Fátima is incredible," I tell her.

"Aren't you afraid to be walking in this storm?"

"No, we've walked many times in these conditions," Kate says, full of confidence.

I smile to back her up and give myself the confidence boost I need, but I'm with the lady going to Fátima. I'm afraid of lightning.

We make our way down the road in the dark and rain. It's not as bad as I imagined it would be, but I'm glad not to be alone. We come to a row of shops and the café's welcoming light. There are Halloween decorations in the window. We leave our wet gear outside under the awning and go in. The shop has gone all out for Halloween. There are decorations on the walls and even a silhouette of a murder victim on the floor.

I order my usual: café con leche and pastéis de nata.

"Oh, look how cute," Kate says, pointing to a whole row of cupcakes decorated for Halloween. "I just love Halloween. We have to have cupcakes."

"You're a bad influence on me."

"But we'll walk it off," she says. "And I'm going to get one of those pastries too. I love them."

We take a picture of ourselves with our Halloween treats and post it on Facebook.

> POST: Happy Halloween from the Caminho. Thunder, lightning, rain, and a predawn walk toward Porto—apparently, the Caminho does tricks and treats too. Cupcakes for courage.

I remember Kate talked about eating the whole bag of candy she bought at the store yesterday. She has such a slender figure. She must have a great metabolism.

We fortify ourselves, put on our gear, and set out on the short fifteen kilometers to Porto. As we enter the urban sprawl of Vila Nova de Gaia, traffic streams past, windshield wipers whishing, people hurrying through the rain, faces hidden beneath umbrellas. After the quiet of small rural towns, it feels frenetic.

Kate says, "Bom dia," to a man rushing by with an umbrella and a grumpy expression. He gives her a startled look. I follow up with a "Bom dia," and he smiles. We spontaneously say it to everyone we pass—the grumpier their face, the more cheerful our greeting. We count how many people we can make smile.

Initially, Kate didn't make a very good impression on me, but as I've gotten to know her, I've come to like her more and more. We talk about this. She says she has heard it before. She's a bit of an introvert and aloof when she first meets people. So making people smile as we walk is definitely out of her comfort zone. But she started it. We are here to push our limits.

The first ten kilometers fly by, and as we get closer to the bridge into Porto, our hunger alarm goes off for a second breakfast. I can see that Kate's energy is lagging. We spot a pastry shop, stop, and refuel.

It's magic—after coffee and a pastry, we just about run the final five kilometers. The entrance to Porto is across the

Douro River. I stand in the rain looking at the Dom Luís I iron bridge. The Douro River flows swiftly under its girders, one hundred and fifty feet down.

There are two levels to the bridge: an upper deck for the metro and pedestrians, and a lower deck for cars and pedestrians. We approach the upper deck, walking beside the rails. A train hurtles across, and the whole structure trembles. I feel it in my bones.

Kate dances out across the bridge and stops in the middle to look down at the river. My heart jumps into my throat. I glance behind me. No metro is coming, and I tentatively step out onto the iron structure.

"You gotta see this, Dot," Kate calls.

I take a deep breath, visualize safety and love, and relax my shoulders as I walk out toward her.

"See over there," she says, pointing to the bank we just left. "That's where they make the famous port. The grape juice comes down the river on those boats." She points to boats with round casks on their decks, anchored just off the seawall. "It's so cool to see the boats, just as they've looked for hundreds of years. I love the bright colors."

I position myself halfway between the bridge railing and the metro line. She turns to me. "Are you all right?"

"I'm just a little nervous around heights, but I'm fine."

"Well then, let's get across this bridge."

Safely on the other side, we check our GPS. She's staying in a hostel, and I've treated myself to a private room—actually, an apartment I found for a really good price. Our paths continue together to the cathedral, then split. I'm so glad to get to go to the cathedral first. I've almost filled my credencial with stamps, and I need to buy a new one. I also want a stamp from the cathedral.

Kate agrees to accompany me, and we walk to the cathedral, located on the same hill as the bridge. It dawns on me that this is a city of hills. I won't be able to go anywhere without dealing with heights.

CHAPTER 16

PORTO

The cathedral complex is part of a larger site that includes an adjoining monastery and museum. We line up, just two of many tourists standing in the rain to see the opulence. Not to sound callous, but I have some issues with the Catholic Church charging people an entrance fee. I can understand a donation box or suggesting the purchase of a candle to honor someone, but charging admission feels wrong. I know they do charitable good, but their altars are covered in gold, and their accouterments could feed and clothe the world. Jesus taught us to lift up the poor and not be greedy. I still can't understand how people bow before such riches. This has happened throughout history—people giving homage to kings and queens who grow rich off others' labor and then expect everyone else to bow down to them.

We finally reach the front of the line, pay our entrance fees, and I purchase a new credencial. The cashier tells me I can get it stamped in the museum gift shop on our way out. There's always a gift shop on the way out.

We finish our tour and make our way back into the courtyard in front of the cathedral. My GPS points me back toward the river, and Kate's leads her along the street beside the cathedral. We hug and make plans to meet in the morning at the famous Livraria Lello bookstore of Harry Potter fame.

"I have all the Harry Potter sites mapped out to visit while I'm here," Kate tells me.

The energy of youth. "I'm going to rest."

My GPS leads me down steps beside the cathedral to a narrow, winding passageway between stone buildings. The passageway becomes steep steps cut into the cliff, and the stone walls are filled with graffiti. Voices rise from somewhere below me, and I get a bit nervous.

I pull the scarf tighter around my neck. The problem with being in a place you've never been before is not knowing the safe parts of the city. A group of tourists comes into view, and I step aside to let them pass. They say, "Obrigado," and I start to breathe easier. I didn't realize I'd been holding my breath.

In fact, Scarf, I haven't been staying in a place of love, as I intended.

I take a moment to put myself in a state of love, then tackle the steps downward with confidence.

The GPS says I have arrived. At first, it looks like nothing more than a stone wall pressed against the cliff. Then I notice a narrow stone ledge jutting outward, lined with wooden doors. A small gap separates the stairs from the ledge; to reach my door, I must step across it. A railing runs along the stone once I make it over. I take the step and edge along the ledge until I find the address I'm looking for. A low rumble sounds overhead. I look up. The metro hurtles across the bridge above me.

I enter the code the proprietor sent me. The door opens into a stone passageway with steps carved into the cliff, leading upward. I walk up the dark passageway. The lights automatically turn on as I ascend. I locate the door that matches the photo the owner sent me, and I enter another code to open it. This leads to another set of steps and finally to the door of my small apartment in the cliff face.

I enter the code and step inside. I drop my pack and collapse on the couch. I have always been afraid of heights, and yet here I am, lodged in the face of a cliff.

The rumble returns. I look up and notice a skylight. Through it, I see the underside of the bridge just as the metro roars across. I catch my breath and remind myself that the bridge has been here for years.

In an effort to distract myself, I take stock of the room: a counter with a sink, a small table and chairs, a wooden rack for clothes and shoes. On the table sit two bottles of water and a small carafe of port beside pretty wine glasses. I go over and pour a modest taste. The sweet, strong nectar quiets the flutter in my chest. Potent stuff. I won't drink much of it if I expect to manage those crazy steps.

Just off the living room is a small bedroom with two twin beds and a tiny bathroom. It's absolutely amazing and so cozy. Maybe I should have invited Kate to share this bounty with me. But I'm so glad to be alone.

I take a shower and wash my wet, dirty hiking clothes in the sink. I hang them up to dry, then make my way out of the apartment, down the stairs. There's a larger common kitchen just off the foyer, with supplies for coffee and tea as well as cellophane-wrapped rolls for breakfast. I make a note to stop by a grocery store and get something a little more nutritious.

I go back up to the apartment, put on my rain jacket, pocket my valuables and headlamp in case it's dark when I return. I don't want to negotiate this in the dark. It's time to explore the city while it's still light.

Outside, I continue down the stone staircase beside the cliff. I stop on a landing and look down at the riverfront and boardwalk. I can feel the romance wafting up. There are couples strolling and street musicians playing softly. Cafés are nestled alongside the stone walls and rock cliffs of the city, leaving plenty of room for pedestrians to stroll along the waterfront.

My research tells me this is the historic Ribeira district, a UNESCO World Heritage Site. According to my guidebook, it's very touristy and expensive. In my view, it's charming. A well-dressed young couple stands at the river's edge, trying to take a selfie. I ask if they'd like me to take the picture. They agree. The husband thanks me and tells me they're on their honeymoon.

We exchange pleasantries, and I learn they're from Morocco. He invites me to visit their country. I ask if it's safe for a single woman. He says that as long as I stay in tourist areas and watch my pockets, I'm perfectly safe. He raves about the beauty of his country. Morocco would never have been on my bucket list. I'm going to need a bigger bucket.

He looks down at his bride and smiles. I know that look. I excuse myself. He has done his courteous duty. Now it's on to the honeymoon. My heart aches, and I suddenly feel very alone.

My phone dings, and I check WhatsApp. There's a text from Kate. She has connected with Sally from Australia. They're at the bar in their albergue, having a drink and deciding what to do for dinner. They invite me to join them.

Well, Scarf, not alone for long.

I head over to join them at their albergue.

"Dot, welcome. We're celebrating the conclusion of Sally's Caminho. She heads home tomorrow," Kate says. "What are your plans?"

I order a glass of ruby port from the waiter. "I'm here for three nights, so I plan to go sightseeing and rest. Then I'll start walking again on Monday morning. And you?"

"I'm staying until Tuesday," Kate says. "I have a couple of online calls with clients on Monday."

"Then this is farewell." I raise my glass. "To Sally, saúde!"

"Not farewell," Kate says. "Bom Caminho. We never know where the way will lead us or who we may see."

"So true," Sally says. "We are independent, adventuresome ladies, and our paths will cross again."

"Chin-chin," I say, then realize I have to be conservative in my intake. The path home is treacherous.

"Chin-chin," they echo, and we clink glasses.

• • •

I wake early and head back down to the riverfront. It has a completely different vibe. There are tents set up for the morning market, and the cafés are closed. I walk up a hill to a café that looks open on my app. I realize Porto begins above the riverfront. It's a large, busy, cosmopolitan city.

I stop for breakfast and take out my guide to decide what I want to see. The palace gardens are at the top of my list, along with a few museums and parks. I arrive early at the bookstore where I'm to meet Kate and browse around.

The university is nearby, along with a famous church. Since there's a break in the rain, I decide to people-watch while I wait. I choose a bench across the street to sit.

There are lines of people and signs listing entry times. Our tickets are for eleven-fifteen. It's nearly time, so I'd better get in line and save us a place. I don't want to miss our opportunity.

Kate rushes up to join me. "Sorry, I got a bit lost."

We check in at the door. The employee tells us the ticket price can be deducted from the cost of a book. Kate and I exchange looks. There is no way we are going to buy a book and carry it all the way to Santiago. The store can put the ten euros toward upkeep.

We walk in, and an incredible curved double staircase greets us. Above it, a spectacular stained-glass skylight. I examine it as we wait in a long line of people to climb the staircase. All I can think, as I carefully walk up the stairs with the crowds is that this place was built in 1906, so what if the staircase collapses? What if there is an earthquake and that glass ceiling crashes down on us? I hold my breath until I reach the top and step out onto the crowded floor. To calm myself, I peruse the bookshelves. There's a whole section in English.

Then I remember to stay in love. Standing in front of the bookshelves, I close my eyes and surround myself and any unsuspecting customer that walks by in love.

"I'm hungry," Kate says, joining me in front of the bookcase. "I want to go to the Majestic Café. It's another Harry Potter site."

"Let's do it," I say, and we take off for lunch.

We have a delightful meal, but I think it's a bit overpriced. She leaves to go to the broom shop, and I join a city tour.

The tour finished, I make my way to a different part of town to find a grocery store. I buy my favorite premade chicken Caesar salad and bread for dinner and a yogurt drink, and a granola bar for breakfast. This is much cheaper and healthier than eating out all the time.

The clothes I washed out the night before are slowly drying. They'll be dry in time for me to start walking. In fact, I'm ready to start walking now. But I made arrangements to stay three nights, thinking I'd like to tour this famous city and rest my legs. Well, the only rest my legs are getting is not hauling my pack up and down the hills. Checking my pedometer, I see that I'm still doing about fifteen kilometers a day sightseeing.

I pour myself a small glass of port and glance at my watch—nine p.m. Maybe I can catch Karen. We need to talk. I'm the mom, and I'm the one who sets the limits.

Karen answers. "Hello, Mom."

"Hi, darling. I'm sitting here in my apartment in Porto and wanted to hear your voice."

"Apartment? Are you considering settling in Portugal?" There's panic in her voice.

I laugh. "No, I booked it for three nights on the internet. It's lovely to sleep in my own space sometimes instead of the albergues."

"So how is Porto?" There is a tentative change of subject in her voice.

"It's a beautiful city. Ashley would love all the Harry Potter sights. I'll post pictures."

"You know, Ashley and I were talking. She has fall break coming up, so we've decided that we're going to fly over. I have a hotel booked in Tui. We'll walk into Santiago with you."

I don't know what to say.

"Mom, are you there?"

"Yes, you just caught me by surprise. I never dreamed you and Ashley would want to come and do this. I'm just not sure which day I'll arrive in Tui."

"Well, I've been tracking your progress and figured it out from the guide you left me. I know it may be one or two days on either side. We have two weeks, so Ashley and I can sightsee and get over jet lag while we wait for you. She's so excited."

Well, she got me. I can't turn this down, especially when it comes to Ashley. Scarf, I feel like that metro just rumbled over me. When Karen gets something in her mind, she can't shake it loose. That means I've about five days of being a free spirit left. But who's counting?

"I'm looking forward to seeing you both, too. Well, I'm off to bed. We'll be in contact as I get closer to Tui. Please send me your plane and hotel reservations."

"I will. Bom Caminho," Karen says.

"Bom Caminho, darling."

My phone feels heavier than it should. I stare at Karl's name for a long moment before I press the call button. He answers on the second ring.

"Hey, pilgrim. How's Porto?" he asks gently. His voice settles something in me.

"Beautiful. Imposing. A little too full of itself," I say.

He chuckles. "Karen told me she and Ashley are coming to walk with you."

"Yes. In a few days."

"You okay with that?"

I take a sip of port. "I don't want to slip back into old roles."

"You won't," he says calmly.

"She still tries to manage me."

"I know. Let her try. I've been following you on Facebook. There's an independence I never noticed before—when it was you and Dad together."

I swallow. "I miss him. But I'm also loving who I'm becoming."

"I've always seen the strength in you."

I close my eyes for a moment. "Thank you, son. I just needed to hear a voice that trusts me."

"I do," he says simply. "And so does Karen. We just show it differently. Bom Caminho."

"I love you."

"I love you too."

We hang up. I tuck the phone away and pull the soft fabric of the scarf tighter around my shoulders.

• • •

I wake to the sound of sirens. As I leave my apartment, the fog is so thick I can't see the river. I carefully make my way down the steps to the waterfront. The transformation is startling. There are barriers set up, and no cars are allowed. There are signs marking kilometers. I stop a policeman and ask what's going on. He tells me that this is the annual Porto Marathon, and it ends here at the Iron Bridge. I just can't imagine running up and down these steep hills. There are tents lining the course with all kinds of running gear and food.

I decide to get out of the crowd and make my way to the palace gardens on top of the hill by the sea. The gardens are sleeping for the winter, so there's not much to see. A few families are out with their kids, enjoying the playground. I smile, thinking about taking my own children—and later Ashley—to the playground. I loved hearing their laughter. Maybe it's not such a bad thing that they're coming. But how do I reclaim myself while remaining part of the family?

I walk over to a fountain surrounded by benches and flower beds. There's a familiar form sitting on a bench.

"Sydney?"

"Dot?" She jumps up and hugs me. Her eyes are red. Tears stain her cheeks.

"What's the matter?" I motion to her that we should sit.

"Sean left. Ian couldn't seem to shake the bug he had and decided to go home. Sean went with him. I thought I meant more to him than that."

"I know, it hurts." I take a breath and send her love. "Where are you staying?"

"I'm at the Hostel Porto. There's a group of us. It's not like I'm alone. But I feel that way. How did you know Roy was the one?"

"It was a long time ago, and looking back, it was something that grew slowly through shared experience. But there was a strong attraction. It was a feeling of much more than friendship. But for me, it wasn't love at first sight."

Sydney studies the fountain in front of us. "I thought Sean was the one."

"I've felt that certainty before," I say quietly. "Passion can be very convincing. It feels like destiny. But sometimes it's simply intensity." I pause. "Intensity doesn't always endure."

She turns to me. "So how do you know the difference?"

"You don't," I say gently. "Not at first. You live it. And if it ends, you learn from it."

We sit quietly for a while. I think about Peter and how I thought I'd ruined my life when I got pregnant. And then, when I saw him again, my expectation of the moment was not shared. I realized the truth. It doesn't matter who Karen's father is. She is my daughter.

Wiping her eyes, Sydney checks her phone. "I'd better get back. I'm going across the river to learn about port with some of the girls in my hostel. We're leaving Porto tomorrow along the central route. But I haven't forgotten your party in Santiago."

"See you in Santiago then," I say, and hug her.

I leave the garden and walk to the Clerics' Church, the church of the clergymen. It's nice to honor the regular clergy. They deserve it as much as the saints. There is an attached tower that can be seen throughout the city. The plaque says it is seventy-five meters tall and was built in 1763. They charge people to go up the tower. I just can't do it today. I've lost my courage.

This cathedral is small compared to the grand cathedrals I have seen, though it's built in the Baroque style. A sign by the altar lists the upcoming events. There is a free organ concert at noon. I check my phone—eleven forty-five. Perfect timing. I send Kate a message about the concert. She replies that she is in the church and tells me to look up above the altar. She is waving to me from the small balcony above the altar. A smile spreads through my whole body. Kate just spreads joy wherever she goes. She wasn't who I thought she was when we first met.

When people first meet me, what judgments do they form? And what judgments do I make about myself because of them?

I close my eyes and let the church's atmosphere settle over me, quieting my mind. This is one of my favorite things to do in churches: soak up the faith and love of everyone who came before me. It's like going to the well for water.

Kate slips in beside me as the first strains of the organ fill the church. We sit and drink in the beauty.

The concert ends, and she announces her hunger. She's always hungry.

"What do you want to eat?" I ask.

"I want to try the *bolinhos de bacalhau*."

"Isn't that the fried fish cakes?"

"Yes."

"Well, the guide on my tour yesterday said the best place to get them is just across the street, the Porto do Olival Café. He said that it's the oldest café in Porto, dating back to 1853."

"I just hope the fish is younger than that." Kate winks.

"Me too!"

We go in, order our cod cakes at the counter, and take them outside to sit in the sun. Such a luxury—to sit in the sun and nibble on delicious food.

"I wonder why they call the café Porto do Olival," Kate muses.

"Let's Google it. Isn't that how all you young folk get your information?"

"Let's see... Oh, this used to be where the city wall stood, and it was one of the gates. The back wall of the restaurant is the original wall, dating to 1336. And the gate was where pilgrims entered the city. How cool is that?"

"I love to be part of a tradition that goes back so far," I say.

"Thank you for bringing me here." She licks the last of the crumbs from her fingers. "I have to go get ready for a meeting. What are you doing?"

"I'll explore the famous train station and then find something for dinner before I head back to my lodgings. Then I'll pack and get ready to walk early in the morning."

"Which route are you taking?"

"It's supposed to be beautiful tomorrow, so I'll walk up the coast and then cut across to the central route if the weather deteriorates. I really don't want to walk the coast in storms."

"I don't know if I will catch up to you. You walk really fast."

"I'm not carrying my office on my back." I smile at her. "Let's keep in touch. You never know where life will lead us."

"Bom Caminho," she says and hugs me.

"Bom Caminho." I hug her back. She has been the one constant since Lisbon and has brought me such joy. It's sad to leave her behind.

• • •

The famous train station is under renovation, so the visit doesn't take long. The tiles are remarkable, but other than that, it's a busy train station with people rushing around. The city noise and bustle are starting to grate on my nerves. So many people in this world, coming and going. I forget how many people have lives just as important as mine.

I wander back toward my lodging and the riverfront. The only place I haven't been is the port district across the bridge. Well, that is not totally true. There are many places here I haven't seen. I think I'm on overload. But I may never come this way again, so buck up. I might as well go see what all the excitement is about.

I head down the stairs that go by my lodging and pass all the way to the riverfront. The lower level of the iron bridge takes me across the Douro River, where the famous port, for which Porto is named, is brought down to be loaded onto ships and sent around the world.

There are caverns after caverns of port suppliers, and tasting rooms abound. There are stores full of sardines and other bounty from the sea. Tents with vendors from Africa line the wharf. Carvers of exotic animals, weavers of brightly colored cloth, and jewelry made of both wood and metal. Africa is really close, like almost next door. The Moorish influence. I didn't put it together before. Being from America, I just think of Africa as so far away and exotic, but here it's a part of life—just as Mexico is for us in the U.S.

I walk into an ice cream shop. They are making roses out of ice cream and putting them in cones. I ask for a chocolate one, imagining it magically appearing out of Queen Elizabeth's skirt. I walk out to the river and sit on a bench to watch the crowd. This incredibly populated world—so many different yet similar people—keeps me in awe. We all have the dream of having enough to feed ourselves and a comfortable place to live.

Scarf, that's not asking too much.

"Olá," someone behind me says. It's Sally.

"Join me. I thought you had left."

"Not yet. I fly out tonight."

"Are you ready?" I ask, more for me than her.

"Yes, I have to tie up some loose ends. I'm selling my home. It's too much for me. All I need is something small. Maybe a room or two with my daughter."

"I don't know if I could live in the same house as my daughter. She drives me nuts," I say. Then, because I don't want her to think I am a monster, I quickly add, "I love her, but we are like oil and water sometimes."

"I am a lot like my daughter, and the same thing happens with us. But my plan is to travel a lot, so I wouldn't be there much."

"I like that. Does she worry about you when you travel?"

"No, she's used to it. Actually, I think she's a little jealous of my freedom. I hope I'm a good example to her when she gets old enough to release her responsibilities."

"Does that include you?" I ask.

"Well, yes, I suppose it does. I don't want to be a burden to her. I'll seek a permanent solution when that day comes."

"I have thought about that too. My husband died of Alzheimer's. It was such a horrible, long, drawn-out disease. I couldn't do anything to end it for him. According to his wishes and the end-of-life discussions we had, I didn't prolong things either."

"Well, if we put animals out of their misery, humans should also be granted the same dignity."

I take a deep breath. It is easier said than done. There was no way I could euthanize someone or commit suicide. But I don't want to be a burden. But I need to change the subject.

"So, do you think that this is a good offer on your house?" I ask.

"Yes, I do, but I have to be there in person to make sure."

"I wish you the best."

"I wish you a Bom Caminho. Enjoy Santiago. It's a fantastic city."

> POST: Porto is loud, beautiful, overwhelming—and full of reminders that life is complicated. I walked ancient streets, listened to organ music echo through old stone, crossed a bridge that tested my courage, and asked myself hard questions about freedom, love, and family. Still walking. Still learning.

CHAPTER 17

PORTO TO BALUGÁES

The morning is sunny and clear. I shoulder my pack and make my way to the waterfront to catch the coastal Caminho. I had decided that if the weather was good, I would walk a day on the coast, and if it was bad, I would do the inland route. It's a perfect day for a walk by the ocean.

The road by the river leads to an elevated pedestrian path. Fishermen take advantage of its proximity to the water to catch their dinner. I pause and take a picture as one of them pulls in a large fish. They will eat well tonight. Ahead of me is the Atlantic Ocean. The harbor buoys and a lighthouse come into view. The pedestrian path then makes a turn north, and I'm walking along the Atlantic Ocean.

Look, Scarf, we can almost see across to America. My home. We have been away for three weeks, though sometimes it feels as if I've been walking like this my whole life.

The sidewalk transforms into a boardwalk, and my trail-hardened legs and feet simply dance along to the music of the gulls and the sea, clicking off the kilometers. There's a small café by the ocean, and my stomach growls. I glance at my phone. It's lunchtime. An older woman meets me at the café door. She could be my age—maybe a little younger. She takes me to an outside table with a waterfront view.

I order soup and bread. She smiles and nods, our communication unimpeded by the language barrier. She returns with the soup, calling to a man in the kitchen who seems to defer to her. She sets the soup in front of me and pantomimes, asking if I want a picture. I nod as the man brings out a basket of hot, fresh-baked bread. He retreats, and she snaps my picture. I ask if we can take a picture together. We take a picture with the ocean as a backdrop. She gestures that I'd better eat before the lovely lunch she's served gets cold.

Taking my time, I savor the soup's flavors by dunking the bread into the hot liquid. The warm sun and the lull of the waves on the shore entice me to take a nap. But I have kilometers to go. I pay my bill, shoulder my pack, and head north.

The restaurant owner is in my thoughts. She was in command with her directions to her staff but was such a wonderful host to me. Her quiet confidence as a woman of a certain age running her own place is remarkable.

Scarf, I wonder if I could have thrived in the business world. I am a bit envious of her industry, her joy, along with her seeming lack of stress.

• • •

It's two p.m., and I arrive at a small fishing village where I plan to spend the night. I haven't made any sleeping arrangements. I figured I'd find a place when I got tired, but I'm not. The after-lunch drowsiness has vanished with the joy of walking. So, I keep walking.

The soft give of the boardwalk cushions my steps, and I feel as though I can walk forever. The boardwalk continues through towns, ancient ruins, and empty stretches of pristine beach. The sun is dropping toward the ocean, and I look at my phone. It's getting toward five p.m. I'd better find a place to stop. These short autumn days seem to tire before I do.

My app tells me that I'm almost to the town of Vila do Conde, so I'll find a place there. I search for an albergue near a bank. I need to withdraw cash. It's too late to go to a bank tonight, and I've been warned not to use an ATM when the bank is closed. There's a risk of the machine taking your card, and then where would you be? I'll go in the morning as I leave town.

I arrive at my albergue. It's nice, and I'm in a room with several young women who are walking the coastal Portuguese. They are giggling among themselves. I feel separated from them by age, language, and distance. Their gear looks fresh, and I hear the name Porto several times.

Most pilgrims start in Porto; only two to three percent of us walking to Santiago begin in Lisboa. I feel trail-hardened in their presence. We are in very different places in our journeys. I feel like mine is coming to an end, and theirs is just beginning. I love being alone and walking, without any responsibility to a group, but at times it's lonely, too.

Scarf, I'm so glad I have you for company. It's so comforting that Valerie is only a message away if I need any Caminho advice.

I head out to the grocery store to buy dinner. I don't want to wait until eight p.m. to get a large meal in a restaurant. Purchasing my favorite chicken Caesar salad, I get a yogurt drink and a flaky croissant to go with it. The albergue provides breakfast, so there's no need to get anything else.

I head to the albergue kitchen, sit at a huge dining table, and eat my spartan meal. There are people in the lounge next door watching football (soccer in America) on TV, but this is not my sport, and besides, all the commentary is in Portuguese. I wouldn't begin to understand what is happening. I finish eating, get a shower, and go to bed. There's no real place to wash or dry clothes.

• • •

A new day. I pull on my unwashed hiking clothes and go down to breakfast. I finish eating and go back to the room. The girls are shouldering their packs, looking at their app, and conferring on the best way to get to the beach.

I check the weather, and the thunderstorm forecast hasn't changed. I grab my rain gear and prepare for a soggy hike inland. I don't want to be on a lonely stretch of beach in a storm.

I find the bank and withdraw enough cash for the next week, then head east away from the sea. It starts raining again as I reach the outskirts of the town. I stop to cross a road and become aware of the high arches of an ancient Roman aqueduct overhead. It just blows my mind that there are still things here that the Romans built over a thousand years ago.

I hope I'll be as well preserved as I age, Scarf.

I giggle at the thought. I can just see myself in a toga. I don't think I would have liked to have been alive during those days, an heir-making machine with no rights. We have come a long way, baby. I skip a little down the road.

Depending more on my GPS than the sparse arrows, I come to the imposing facade of the Church of Our Lady of Lapa. I stand a moment in wonder, allowing the beauty, stronger than the rain, to wash over me. I continue walking, strengthened by its presence.

I leave the town behind, and the landscape becomes rolling hills and lush green farmland. There are smells of fresh-mown hay, and cattle are contentedly grazing in the rain.

I reach a stone bridge that the guidebook says dates back to Roman times. Distinct yellow arrows point across it toward stone walls marking a small village. As the cobblestone road climbs into the fortified town, I realize I have reached the main route of the Caminho.

It's like I've stepped back in time. I can imagine the early pilgrims with only the clothes on their backs, a staff for support, and a gourd of water for drinking as they walk through this countryside. A long tradition of faith. I must hold onto the pilgrim's faith that I, too, will make it all the way to Santiago.

I catch up to a young female pilgrim ahead of me. The way she moves and how new her gear looks tell me she hasn't been walking very long. There's a difference between those who have been walking for a long time and those who haven't. I hope she keeps going.

"Bom Caminho," I say as I pass her.

She mumbles it back. Probably all she can manage.

I stop at a bar and learn that I'm in Arcos. There are five

pilgrims there, two couples and a single man. I give the single man a once-over, but he's so absorbed in his coffee that he doesn't notice. His gray hair and sun-kissed face are attractive. The rest of him is a mystery beneath his rain gear. At my age, what matters most is rarely visible anyway.

A cup of café con leche and pastéis de nata will do nicely. Desire, these days, is simple. Warmth. Sweetness. A small, perfect indulgence.

After my second breakfast, I put on my pack and rain gear and head back into the fray. The terrain gives way to more rolling hills, some steeper than others. I remember reading on the Caminho Portuguese Facebook page that there is a steep, rocky mountain I will have to conquer in the next couple of days. Many people find it daunting and warn about it. It will be terrible in this rain.

I push myself to reach Barcelinhos, covering thirty-two kilometers. I think I have Santiago fever; it feels so close now. I only have about two hundred kilometers left to walk. The rain starts pouring down as I enter the town. I hadn't arranged a place to stay. I sit on a wall, letting rain drip off my nose onto the guidebook. I check the apps on my phone and learn that there is an albergue right across the street from where I am, but nothing in my book indicates it as a good place to stay.

I reexamine the guidebook, hoping it will make a decision for me because I can't.

Scarf, I can't sit here by the side of the road in the rain all night.

The streetlights flicker on, and thunder rumbles overhead.

I take the path of least resistance and cross the street to the albergue. There's no one in the office, but the door is wide open. Finally, a woman emerges from another building.

Am I in the right place?

She approaches me and starts speaking in Portuguese. I give her a blank look. I'm so exhausted. She makes a call and hands me the phone to talk to the albergue owner, who says the woman will stamp my passport and show me to a bed. She stamps my passport, documenting that I've made it this far, then takes me to a room with four beds and a bathroom. There's no one else there. I pick the bed closest to the bathroom and set down my gear.

A friend of mine who is in Alcoholics Anonymous told me several years ago about the acronym H.A.L.T.: don't let yourself get too Hungry, Angry, or Tired. I can't recall what the 'L' stands for, but I do know I'm hungry and tired. I can fix these.

By studying my app, I find an open restaurant nearby. I pull my rain gear back on and walk the three blocks to the restaurant in the dark.

The proprietor welcomes me at the door. I'm the only person there. She seats me and, with the help of her phone, explains the menu. She tells me that the complete pilgrim's menu is ten euros. She serves my meal, fussing over me like a VIP. I finish my delicious dinner, and she offers to stamp my credencial. I pull it out of my pocket. It's inside a baggie so that it doesn't get wet. She stamps it, then shows me her certificates on the wall from when she and her husband walked to Santiago. She also tells me that they are part of a pilgrims' support organization. Her kindness brings a smile to my face. My belly is full, and my heart is happy.

I walk back to the albergue, not minding the rain, but I still don't see the owner. I had locked the door and taken the key with me. I'd been a bit concerned about being so presumptuous, but there is no one else around.

I lock the door behind me and take off my wet clothes. The shower is perfectly hot, and the albergue provided fluffy towels. What a treat. I don't have to get my own wet and hope it will dry by tomorrow. I was led to the right place. I have to believe that I will be okay and not end up curled up under a bridge somewhere. I must trust in divine guidance. So instead, I get to curl up in my cozy bed and look at my guidebook.

Tomorrow I will get to Casa Fernanda. I've been told this is a must-stop. And it is only twenty kilometers. I message them on WhatsApp and try to call. My app said they are closed. This could be a problem.

There's a knock at the door, and it's the owner of the albergue. I give him my fifteen euros and ask him if he knows anything about Casa Fernanda. He says yes and calls them. Fernanda answers and apologizes, saying she had been taking care of pilgrims, so she hadn't had time to respond. She will have a bed waiting for me. With only twenty kilometers to walk, I'll be early.

I thank the owner for his help and go back to my lonely bed.

Lonely.

That's what the L in H.A.L.T. stands for—lonely. The one I blanked out was the feeling I was experiencing. I didn't want to admit it to myself. I am lonely. Spending some time with women my age had whetted my appetite for companionship. But now they're going their own way, and I'm alone again. I've always loved my alone time, but I guess you can have too much of a good thing. Tears are trying to rise from my heart, through my throat, to my eyes—but it's too far for them to travel.

Scarf, I think these two lovely people were put in my path to remind me to stay in a place of love.

I have kind of let that drop. I was definitely shown love tonight. I think about walking into Porto with Kate, sharing our love through "bom dias" with people on the street. I believe I will share the feeling of love with others rather than keep it all to myself. But I guess I had to start somewhere.

> POST: Walking the coast today—sun, sea, boardwalks, and a kindness-filled lunch by the ocean. Ended the day on the central route, tired, a little lonely, and deeply grateful for strangers who show up exactly when needed. Still walking. Still learning. Sending love.

• • •

From my bed, I hear the thunder and see the lightning flash through the closed curtains. The weather app tells me it should pass in about thirty minutes.

I remember Halloween morning with Kate. I wonder how she is doing. She was staying an extra day in Porto. I love that we can walk our own walk without feeling as though we have to be connected at the hip. We can respect another's Caminho and not force ours upon them.

The storm cell passes by the time I get ready to leave. I follow the yellow arrows and come upon an open café. It's crowded with locals grabbing a coffee and a pastry before work. I can tell they are not pilgrims by the way they are dressed. Many families with school-age children are buying breakfast or a loaf of bread for the day. A few professionals are getting their energy up for a day's work, and I'm getting mine up for a day's walk.

I watch the café owners, who appear to be husband and wife and a very good team. He is running the cash register and serving the patrons. She is preparing the orders. The décor has a woman's touch, with pretty flowers, plants, and beautiful sayings and pictures on the walls. I can see how hard they work.

It's raining again when I leave, but with a full stomach, I can handle it. I cross the medieval bridge into Barcelos. What a pretty town. I would have loved to have explored it in the sunshine. The way takes me through the town center and out the other side. The road starts to rise, and there's a pilgrim in front of me. I catch up and see it's an older man. He nods but focuses on his feet as he treads carefully on the wet cobblestones. I come upon another male pilgrim, and the same thing happens. If they started in Porto, then they are on their third day of walking. It's a day of soreness, just trying to make each kilometer while your pack cuts into your shoulders as you keep trying to find the perfect position. I remember that feeling, and I'm glad I'm long past it.

Now there are two women walking in front of me, in full rain gear. One is digging into the other's pack and produces an umbrella. I'm not catching them as quickly. They seem a little more prepared. I challenge myself to catch up with them, so I put my legs into the next gear. I need a little competition now to keep my interest in walking. There's not much else to focus on in the rain.

I finally catch them and learn that they are from Newfoundland. These women are tough. You have to be to live in such a cold climate. One is walking strongly, and the other is limping a bit. The strong one tells me her name is Ginger. She quickly pulls out a lock of red hair, then tucks it back under her cap before it gets soaked.

I ask the one who is limping if she is all right. She introduces herself as Isabella. She has olive coloring and does not show me her hair. I believe it is all she can do to walk. She says she has blisters but will make it. My guess is that they're friends committed to walking together, even if they move at different speeds. It is something they will have to work out.

We walk together in silence, rain coming and going. We reach a fork in the road. They want to go see the church, while I prefer to walk the path of the wooden cross. The biggest reason I didn't walk to the church with them is that I want to walk at my own pace and not get involved with anyone. I just want to get to Santiago.

But in the Caminho spirit, I say, "From what I've heard on Facebook and from friends who've walked this way before,

Casa Fernanda is not only a lovely place to stay but also offers delicious food and entertainment. It's just a few kilometers past the church."

"Thanks for the tip, but we want to walk further. Isabella has to get to Santiago in time for her flight in about a week."

The cross stands atop a hill, beautifully carved from wood. The plaque says it was made in 1928. The locals built a strong shelter to protect the delicate wood. There are a few prayer stones at the foot. I have so much respect for the people who build and maintain these artifacts of history.

The road flattens out and winds through a village. A clap of thunder and a bolt of lightning flash a couple of blocks away. There's no place to go. I keep walking as close to the buildings as possible, hoping they will be hit by lightning before I do. The wind picks up, driving the rain down the street and into my face. I lean forward, trying to make headway and protect myself as best I can.

What if this happens when I start up the mountain?

Scarf, I'm scared of being alone on that mountain. If it's going to be a pretty dry, sunny day, that would be one thing. But the weather forecast predicts storms over the next few days.

CHAPTER 18

BALUGÃES TO SÃO ROQUE

I breathe deeply, remembering to stay in a state of love. I have to trust that I'll be all right, that something will work out—just like it did when I found that lovely albergue and restaurant last night. But the mountain keeps intruding into my thoughts.

After what feels like forever—though it's probably only fifteen minutes—the storm cell passes, and the rain diminishes to a drizzle. The arrows lead me out of town and into farmland. Out here, there's nowhere to hide. I'm the tallest thing around. What if another storm comes through? I'm soaked, and I doubt my wet rubber-soled shoes will offer any protection. I've heard you should curl into a ball during lightning because you're less likely to be struck. I don't know if that's true, and I am definitely not pulling out my phone in the rain to look it up. I keep walking.

I come to a gate with an arbor of flowers overhead. There's a sign: Casa Fernanda. Welcome, pilgrims.

I'm here. I'm safe. I want to celebrate.

I open the gate under the arbor and walk through it. A welcoming committee of several cute, friendly little dogs runs up to greet me. They don't seem to mind the rain. A man meets me on the path and introduces himself as Jacinto, Fernanda's husband. He says she'll be with me in a minute and invites me into a pavilion to get out of my wet gear.

The pavilion is covered but open on three sides. The fourth side has a door leading into a building. Underneath the pavilion roof are couches, a kitchen and grilling area, a potbelly stove for heat, and, at the far end, a laundry sink and clothesline. I hang my wet poncho on the clothesline and set my soaked shoes on the rack by the door. There are newspapers available to stuff into the toes to help them dry. It's thoughtful—and comforting.

Jacinto opens a door to a short hallway—one full bathroom on each side—leading into a sleeping room. There are four beds. A curtain leads into another sleeping area. Jacinto tells me to pick out a bed in the first area. I pick the one closest to the bathroom. He leaves me to get out of my wet clothes, shower, and warm up.

Now clean and warm, I carry my wet clothes back out to the covered area. Fernanda has arrived. She grabs my wet clothes out of my hands and takes them to the clothesline and hangs them up. She makes me a cup of hot tea, takes a tin of cookies from the kitchen shelf, and brings them to me.

"Eat," she commands. "Dinner will not be served for a couple more hours, and you must be famished."

This place is living up to all of its accolades.

There's a noise at the gate, and two men come toward the shelter. One of them uses the translate app on his phone to communicate with Fernanda. They need a bed for the night. They look and sound Asian.

They are welcomed, relieved of their wet rain gear, just as I was, and shown into the sleeping room. I go into the sleeping room, under the pretext of doing something, and they are on the other side of the curtain, in the other sleeping space. I like that the sleeping arrangements are separated by gender. I will choose my own sleeping partner, should I get so lucky.

I go back out to my cookies and hot tea.

The two women from Newfoundland come in. We greet each other like old friends, and they are shown to beds in my section. Jacinto is making a fire in the potbelly stove, and he offers to refill my tea. As they take turns getting clean and dry, the rest of us gather in front of the stove, soaking up its warmth. The Newfoundlanders tell me that they got to the church as that bad storm cell came over and took shelter there. I tell them I was not as lucky.

Ginger gets her wet shoes and puts them on the tiles in front of the stove. What a great idea. Soon, three pairs of wet shoes line up, and they begin steaming.

Dinner is announced, and we go into the main house, where there's a long table set up in the kitchen. Fernanda has water and wine on the table, along with bread and a carafe of olive oil. She says her neighbor makes the bread, and the wine is their house wine—made right here.

We sit down, and Isabella offers to say grace. It's lovely. We always said grace in our family before every meal. Roy would have loved this.

Fernanda serves us a soup made with vegetables from her garden. I savor each bite. The strength of the earth settles into my bones. She clears the bowls and serves the main course. She tells us that the chicken, potatoes, cabbage, and carrots are from their farm. She says these are the last potatoes of the season. Talk about farm-to-table. We tuck in, and soon there are only empty serving plates. Jacinto clears the table while Fernanda brings out cheese and jam for dessert. What a team. I thought I was full, but there's always room for dessert.

Then the fun begins. Fernanda gets out her special liquors, which are also made in the area by her or her family. One is what I'd call white lightning. I've had enough lightning for one day; I am not about to drink it from the bottle. One of the Asian men takes the bottle and fills up his small shot glass. He sniffs it, then knocks it back.

"If you keep drinking it like that, you'll be speaking Portuguese in no time," Fernanda says.

He laughs, and then I see his translation app open on the table. We all crack up.

"Fernanda, I hear that you sing and dance," I say.

She knocks back a shot of the strong liquor to lubricate her vocal cords, strikes a flamenco pose, and begins to sing and dance. We all start clapping along with her. She finishes her song and pours another round. The evening becomes quite jolly, but soon it is time to go to bed. Walking comes early in the morning.

I'm sharing the room with the two women from Newfoundland. The liquor gives me courage.

"May I walk with you for the next couple of days?" I ask tentatively. I don't want to intrude upon their Caminho.

"Of course," Ginger says.

"There's a mountain coming up the day after tomorrow, and I really don't want to walk over it alone in the rain."

"Of course you shouldn't," Isabella says.

We consult our guidebooks and decide to walk as far as Labruja tomorrow, to get a start on the mountain the next day. I had heard wonderful things about a town in between, Ponte da Lima, but with the weather, it makes sense for us to push on.

Isabella turns out the lights, and I feel myself begin to drift off.

Suddenly, I'm jolted out of a deep sleep. Noise and a light come from the other room. One of the Asians comes through to the bathroom. He's in there a long time. The other guy is snoring loud enough to raise the roof. He wakes up as his buddy comes out of the bathroom, and they trade places, talking loudly in their own language as they pass each other. This is not going to be a restful night.

• • •

We are up with the sun, and Jacinto makes us a delicious breakfast of farm-fresh eggs and toast. The Asians leave first, then the three of us leave together after hugging goodbye and taking a picture with Fernanda. This is a stop to remember.

We walk into Ponte de Lima with only intermittent light showers. We see a restaurant and go in for lunch, and who should be there but the two Asian men. We all laugh.

Isabella needs to find a bank to get some euros. We walk out of the restaurant and see an ATM attached to a bank next door. Ask, and you shall receive.

On our way out of town, we stop at a shop with a half-door where a man stands behind the lower half that has pilgrims' paraphernalia hanging from the back of the open top. He introduces himself as Manuel. In the shop behind him, there is someone refinishing furniture.

Then it hits me—Manuel. I've heard about him on Facebook, but I had forgotten that he was in this town. Isabella and Ginger buy a souvenir. He stamps our credencials then reaches into a box and carefully draws out three slips of paper. He looks at a slip, folds it in half, and hands it to me. Then he looks at another and hands it to Isabella. He puts the third slip back in the box, gets out a pencil and paper, and then writes a message to Ginger. He tells us we can't read them until evening. I try to give him a donation, but he declines, asking me to pray for him and his family in Santiago. I promise to do so.

The trail turns into a narrow path of steppingstones beside a creek. Due to all the rain, the creek is overflowing onto the path. There's nothing to do but get wet. We're already wet, but there's something about intentionally stepping into the cold, flowing water of the creek that makes me shiver. The creek ends at a stone wall near a road. We step out onto the left side of the narrow farm road and squish along. With this weather, there's no way our shoes will dry.

The night before, we looked up a few albergues in Labruja and chose one with a washer and dryer. Dry clothes in the morning have become a luxury—even if they don't stay dry for long. No matter how good our rain gear.

Isabella is really starting to limp. She says she now has blisters on top of her blisters. But she is determined to keep going. I hear her reciting the rosary for strength. The road goes up the beginning of the mountain we will walk over tomorrow. Isabella falls farther and farther behind. Ginger and I stop to look at our maps and guidebooks. We need to find a place to stay sooner rather than later so Isabella can rest. The place we picked out last night is too far away.

The map indicates an albergue just beyond the next curve. We exchange a look and silently agree. We come to a long gravel driveway that ascends to a farmhouse. We halt at the end of the drive and wait for Isabella to catch up.

The owner lets us in the front gate and leads us to the rear of the house. On the porch, the two Asian men sit with a young female pilgrim. This is becoming a habit.

We sign in and pay for dinner. Breakfast is included. The owner leads us across the yard to the house, where we take off our shoes on the porch and drop our poles in the receptacle. She takes us upstairs. Why is it always upstairs? She directs the three of us into one room, and the two men and the young female pilgrim into the other.

After dinner, we retire for the night. I pull out my slip of paper that Manuel gave me.

May the Camino give you exactly what you need. Have faith.

• • •

I wake up, and I'm tired. The men's noise in the bathroom next door and the rain had kept me from dropping off as easily as I normally do. And, if I admit it, despite having support for the walk over the mountain, I'm still nervous.

Isabella is sitting on the edge of her bed, dressing her blisters. I wish there was something I could do to take the pain away.

Ginger is in the bathroom, so I go into the kitchen to get breakfast. The young female pilgrim, who bunked with the Asian men, is already up making coffee. We introduce ourselves. She is from Barcelos, Portugal, and she started walking from her front door. She was taking a short vacation from work, had always wanted to walk the Caminho, and the timing was perfect.

"Are all albergues like this?" she asks in halting English.

"Well, they are all a little different. Why?" I ask.

"My room was a bit noisy, and I am not sure I like sleeping in the same room as men."

It dawns on me I've been so wrapped up in my own fears, I let this young woman sleep in a room with those noisy men. Of course, she had a rough night. I feel so bad. It's horrible not to think of others and to think only of yourself.

"I'm so sorry. I should have thought and invited you to sleep in our room. We had another bunk. By the way, I'm Dot."

"I'm Beatriz. I didn't know I had a choice. I was so tired, I just went where I was directed."

"Well, you do have a choice. Would you like to join us walking over the mountain today?"

"Will it be all right with your friends?"

I laugh. "I just met them yesterday. I don't think it will be a problem."

We finish breakfast and our morning routines, meet on the front stoop, and put on our damp shoes and rain gear. Walking down the driveway to the road that leads through the village, Isabella is still limping.

"Do you have poles?" I ask, trying to be more mindful of others' needs.

"They are in my pack. I don't think I'll need them. Actually, I never use them at home, and a friend insisted I bring them."

"Why don't you try them and see if they will take the pressure off of your feet?"

She pulls them out of her pack. I show her how to extend them to the correct height and put her hands through the straps for support. After trying a few steps, she looks at me in wonder.

"This helps."

I smile back.

Beatriz and Ginger wait for us to catch up.

We start walking, and the arrows point us up a dirt path through the trees. Here it comes—the mountain. I take a deep breath. Beatriz steps in front of me as we come to the first scramble over wet rocks. She climbs over the rocks and reaches out her hand to help me. I thank her but refuse the hand.

We get to a log—it's over or under. Beatriz quickly vaults it. I don't want to crawl through the mud, so I push myself up to sit on it and swing my legs across. She watches to make sure I'm safe. And so it goes—up and up—water streaming down the path, the rain eroding it under our feet.

The sky finally lightens as we reach the summit. We pause, take pictures, and post them on Facebook.

> POST: Today, the Camino reminds me why we walk. I was afraid and alone. Then I found laughter, shared meals, warm fires, and companions for the road ahead. Grateful for mountains climbed—inside and out.

Now it's downhill. Not my favorite part. Beatriz continues to act as my bodyguard, making sure I have good footing. The path dumps us out on the outskirts of São

Roque, named for Saint Roque, the healer often depicted with a dog at his feet—a fitting name for a town set high along the Portuguese Caminho.

We come to a crosswalk at a busy street, and Beatriz sticks her arm out in front of me and leans forward to look both ways. This is getting ridiculous. She is young enough to be my granddaughter, yet she treats me as if I were as old as Methuselah. Once safely on the other side, we head into a café for a quick bathroom break and a pick-me-up.

I pull Beatriz aside. "I really appreciate your concern, but I was able to make it this far from Lisboa. I must be doing something right."

"I'm sorry. I don't mean to offend you. I want to make sure you are safe. We are taught to care for our elders here in Portugal."

I start laughing. I had not thought that this mop of silver curls would command such respect and concern.

"You were so afraid of the mountain, I wanted to give you comfort."

Scarf, I am once again an idiot of my own making. I had no idea that my fears had telegraphed themselves so effectively. In fact, my fears were unfounded. That mountain was not any worse than the hills I walked over around Fátima and Tomar. What an old fool I am, making a mountain out of a molehill.

Scarf, how does this happen? I was worried and alone, and then three lovely women were put in my path. "Have faith" was Manuel's message. My heart rejoices.

"You are so kind," I say. "I believe it was the combination of the storms and the hype about the mountain that fueled my fear. I felt comforted by your presence and by Ginger's and Isabella's. It's nice to be with people who are watching my back. But I don't want to impose myself unnecessarily on you."

"It is not an imposition. It is my honor. But if it makes you uncomfortable, I will let you get run over," she says with a wink.

I laugh as we make our way back to the table. "You see, my daughter and granddaughter are arriving in Tui today. We will walk together to Santiago. I'm going to be straitjacketed soon enough."

"Straitjacket?" Ginger asks.

"Well, that's a bit dramatic. My daughter thinks it's time for me to go to the nursing home. And I'm out here to prove her wrong."

"Why does she think that?" Isabella asks.

"Well, after her father died, she just figured that it was the next step. I believe she sees me in the same frail light. And I don't think she can face another round of caregiving. I'm also not ready to become her patient."

"That's why you were so upset about me hovering over you," Beatriz says.

"Yes, you're right. I didn't realize that you were pushing the same buttons that I'm afraid Karen is going to push when she arrives. And I was ashamed of my fear of going over the mountain. I have to believe in my ability—for Karen to believe in me, too. And I'm not sure I'm strong enough."

"Not strong enough?" Isabella exclaims. "You have walked almost five hundred kilometers, carrying your backpack in all sorts of weather. Don't sell yourself short."

I let out a quick breath. "Thank you for reminding me. I do sell myself short sometimes."

"Well, it has no base in reality," Ginger says, then changes the subject. "Isabella and I have decided to take a bus to Valença."

"Are you all right?" I ask. Once again, I have gotten lost in my own pain and failed to see others' pain.

"It's really my fault. My pack is too heavy, and my feet are suffering. I can't walk anymore today. I want to qualify for a Compostela, and I am afraid that if I don't take a break, I may not make it to Santiago," Isabella says, getting tearful.

"Yes, to qualify for your Compostela, you must walk from Tui to Santiago. But it's not worth damaging yourself," I say.

"I know. That's why we are going to take a break this afternoon," Isabella replies. "Will you be all right, Beatriz? We don't want to abandon you."

"Dot will look after me." Beatriz winks. "You take care of those feet. It's still a long way to Santiago."

"Well, I meant, what are you going to do when you reach Tui, with Dot going off with her family?" Isabella asks.

"I thought I would stay at the albergue next to the cathedral."

"We're staying there too," Ginger says. "We'll save you a bunk."

"That would be lovely," Beatriz says. "Well, it's all settled. If we're going to get to Tui before dark, we'd better start walking."

CHAPTER 19

SÃO ROQUE TO PORRIÑO

Beatriz relaxes a little as we keep walking. We have about eighteen kilometers to go, and staying on alert that long would ruin anyone's day. The terrain tilts into another climb, and then it drops into the Minho River valley. The river marks the boundary between Portugal and Spain.

We walk into Arão around four p.m. My phone dings. A picnic table sits beside a food truck. I sit while Beatriz goes to see what's available.

Karen: *We've arrived, and we're at the hotel. Where are you?*

Me: *I'm just outside Valença, and I'll get to the hotel late this afternoon—about three more hours of walking. And I'll lose an hour at the border, so it might be eight by the time I arrive—just in time for dinner.*

It probably won't take me that long to walk the next five kilometers, but I don't want her to worry.

I join Beatriz at the food truck. I need fuel. The owner is telling Beatriz how she makes her food, and how she's out of her famous soup and has only one famous sausage sandwich left.

"Want to split a famous sausage sandwich?" I ask Beatriz.

She grins, and I order the sandwich. We both get chips and a soda to go with it. While the owner fixes our food, she tells us it's all from scratch—nutritious, the best ingredients—and that we'll have to come back for her soup.

We pay and walk back to the picnic table. The owner follows us and starts telling us how she emigrated here from Russia to make a better life for her family. At first, I listen, thinking of the courage it must take to leave your country and start over. But then she repeats herself—recipes, nutrition, her family back in Russia, how hard she's working. I hate to be unkind, but time is marching on—and so must we.

I pull out my phone and make a show of reading messages. "We should go," I tell Beatriz, whose eyes are starting to glaze over.

We shoulder our packs, and the owner follows us a few meters down the road, still talking.

I give her a firm, "Bom Caminho."

She must realize that she's left her food truck unguarded because she finally waves goodbye to us and hurries back to her truck, ready to catch the next unsuspecting pilgrim.

We walk through Valença, with its ancient fortress. The rain puts a damper on our desire to stop and admire it. We approach the bridge over the Minho River into Tui, and the sky darkens. The first fat drops of rain hit my face.

Scarf, we made it! Spain.

We pause under the royal-blue sign, a circle of gold stars surrounding the proud word España.

"I'll take your picture, and then you take mine," Beatriz says.

We resume walking and reach a turnoff. I have to keep going up the hill, but Beatriz turns right toward her albergue. I'll miss walking with these women. We've only known each other a couple of days, but we've formed a bond—born of needing help and offering it.

The rain builds until I'm caught in a deluge. I duck under a portico and look at my map. Another kilometer to the hotel. The rain has been the bane of my Caminho since Coimbra. I think of Coimbra as the turning point of my Caminho—from being alone to meeting people. From no rain to rain, from flatter terrain to hills. From introspection to interaction. From keeping love to myself to sharing it.

Please, God, help me share the love with Karen. Ashley is easy, but Karen knows how to push my buttons—in the way only a child can push her mother's buttons.

There are the hotel's glass doors. I make my way into the lobby, dripping all over the beautiful floor. I apologize to the man at the desk, and he just waves it off.

"We've been mopping up rain all week. And we'll be mopping all next week, if the weather prediction is correct," he says. "Do you have a reservation?"

"Yes." I give my name, then text Karen that I've arrived. "What time is it? I know the time changed when I crossed from Portugal to Spain, but I want to make sure I'm on local time."

"It's seven p.m. We're used to this, but pilgrims are always a bit disoriented. May I stamp your credencial?"

"Yes, please." I look at my phone again, and the time is correct. Amazing. I don't even have to change it.

"Gran!" Ashley rushes toward me.

It's hard to reconcile the child who once ran everywhere instead of walking with the grown woman she has become. But it's the same smile and loving glow.

I open my arms. "Ashley, welcome to Spain. But be careful, I'll get you soaking wet."

"Oh, I don't care. I'm so in awe that you walked all the way here from Lisbon and through the pouring rain."

"It didn't rain the whole way." I laugh at her exuberance.

"Well, you know what I mean." She giggles.

"Where's your mom?"

"She's napping. I saw the text come through. I didn't want to wake her. I don't think she slept a wink on the plane. She'd have been up there telling the pilot what to do if they'd let her."

"Now, Ashley, be kind. Your mother only wants the best." I sigh. Not much has changed.

The man at the desk motions to me. "Excuse me, ma'am.

Here's your key. You're in room number 112 next to your granddaughter and daughter. They're in 110."

"Thank you," I say, relieved that I have my own room. "Let's go, Ashley. I have to get out of these wet clothes. As good as my rain gear is, nothing can stand up to a deluge."

While I'm showering and rinsing out my rain-soaked clothes, Ashley goes to wake up Karen. We plan to meet in the lobby at eight p.m. to find a place for dinner.

I see it is a quarter to eight. I have fifteen minutes to rest. There's a knock at the door. I haul my tired body off the bed.

"Mom," Karen says when I open the door. "Why didn't you wake me when you arrived?"

"It's wonderful to see you too, darling." I embrace her. Stay in love, I remind myself. "I just had to get out of my wet things and into warm, dry clothes."

She steps back from the embrace and looks me up and down. "You look different. In fact, you look so strong and healthy. I haven't seen that glow on your face in years."

I welcome her in and close the door. "Oh, darling. I feel better than I have felt in years. As much as it was a pleasure caring for your father, it took almost everything out of me. And I know it was hard on you, too."

She appears to be fighting for composure.

To not provoke a deluge of tears, I say, "I'm starving. Let's find dinner."

We wander the streets with our rain gear and umbrellas and happen upon a small café near the cathedral named Emma's. The waitress comes over to take our drink orders. I request the house white wine, and Karen joins me. Ashley looks at us questioningly.

"Please bring a carafe and three glasses," I tell the waitress. "Ashley, at nineteen, you're old enough to drink wine if you would like some. It's part of the culture."

"Yes, please. I want to experience everything."

There's a shout from the restaurant's door. It's Ginger, Isabella, and Beatriz. I get up and greet them. I ask them to join us, and the waiter makes arrangements at our table. I request three more glasses. The serendipity is amazing.

I introduce everyone, and we toast to the women on the Caminho and peruse the menu. We decide to each get something different and share.

Karen leans over toward Ginger and quietly says something. I bet she is checking up on me. Ashley is pumping Beatriz for details on the Caminho. I sip my wine and enjoy the conviviality of the moment.

The waiter brings our food, and Isabella asks for grace. Karen's expression tells me that she approves. A relief flows through me. It is a meal of wine, women, and laughter.

We take a selfie, and I open Facebook.

> POST: Serendipity on the Camino. Walked into Spain soaked to the skin... and somehow ended up at a table full of strong women, shared food, shared stories, and shared laughter. The Camino has a way of reminding you that you're never really walking alone.

I ask Ginger where they're staying tomorrow night. She says that they're staying at an albergue in Porriño. I make arrangements for three beds. We're all set. It'll be nice to have a buffer. And it will get my girls into the Camino familia spirit.

We finish dinner and make plans to meet tomorrow morning at the cathedral. Karen and Ashley need to buy credencials, and we all want stamps. Then we will start walking the twenty kilometers to Porriño. It will be good to start them with a short day. I don't want to stress them by walking too far the first day. And it will be good for Isabella to help her feet heal, though she said at dinner that they felt better after taking the afternoon off.

• • •

We leave the cathedral under overcast skies. I don't want it to rain on the girls' first day. Like, I have control over the weather. Leaving Tui, we have a sharp downhill run, then the Camino flattens out. The arrows point to a dirt path through the woods. I'm so glad we are not on narrow roads with cars bearing down on us. Karen would have a fit.

Our hunger alarm starts going off. Our breakfast of coffee and pastries was not enough to keep us going. The path dumps us out into a small town, and we stop at a small café where there are other pilgrims gathering.

"We call this second breakfast," I tell Ashley and Karen. "The café con leche is to die for. Unfortunately, now that we are in Spain, there are no more pastéis de nata. We will have to find another source of fuel."

"Ooo, look at those pastries full of chocolate," Ashley says. "I want one of those."

"Is there nothing here that's healthy?" Karen sweeps her critical eye over the case.

"You can get a bocadillo, a sandwich," I suggest. "You're burning more calories than you realize, darling. We still have nine kilometers to go."

"How far is that in miles?" Ashley inquires.

"That is just about six miles—two to three hours of walking," I tell her.

She looks at me in amazement. "Oh my, and you have been doing this every day."

"You get used to it, and then you fall in love with the simplicity and the rhythm of it. I'm going to join you in one of those *napolitanas de chocolate*. Karen?"

"When in Rome... a napolitana for me too."

I turn to the bartender, order three café con leches and three napolitanas, and pay. Pulling out my credencial, I tell Ashley and Karen to get theirs out, too. We must get two stamps a day between here and Santiago to earn our Compostela. He quickly stamps our credencials then moves on to the next customer.

All the tables are small, and the girls had put two together. We join them, and the bartender brings our completed order.

Karen takes her first sip of café. "Heaven," she says, relaxing into her chair.

This is the first time I've seen her relax since she arrived.

Ashley takes a bite of her napolitana and looks at her mom. "Agreed," she says.

An old saying pops into my mind, "*Solvitur ambulando.*" It is solved by walking.

Well, Scarf, so far, so good.

"What are you smiling about, Mom?" Karen asks.

"You know, I was a bit nervous about you all joining me. I shouldn't have been. I love that you are here."

The pilgrims around us begin putting on rain gear. I glance out the window. It has begun raining.

"Suit up, ladies, we're in for a gusher," Beatriz says as she dons her poncho over her pack.

"Oh my God," Karen mumbles, and begins rummaging in her pack.

"What's wrong, darling?"

"I can't seem to find my poncho. I'm sure I packed it." She goes through the main pack again.

"You girls go ahead. We'll be along shortly," I say, not wanting Karen to have witnesses. I turn to her and ask, "Did you put it in a side pocket?"

She unzips the bottom compartment. "Oh, wait, yes. Here it is. I can't believe I forgot where I put it."

"It's jet lag. It took me a while to get oriented too. It's amazing how you can lose things in such a small space." I help her put it over her pack, making sure that it covers everything.

She glances around the room. "Where's Ashley?"

"She went ahead with the girls. Ready?"

"As I'll ever be. I can't believe we are going out on purpose to walk in the rain."

"There's no other way to Santiago. It's part of the magic of the Camino. You can't just stay in one place. You must always move forward."

Karen does not respond. She is focusing on her footsteps and getting into a rhythm with her poles. I remember when she was a baby, just learning to walk. Her focus and concentration were second to none. She's going to master the Camino, too. She's done this with everything in her life, from one challenge to the next. Nose to the grindstone. Roy was a bit of a workaholic, too. Those hikes in the hills, even though physically challenging, were one of the few times he would relax. I sigh.

Scarf, what we unknowingly impose upon our children.

We walk in silence. I love that we can be silent together. I remember those special nights after feeding Karen, I would rock with her quietly in my arms. I smile as the memory flows warmly through my body.

• • •

When we stumble in, Ashley is sitting in the bar attached to the albergue, looking fresh and clean. She runs over to us.

"You made it!"

"Was there any doubt?" Karen says. "We sauntered, as John Muir advised when walking through nature."

We check in and go to take showers.

"Hand me out your dirty clothes, and I'll throw them into the washer with mine," Ashley offers. "The girls have gone out to find food, so it's just us."

"You did a good job with her, Karen," I tell her through the shower wall.

By the time Karen and I get dressed and are ready to go out, Ashley has managed our laundry.

"Let's go explore," Ashley says. "The rain has stopped, and the sun is out." Her youthful energy is contagious. "I'm hungry. I hear they have some tapas at a restaurant down the street. Real tapas in Spain, how cool is this?"

"Vamos," Karen says, rising to the occasion.

We walk into a small plaza in front of a church. Karen tries the door, but it's locked. She looks at me in question.

"Many of the small churches are closed," I tell her. "Their insurance will only allow them to be open if there is someone available to monitor it. This is because of vandals. It's a shame that someone would vandalize a church, but not everyone in the world is a kind, respectful person."

Ashley stops in front of a café. "Gran, Mom, look at this." There are tables spilling out into the pedestrian cobblestone street. "I've seen this on travel shows. This town must be ancient."

I laugh. It feels so good to be laughing with my family. It wasn't so long ago that we were crying together.

"You know, Ashley, I have gotten so used to this that it's almost lost its charm. Every town in Portugal and Spain has these lovely pedestrian-only centers with restaurants and shops. Thank you for bringing back the magic. There are quite a few people here. That's a good sign. Let's look at the menu." I peruse the choices and prices. "They have a pilgrim's meal for just twelve euros."

A waiter comes out with his hands laden with food. The aroma makes me swoon. He delivers his burden, then asks us if we would like a table inside or outside.

"Outside", we say in chorus and laugh. He shows us to a table where we can people-watch while we enjoy our meal and hands us menus.

"The pilgrim's meal comes with a starter, an entrée, and dessert, along with wine and bread," I explain. "You choose each course. I love the soup here, so I'll start with that and then have the chicken. Ashley, do you see anything you like?"

"I'll have what you're having."

"Karen?"

"I'll try the salad and the beef. I want to lose a few pounds while I'm here," she says.

The waiter comes with wine and bread.

"I'd like some water," Karen tells the waiter.

"Gas or still?" he asks.

The look of confusion on her face is priceless. Struggling not to grin, I interpret for her.

"Would you like soda water, which is the gas, or just regular water in a bottle, which is still?"

"I just want plain ice water."

"Still," I say to the waiter. "And three glasses, please."

He returns with three glasses and a liter bottle of water, which he opens and pours.

"Where's the ice?" Karen asks, her jaw tightening.

"Oh, darling, I forgot. They don't routinely serve water with ice in this country. You have to request it." I ask the waiter for a glass of ice. He smiles and nods. I'm sure he is used to Americans and their requests for ice.

"How strange not to bring ice for the water," Karen says, her tone putting me on alert. When she was a child, that tone foretold a temper tantrum. I thought she had grown out of them.

Then the food arrives, and we tuck in.

"Delicious," Karen says.

I relax.

Families are strolling down the street, the children darting in and out, playing.

"It's the paseo," I explain. "Everyone comes out in the evening and strolls the town center, enjoying their friends and neighbors while the children play."

"It's lovely," Ashley says, embracing the custom.

"But shouldn't those children be in bed?" Karen asks. "I never let you stay up so late, Ashley. It's after eight p.m."

"It's a different culture, Mom."

We finish dinner, and I suggest we stroll a bit.

"Mother, we really should go back and get to sleep. We have a long walk tomorrow. Where are we staying tomorrow night anyway? I don't think I want to stay in one of these albergues again. I'm not sure I'll be able to sleep in a room with all these people tonight. You've been doing this, but I'm not used to that."

"Sometimes I stay in hotels, but it gets awfully lonely. You meet such lovely people staying in an albergue."

"Well, we're here now, so you won't be lonely. We've already paid for tonight, but let's find a hotel for tomorrow night."

"No problem." I know enough when to give her some semblance of control. I turn down the street toward the albergue.

"I want to see more of the town," Ashley says. "And find the girls."

"You know your way back to the albergue?" I ask.

"Yes, Gran, I do."

"Well, enjoy."

Karen stops walking. "Wait a minute, you can't go walking the streets by yourself at night. It's dangerous."

"Well, no, it's not," I say. "Just stay in the well-lit areas."

"Mother, please don't encourage her. You are coming back to the albergue with us."

Ashley and I exchange looks, and I shrug. Ashley, sullen now, joins us as we walk back, passing smiling groups of families and young people. I can feel her disappointment deepen with each smiling face.

Beatriz is in the lounge when we walk into the albergue.

"Welcome. The other two have gone to bed early, but I'm not ready to sleep. I want to go out and see more of this sweet little town. Did you know it's famous for its pink granite? I want to see the town hall—it was designed by the architect Antonio Palacios."

"Mom, can I go with her? I won't be alone."

Karen nods wearily, and Ashley rushes off with Beatriz before she can change her mind.

"Let's sit and look at the guidebook," I suggest to Karen.

We sit at one of the tables and review the guidebook. The next large town is Redondela, which is only sixteen kilometers away. We search for a hotel with a room for three, find one, and book it. There is fatigue etched all over Karen's face. Between the jet lag and the walk today, she must be worn out. I soften toward her controlling nature.

"I'm tired," I say. "Let's go to bed."

"I think I'll wait up here for the girls."

"Karen, they'll be fine. Spain is safe, and they are together. Beatriz is a native, knows the language, and her way around. She couldn't be in better hands." I smile, remembering how Beatriz treated me on the first day we walked together.

"I'll just stay up for a while longer. I want to read about Redondela."

"All right." I don't want to engage in an argument. "I'm whipped, so I'm off to bed. Just remember not to shine any lights around when you go into the dorm. I point my phone light to the ground so I don't bother anyone."

"Please, Mother, give me credit."

"Sorry, darling." I kiss her on the head and go into the dorm.

CHAPTER 20

PORRIÑO TO PONTEVEDRA

I wake with the sun. Karen is still sleeping on the bottom bunk, and Ashley is on the top. I wonder how late they stayed up. I get up quietly and do my morning ablutions. In the lounge, the coffee is on, and breakfast is being served.

I order a café con leche and take it to an outside table to enjoy the morning. The birds are chirping, the only thing stirring in the town. The pinks of the sky begin to fade in the rays of the morning sun.

"Hey, Gran." Ashley joins me with a cup of coffee and a napolitana.

"How was your evening?"

"It was wonderful. Beatriz is so much fun and knows all the best places. Thanks for going to bat for me with Mom."

"Well, it's a new experience for her, and most Americans don't realize how safe Spain is. Speaking of safety, do you have the AlertCops app?"

"Of course. Mom made sure we both downloaded it before we came, and when we got to the hotel in Tui, she made sure we activated it."

"She loves you, sweetheart. And sometimes love makes us extra cautious."

"I know, but I don't want it to straitjacket me."

I laugh. "Oh, sweetheart, I'll do my best not to let that happen."

Karen joins us with her cup of café con leche. "What are you two laughing about?"

"The beautiful morning and Ashley's wonderful experiences last night. Let's order a more substantial breakfast."

We finish breakfast, shoulder our packs, and start walking. I can see that Karen is struggling with sore muscles. I remember the first few days were tough. Ashley is just tripping down the road.

Ah, youth, Scarf. What would it be like to feel that again? Though I don't want to relive the painful lessons.

Karen's pace slows, and Ashley gradually gets ahead of us. I slow down to walk with her. We catch up with Ashley, who has stopped to look at a mural of a pilgrim at sunset painted on the wall of an underpass.

"This graffiti is incredible," she says.

"Yes, it is. I love that people paint beauty," I say.

Karen does not comment and keeps walking. I can tell she is hurting. I bet she stayed up too late waiting for Ashley. I'm glad we have a short day.

Ashley and I catch up easily and pass her. We get beside the next mile marker; I stop and read out loud.

"One hundred kilometers to Santiago—woo hoo! Ashley, please take my picture. I can't believe that's all we have left to go."

Karen groans as she walks up, shakes herself, and puts on a brave smile. She points to the darkening sky. "I hope the rain holds off until we reach Redondela."

"Now you and Ashley pose beside the marker. We must send this to Karl and Marty."

"Yes, Marty, my obnoxious husband," Karen says. "He thought I was crazy, chasing you across Spain and dragging Ashley with me."

I silently agree.

"Come join us, Gran. We'll do a selfie of the three of us."

A pilgrim stops and smiles at us. "Do you want me to take the picture?"

"Yes, please." I hand him my camera. He has a nice head of gray hair and is fit. There are crinkles of laugh lines at the edge of his blue eyes. His tan face really sets them off.

Scarf, now that the kids are here, I may never get a chance at exquisite sex.

The pilgrim hands me my phone. "I assume you are headed to Santiago. Where did you start?" he asks as we all start walking again.

"I started in Lisboa. My daughter and granddaughter joined me in Tui."

"Amazing. I just started in Porto."

I bask in the admiration. "Wasn't Porto lovely?" I want to keep the conversation going.

"Yes, a beautiful town. I'm so sorry I had to experience it alone. I'm a widow."

"I understand. I lost my husband a few months ago."

Karen clears her throat.

"I'm so sorry, I haven't introduced myself. I'm Dot, and this is my daughter, Karen, and my granddaughter, Ashley."

"I'm Luciano, from Madrid. You all sound like Americans."

Ashley speaks up. "We're from California. I'm so sorry to hear about your wife. When we lost Pop-pop, it was so hard. I'm glad Gran is out here walking through the grief."

"Yes, the Camino has a long history of people walking it to heal. It has been helpful to me. And it is also helpful to meet such lovely peregrinas."

Ashley falls in walking beside him. "What's a peregrina?"

"Ah," he says, "a female pilgrim."

"You have an awfully small pack. I know Gran told us to pack light, but that's amazing."

"I hired a company to plan my route and carry my suitcase forward to the next hotel. It's very convenient."

"I didn't know you could do that."

"There are many ways to walk a Camino."

The rain starts to fall in a fine mist. We don our rain gear. Luciano pulls on a jacket and takes an umbrella from his day pack. He graciously shares the shelter with Ashley, who drills him on Spain and the Camino.

We get to the edge of a small town, and Luciano pulls out a small book.

"This is the itinerary the tour company gave me. They suggest I stop here and have a bite to eat." He points to a small bar just down the street. "The food is supposed to be amazing. Would you like to join me?"

"Yes, please," says Ashley.

Karen and I nod. There is gratitude in Karen's eyes for a break.

A harried waitress takes our order. It is one of the few places between Porriño and Redondela where we can get a meal. We get the pilgrims' menu of lentil soup, chicken and rice, a beverage, and dessert.

"My Pop-pop died of Alzheimer's," Ashley tells Luciano. "It was a long and drawn-out process. I was worried about Gran. She looked worn out. And now she looks great. You are right. The Camino must be healing."

"My wife had dementia from a stroke, and it, too, was a long struggle. It was exhausting for both of us. I hope to have recovered by the time I reach Santiago."

"I'm so sorry," Ashley says.

• • •

She has taken him under her wing. This child has a heart as big as the sky. She was there every step of the way with her Pop-pop. I remember that once we explained the disease to the grandchildren and told them what they could do to help, they were great. Sometimes they saw parts of the disease I wish they hadn't, like his unreasonable expectations, being argumentative, or when he insisted on driving somewhere and I couldn't let him. Then he lost the ability to eat with utensils and just wanted to wander everywhere. But they understood and would jump in to distract him, get him involved in their activities, and give me room to breathe.

The rain comes down in earnest when we leave the restaurant. I envy Luciano's suitcase of dry clothes waiting at his hotel.

"Where are you staying?" he asks, as if reading my mind. We have fallen into step while Karen and Ashley trail behind.

"We're staying at the Rúa do Medio tonight."

"That's where I'm staying. We'll have to go explore the city together."

• • •

Now that we're cleaned up, we meet Luciano in the foyer.

"Wow, he's so cosmo," Ashley whispers to me.

"Cosmo?" I ask quietly as Karen greets him.

"Yeah, sophisticated and worldly," Ashley whispers back.

"Yes, he is. And I feel like an old crone."

"Gran, crone used to mean an old, ugly witch. Now we use it to mean a wise and wonderful woman. And you are that woman."

I pull her into a big bear hug.

"What are you two up to?" Karen asks.

"I was just telling Gran how beautiful she is. Don't you agree?"

They look at me with scrutiny, and I can feel the blush of red all the way to the roots of my curly hair.

"I believe we have a tour to go on," I say.

"Yes, I would be honored to be accompanied by three such lovely ladies." Luciano directs his smile at me and offers me his arm.

Karen whispers to Ashley, "What was that all about?"

Luciano starts telling me that Redondela is famous for its ancient Roman aqueducts, so I don't hear Ashley's reply.

CHAPTER 21

REDONDELA TO CALDAS DE REIS

Upon waking, we go to the breakfast room. I love it when breakfast is included in the room rate. There is the usual coffee, toast, and pastries, but this hotel also has put out some lovely cheeses, meats, and fruit.

"I have room," Luciano says, inviting us to join him at his table. "What do you ladies have on your agenda today?"

"We're walking to Pontevedra... Oh my, we didn't make arrangements for a room tonight."

"I'm staying at a hotel in the old town, close to the Sanctuary of the Virgin de la Peregrina. Let me call and see if there's availability."

"That would be lovely," I say.

He calls once we finish our breakfast, then turns to us and smiles. "I was able to reserve a room for three at the special pilgrim's price. You pay when you arrive."

"Thank you," Karen says.

I see that she is truly grateful for his intervention.

Maybe there's hope for this crone after all, Scarf.

We agree to meet in Pontevedra, if not before, then we go to our rooms to get ready to leave.

We walk out of town, and there are the girls. It's good to see them. I don't want them to think I'm ghosting them for my family. They wait for us, and we fall in together and walk in the weak autumn sunshine. The overcast sky promises more rain.

"How's 'Umbrella Man'?" Beatriz asks me with a smile.

"Umbrella Man?"

"You know, the gentleman with the umbrella who seems to be sticking close to you."

"Oh, Luciano..." I start giggling. I have the sudden picture of Luciano surrounded by a tour group, holding his umbrella high.

"Let me in on the joke," Ginger says.

"Beatriz has given a trail name to our new walking companion, 'Umbrella Man'. And it is well earned. He took us on a lovely tour last night and also arranged a hotel for us tonight. By the way, Ginger, what were you and Karen whispering about at dinner in Tui?"

"She asked me how I thought you were doing. Then she followed up by telling me that her friends admonished her for letting her eighty-year-old mother go and tramp all over Europe by herself. I told her you are our hero, and there's no need to worry."

"Thank you," I say, warmth spreading through me.

You know, Scarf, sometimes it feels like Karen is truly concerned for me, and other times it feels like she's just doing her duty. I will not be a burden.

The six of us women stop for lunch at a small restaurant and get the hearty pilgrim's meal. It starts to drizzle. We gear up before we head back outside. The arrows point the way out of town, then show us the turn into the woods. The dirt path is interspersed with large, flat stones, the remains of the old Roman road. The rain is making the ancient stones slick. I depend on my poles to keep my balance. We are a quiet group, lost in our own thoughts. Even Ashley seems subdued.

We enter Pontevedra in a downpour. I'm so grateful we're going to a hotel. The girls wave goodbye as they peel off at their hostel. We check in. I was concerned about the price because I hadn't asked Luciano, but for three, it's quite reasonable.

Karen whips out her credit card. "This one's on me. You've been paying for us since we arrived. We didn't come here to be a burden on you."

I smile and let her pay. I didn't invite her to this party.

Luciano comes in as we are heading to our rooms. He suggests we meet in the lobby in about an hour and offers to take us on a tour of the city. I smile at him, and the words

"Umbrella Man" have me full-on grinning. We agree and head to our rooms.

I take time to drop a post to the Camigas.

> POST: Finally dry and off the road for the day. Rainy miles, sore muscles, family, friends, and some unexpected kindness along the way. There are many ways to walk a Camino. Some days call for endurance. Some days for trust. And some days for letting someone share an umbrella.

Our first stop is the Sanctuary of the Virgin de la Peregrina. It's small but tall. A volunteer greets us at the nave door and stamps our credencials. He tells us we can visit the nave for free, but if we want to walk up into the dome, we each must pay a euro. Luciano quickly pulls out the coins and drops them into the volunteer's hand. I'm sunk. I was going to sit out the trip up to the dome, but that would be rude. And I can't let Karen see me sweat.

We mount the spiral staircase—Ashley first, then Karen, then me. Luciano is bringing up the rear. I'm sure he will catch me if I fall. Ashley gets way ahead of us and lets out a muffled scream. We race up the steps and step into a room full of memorabilia. There are three lifelike dolls peeking out from between two cases filled with silver chalices. The dolls are about two-and-a-half feet tall and dressed in traditional costumes.

There is something spooky about how much they resemble live toddlers playing dress-up.

"Oh, honey, they're just dolls," I say and put my arm around her shoulders.

"They just took me by surprise. They're creepy-looking," Ashley says.

"Yes, they are. But in context, they are props that are used at the festival of the Virgin. I am sorry they scared you. Come to the balcony and look down into the church," Luciano says.

Ashley joins him at the rail. Now it's my turn to feel fear. Karen and I stand behind them.

"Do you notice anything about the floor plan of the church?" he asks.

"It is a strange shape, round, not a rectangle like most churches. Oh... it's a scallop shell," Ashley says, turning to him.

"Yes, this church is dedicated to the Virgin who watches over pilgrims. It's amazing, no?" he says, then steps back to make room for Karen and me at the railing.

I motion Karen forward and keep my distance.

"Are you still afraid of heights?" she asks.

"Yes, and I'm very comfortable standing right here."

"Oh, Dot, I'm so sorry," Luciano says. "I should not have presumed you would like to come up here."

"It's all right. I could have said something, but this Camino is about facing my fears and building my confidence. I wanted to come up here. I just don't want to stand next to the railing."

He offers to walk in front of me as we go back down the stairs. It feels nice to be coddled.

We leave the church and head to the Convent of St. Francis.

"Did you all know that St. Francis walked the Caminho Portuguese in 1214? As a result, the Franciscan order settled here and built a convent and church in the 1300s. It is built on an old Templar site," Luciano explains, swinging his umbrella as he walks.

"I went to Almourol Castle and the Convent of Christ when I was in the Tomar area," I tell him. "They were fantastic."

"I trace my heritage back to the Knights Templar. Even though we have undergone many iterations over the centuries, we still live by the code of honor and duty to pilgrims. I am so glad you are interested in our heritage." He grabs my elbow to assist me up the steps of the church. At the top, he does not let go immediately.

"I find it all so fascinating," I say, looking up into his liquid brown eyes.

His gaze lingers, warm on my face.

"Mother," Karen calls from the doorway. "You must see inside this church. The stained glass is amazing."

I follow her, a little annoyed at the interruption. But she's right. It's beautiful. We wander through the church. I sit in a pew for a minute, closing my eyes and letting myself relax and fill with love.

Oh, Scarf... how do I reclaim myself and still stay close to my daughter?

The group is heading back to the door, and I follow. Outside, the sun has set, and the illuminated square is lovely.

"Dot," someone calls. The girls cross the square and come toward me.

"We just missed you," Ginger says. "Isn't it magnificent?"

"It is," I reply.

"I'm hungry," Beatriz tells us.

"Me too," Ashley adds.

"After that lunch, I really don't want a big meal," I say, glancing at my watch. "And it's a bit early for dinner."

"How about dessert?" Luciano suggests.

"Chocolate and churros would be perfect," Beatriz tells him.

"What's that?" Ashley says. "If chocolate's in the title, it's for me."

"It is fried dough dipped in hot chocolate. Just perfect for a cool evening," Luciano explains.

"Lead on," I say.

We walk through the square and head down one of the side streets in the city center. We arrive at a café with sumptuous pastries on display, and we pull a couple of tables together. The waitress comes over, and we order chocolate and churros all around. She brings out hot mugs of rich, thick chocolate and several large plates of churros—doughy logs, crisp on the outside and soft in the middle, fresh out of the fryer. All I hear are little sounds of satisfaction as we dunk churros into chocolate and let the gooey sweetness melt on our tongues.

"In three days, we will be in Santiago," Ginger says. "I can't believe we are so close, yet I don't want it to end."

My eyes mist over. "I know what you mean."

Scarf, it has been quite a journey.

"And three days until your eightieth birthday, Mom," Karen adds.

"You could have just said birthday and not included my age."

Beatriz turns to me. "You're turning eighty the day we reach Santiago?"

"That I am. And you're all invited to the party."

"Unbelievable," Beatriz says.

"I'll drink to that." Ashley tips her cup of hot chocolate into her mouth, not letting any of the goodness go to waste.

We look at the guide and find an apartment in Caldas de Reis with six beds to rent for the night. I glance at Luciano.

He smiles. "Oh, don't worry about me. I'm already booked through the tour company."

"I brought my swimsuit," Ginger says, and she reserves the apartment. "The hot springs there are supposed to be wonderfully healing."

"Hot springs?" I inquire.

"Yes," Luciano says. "Caldas de Reis means 'Cauldron of the Kings.' You must take the waters."

Ashley frowns. "I didn't bring a suit."

"No worries. Go in your bra and shorts, like we did in the old days." I give her a wink.

We settle our check and walk back to our lodging, discussing the rest of the journey.

CHAPTER 22

CALDAS DE REIS TO PADRÓN

Luciano isn't at breakfast. His loss. Karen, Ashley, and I eat, then walk through town, searching for the arrows to lead us to Caldas de Reis. The dawn breaks without clouds for the first time in days.

"Look, sunshine and blue sky," Ashley says.

"Let's grab something for a picnic." I point to an open café.

We go to the counter and buy bread, cheese, cookies, and cans of Aquarius, my favorite electrolyte drink, and distribute them between us. We leave the Lérez river basin, and the yellow arrows guide us inland. We make a steep curve up a hill beside a cemetery. Most of the tombstones look ancient, but a few are newer. This church is still active but locked. The grey stone cemetery wall becomes the church wall, and as we round the corner, there is a bench with a sculpture of a small, rotund man in glasses resting on it. A sign informs us that he was the parish priest. It's so lovely. We follow the wall and come upon a large sign that says, *Yo soy el camino, la verdad y la vida.* I don't need Luciano to interpret: "I am the way, the truth, and the life."

I look at my daughter and granddaughter as they explore the church grounds, and I smile.

Yes, Scarf, I am glad they are here.

Ashley comes and stands beside me. "What are you smiling about, Gran?"

"You and your mom. I wasn't sure about having you join me, but I'm finding such joy in your presence."

"Why weren't you sure?" she asks.

"Truth?" I say, nodding to the sign. "When I married, I made compromises, and it was worth it. During your grandfather's illness, it was heartbreaking not only to watch his strength fade, but also to feel, day by day, that we were slowly losing him. There were times, sitting quietly beside him, I would wonder what my life might have been like if I'd never married him. I know that sounds cold, but the pain of that illness for both of us was almost too much to handle at times. I believe I came to Portugal to seek a lost part of my youth. I'm struggling to find out who I am apart from Roy, while still honoring him and our life together. Am I making sense?"

"Oh, Gran...oh yes, you are. I always wondered what you were like at my age."

"It was a long time ago, but my memory is of an innocent young girl who lived as she was supposed to live, wearing the right clothes, having the right friends, and marrying the right man. I'm so glad that those restrictions are not on young women of your generation."

"There's still plenty of that brainwashing, but we also have more examples of women actually following their dreams. Do you see how fascinated Mom is with history? Her letters to me in college were so well written. But she works as an elementary teacher's aide, so she could be home to care for us. I wonder what her reality would have been if she had not followed tradition."

I smile. "Yes, your mother always did have a talent for writing and a curiosity about life. She could have been another Jean Auel. And maybe she will be one day. Her life is not over by a long shot. She still has time to pursue her dreams."

"What were your dreams, Gran?"

"I always wanted to be a concert pianist, to travel the world. I was very good in college. I was also steered to take courses in music education so I would have something to fall back on." I laugh. "To me, 'to fall back on' meant not making it as a pianist. And it also meant 'in case you didn't find a husband.'

That ship sailed long ago, but I still play for my joy and the joy of others. Now, I am searching for something to fulfill me, to justify my time on this earth—beyond childbirth. Don't get me wrong. I loved having children, and I love having you all in my life. But I want to reclaim that idealist, that passionate young woman I was, but with the wisdom I have today. What sets you on fire, my love?"

She pauses a moment. "So many things. There are so many things I want to do. Sometimes I think it would be easier if someone told me what to do."

I laugh. "Easier maybe, but it would extinguish your fire."

"You know, Gran, this sounds silly, but I want to figure out how to improve recycling and renewable energy. I love my science classes. And even in this day and age, I notice how the boys are given a little more preference over the girls and how hard I have to work, and it makes me angry."

"Good. Anger is energy. Use it wisely."

Karen joins us. "What are you two talking about so seriously?"

"Life," I say. "Shall we stroll on?"

The arrows point us to an uphill path through the woods, with evidence of an old Roman road. At the summit, there's a lovely park, and the girls are sitting down for a picnic lunch.

Beatriz calls out for us to join them. We join the girls and pull out our food.

I pull out my phone and look at the picture of Ashley and Karen at the church. I open the Camigas Facebook page.

> POST: Walking today with my daughter and granddaughter, past an old church and an even older cemetery. I keep thinking about the roads we take—and the ones we don't. Loving deeply means choosing, and choosing always means leaving something behind. Today I feel grateful for the life I've lived... and curious about the woman I'm still becoming. Buen Camino.

"Trade you a tangerine for a cookie," Beatriz says to Ashley.

"You're on."

Ginger is looking down at her phone. "The apartment we're staying in tonight has a kitchen, a washing machine, and a dryer."

"Let's cook dinner," Isabella says. "We can pick up one of those premade lasagnas at the market, a couple of salads, bread, wine, and dessert."

"Sounds lovely," I say.

"And if we see Umbrella Man, we can invite him to join us," Isabella adds.

"Let's see...that's six to one. He'd be a fool not to join us." I laugh.

"Make that five to one. I'm a happily married woman," Ginger says.

"Me, too," Isabella and Karen say in unison, laughing.

"And we're too young." Ashley high-fives Beatriz.

"Well, that just leaves you, Mom." Karen gathers up the remains of her lunch, shoulders her pack, and starts walking.

I sit, stunned. Ginger winks at me.

We clean up, making sure we leave no trash behind.

The arrows lead us to a park, then to a glen with wooden sculptures. There's an owl, a totem of a wood sprite, and a chair.

Isabella sits in the chair and leans back. "Just leave me here," she says.

I snap a picture of her. "How are your feet?"

"They're better but probably won't heal before Santiago. I'll manage."

"Yes, you will. As long as they are not infected."

"No signs of infection," she says.

The weather starts to deteriorate as we walk into Caldas de Reis. A cold breeze picks up. I'm not sure I want to swim, even in a hot spring. We check in, put on swimwear, pull on long pants and jackets, and head out to find the hot springs and a store. There's a covered pool on the next corner near the river, steam rising from it. I dip my fingers into the water. It is delightfully warm. I'm not sure I want to submerge, but it would feel wonderful on my feet.

"I'm just going to soak my feet," I say.

"Good idea," Isabella tells me. "I'm not sure I am up for a swim."

The dark clouds let go of the first few drops of rain, but we are protected under the shelter. I strip off my shoes and socks, roll up my pants, and sit on the edge of the pool. Carefully swinging my legs over the edge, I rest my feet on the slick, moss-covered bottom. The girls all do the same, and soon we are in heaven, soaking our tired feet.

Ashley makes her way to where the spring is bubbling out of the wall. "It's even warmer over here."

"Don't slip," Karen says as Ashley takes a step and loses her balance, plopping down into the pool.

"Are you all right?" I stand to go help her, but my feet slide out from under me, and I sit down in the warm water.

"Are you all right, Gran?" Ashley asks, making her way over to me.

"Yes, I am. I just slid down the wall."

"Thank God," Karen says.

"Come on in, Mom, the water's fine," Ashley tells her.

"I believe two wet women in the family are enough," she says.

Luciano is walking by, umbrella unfurled. "Hey, Luciano, join us," Beatriz calls.

He steps under the shelter and laughs at Ashley and me splashing each other, with the rest of the group looking on. "I was just on the hunt for a restaurant."

"We're cooking dinner tonight at the apartment we rented. Join us," Isabella says.

“That sounds wonderful. May I bring the wine? There are some lovely Spanish wines you should try.”

“Perfect.” Isabella pulls her feet out of the water and starts to dry them off.

“I’ll go with the girls to the store, and you two go back to the apartment and get dry,” Karen says.

Ashley and I get out of the pool and make our way, soaking wet, back to the apartment.

“That was a blast, Gran,” she says through chattering teeth. The cold wind cuts right through us.

Thank goodness the apartment has two bathrooms. We shower and put our wet clothes in the washing machine, as the girls come chattering through the door with Luciano and wine in tow.

I start heating the lasagna, and Luciano joins me in a glass of wine as the girls clean up.

Dinner is lovely. Now we are replete and drowsy. Ginger pulls out the guide and tells us that we must make plans for tomorrow night. We find an albergue just across the river from the Iglesia de Santiago in Padrón.

“This church, the Iglesia de Santiago, is where the stone boat carrying the remains of St. James is said to have docked when it arrived from the Holy Land.” Luciano takes a sip of wine. “Legend has it that St. James’ body was placed on the altar. An altar was called a Padrón, a place of pardoning your sins. Under the altar, you can see the Pedra de Padrón. This is the stone that the boat was tied to. It's a very sacred place in our history."

The wine, food, and warmth of the kitchen after my plunge are taking their toll. I stifle a yawn.

"I'm sorry. Am I boring you?" Luciano asks.

"No, the swim wore me out." I smile at him.

He looks at his watch. "I did not realize it was so late. This has been a wonderful evening. I was concerned that by traveling with a tour company and staying in hotels, I would not meet many pilgrims. You've made my Camino."

I walk him to the door.

He smiles at me and says, "Until tomorrow."

• • •

The rain continues through the night. In the morning, we leave the apartment with it still coming down. Our nice, clean, dry clothes will not stay that way long, but it was wonderful to put them on this morning. The washing machine alone was worth the price of the apartment.

We find a little café on our way out of town and stop for breakfast. There's no sign of Luciano.

As we leave town, a wizened old pilgrim with a much-loved backpack on his back stops us. He pulls plastic yellow hands and arrows out of his pocket, blesses each of us, and gifts us these mementos.

Wishing us "Buen Camino," he walks in the direction from which we came.

"I read about him," Beatriz says. "This is really special. You cannot buy these. They must be gifted to you."

I zip them into my skirt pocket, feeling very special indeed.

We walk up a hill and back down, along paths through woods and roads through towns. We enter Padrón through a city park by the Rio Sar—the river said to have carried St. James inland toward Santiago.

Ginger has her phone out. "It's over there."

"What's over there?" I ask.

"The Mexican restaurant 'A Cantina.' It's where we can get a wax stamp."

"Let's go," Beatriz says.

Even though it's early for dinner, the restaurant is open. We hang our wet rain gear on hooks by the door. A man greets us and takes us to a large table.

"I want a margarita," Ginger says.

"That sounds wonderful," I say. "Make that two."

The rest of the girls chime in, and there are margaritas all around. We peruse the menu, and when he returns with the margaritas, we order.

"Where can we get your special stamp?" Ginger asks.

"Come with me," he says. "Two at a time."

He leads Ginger and Isabella to a table in the back. When they return, Beatriz and I take our turn. He looks me over, then takes my credencial and lays it out carefully on the bench. On his bench is a small propane burner with a pan on top, brass spoons filled with wax remnants in different colors, pieces of wax, glitter paint markers, and small shakers of glitter. A stamp sits within reach beside a tool that looks like a scalpel. He melts red wax in a spoon and pours it into my credencial. How does he know red is my favorite color?

He takes the stamp and presses it into the wax. Using a scalpel, he cleans up the edges of the impression. Then he takes a gold glitter paint pen and carefully draws around the stamp. To finish, he shakes gold glitter onto his creation. He motions us to keep our credencials open so the stamp hardens completely. I drop a donation in the box on his table.

We finish our lunch, then walk along the river to the bridge by the church and cross to our albergue. It's small, and we're the only ones there. The hospitalero greets us and shows us the washer and dryer, and a shoe dryer. It looks like an old-fashioned hair dryer, but with hoses sticking out to plug into our shoes.

"Is there a way I can send my pack forward tomorrow?" Isabella asks.

"What a great idea," Karen says.

"We have twenty-five kilometers tomorrow—all uphill to Santiago. And it's going to rain all day again. Does anyone else want to have their pack transported?" Isabella asks.

We all nod. The hospitalero gives each of us an envelope tag with a perforated edge. It has the bag-transport company's number on it. Isabella calls the transport company and tells them there will be six bags transported to San Martín Pinario, our destination in Santiago.

Before we peel off our damp clothes, we go to the church. Luciano is sitting in a pew, head bowed. Karen, Ashley, and I walk up to the altar and quietly pay homage to the saint—staff and gourd in hand. I walk over to a large statue of St. James on a white horse trampling figures beneath him. It's gruesome.

Luciano joins me and tells me that when King Alfonso II died, the Moors came to collect what they believed had been promised: one hundred virgins. Ramiro I, his heir, refused, and a battle followed. St. James is said to have appeared out of the clouds on a white horse and begun slaying the invaders, driving them out of Spain. St. James became Santiago Matamoros, St. James the Moor-slayer.

"That St. James sure gets around," I say.

He laughs. It's a nice sound. "Where are you staying in Santiago?"

"We'll be at San Martín."

"So am I. I'll see you there, or at the cathedral if we walk in together."

"That would be lovely," I say and smile up at him.

"Mother, this is a church," Karen says as she approaches us. "You're being awfully loud."

"I must take my leave. I'll see you tomorrow." He gently touches my arm.

"Karen, that was rude," I say quietly. "He was just telling me the legend of Santiago Matamoros."

She doesn't say anything more, but her eyes convey her irritation with me.

A tour group arrives, and the tour guide begins telling everyone about the church's history. They're not exactly quiet, either. I jerk my head toward them and give Karen a sidelong look. She has the decency to blush.

I join the girls at the church entrance, and we head back out into the storm to our albergue. We eat leftovers from lunch and prepare for bed. Isabella tells us we must leave our packs by the door by nine a.m.

Settling in my bunk, I think about that little interchange with Luciano. Am I ready for a relationship? Luciano is a nice man, but geographically it's impossible. With Karen all up in my business, there's no way I could even have a fling if I chose. Do I have to wait until my children are ready before I can move on? If I do that, I may never reclaim myself.

"What time are you getting up?" Ginger seems to direct the question to all of us.

"It won't be light until seven-thirty, so probably about six-thirty," Karen says. "The hospitalero said the bread is delivered at seven, so we can eat before we leave."

"That sounds perfect," Isabella answers.

I roll toward the wall. My pack. I don't think I can leave it with a transport company. I stare at the ceiling. Tomorrow is my last day, and I've carried that pack every step of the way. I turn back to the wall, shielding my eyes from the light. I want to carry it tomorrow.

Oh, Scarf, what's wrong with me? It's such a simple thing to ship it ahead. Everyone does it. It would be so freeing to walk without it. I won't be cheating or anything, but it feels that way. I roll back over on my back.

"Gran, are you all right?" Ashley says from the bed above.

"I'm fine, just restless. Sorry to disturb you."

"No problem."

I stay on my back, feeling rigid. This is ridiculous. I stifle the urge to turn again, not wanting to rock the bunk and disturb Ashley.

CHAPTER 23

PADRÓN TO SANTIAGO

The next thing I know, Karen's alarm is going off.

Then, as we're finishing our morning routine, there's a knock on the door below. Isabella answers it.

"Bread is here."

We trickle downstairs, make coffee, and eat breakfast. On our way out, we set our packs by the door. I look at my pack. It feels like I'm deserting it after all this time. I can't do it. I grab it, rip off the tag, and shove it into my pocket. Shouldering my pack, I follow the girls out the door.

"Mom, why do you have your pack?" Karen asks.

"I don't know. I just couldn't leave it." A tear mixes with the rain on my cheek.

"Mom, are you ok?" she asks.

"Just being silly, darling."

Ashley joins us. "I don't think you're silly, Gran. If you want to carry your pack, then carry it. If you get tired going uphill, I'll help."

"Thank you, sweetheart, but at this stage, I believe I can manage the hills."

"Well, Mom, I think this is ridiculous," Karen says. "You haven't been acting like yourself—flirting with strange men, insisting on being Miss Camino, and making us feel like wimps."

"Speaking of strange, look at that little house on stilts." Ashley points. "What is that?"

"It's a hórreo. They are used to preserve the grain from the harvest, keeping out rodents and water. Aren't they cute?" I say. Trust Ashley—always the peacekeeper. But I know Karen, and I will need to solve this problem if I am ever going to feel entirely free.

The rain turns our last day into an uphill slog. I'm not even aware of the pack on my back, and I have easily kept up with the girls. In fact, I'm in the best shape I've been in for years. I intend to keep it that way.

Yes, Scarf, I am already thinking about home, and I haven't even gotten to Santiago.

The rural road turns urban as we enter the city's outskirts. There's a viewing spot by a parking lot, atop a hill overlooking Santiago. I can just make out the cathedral's spires below in the mist.

A yellow arrow points us through a wooded area skirting the edge of the city, and we come out onto another road with the first high-rises mushrooming. A scallop shell points us to a sidewalk along a busy street. The street rises, and we soon reach a park.

"We must walk through the park," Ginger says, guidebook in hand. "There's a statue up here of two sisters who walked through the park every afternoon dressed in colorful clothes to protest Franco's regime. They broke the conservative norms of the day, giving the people hope of an independent future."

We come upon them, one in a bright yellow jacket and the other in a pink shawl. We take turns posing with them.

Scarf, I'm an independent woman. But it's hard when everyone around expects me to follow convention.

We cross a busy street and walk onto the stone streets of the old city, following the crowd of pilgrims with backpacks. We spill out of a narrow street lined with shops selling Camino memorabilia into a large plaza full of laughing and crying pilgrims. The cathedral rises in front of us. The sight of it leaves me breathless.

Ashley grabs me in a hug. "We made it!"

Karen comes up to us. I ease out of Ashley's hug and open my arms for Karen. She steps into the embrace, tears in her eyes. "Happy birthday, Mom."

We pull Ashley into the fold.

"Look over here," Beatriz cries. We turn, and she snaps a picture. "Now, everyone together." She stops a gentleman walking by us. "Can you take our picture?"

We pose, the six of us with our arms around each other.

I step away from the others and find a quieter edge of the plaza. The cathedral bells roll across the plaza like waves.

I press Karl's name on my phone. He answers immediately.

"You made it."

"We did," I say, my throat tightening.

"And you carried your pack, didn't you? Karen texted me about the pack issue and that you are acting a little strange."

I laugh through a sniffle. "Of course I did."

"I never doubted you." There it is again—that steady belief. "You sound happy."

"I am. Not because it's over. Because I know I'm not."

A pause.

"How's Karen?" he asks gently.

"She's good. It's a lot of changes for her. We cried," I admit. "The good kind."

"I'm proud of you, Mom."

That lands deeper than he knows.

"For what?"

"For going. For not shrinking. For showing Ashley what eighty can look like."

I look across the plaza at my granddaughter laughing. "I don't want to be anyone's burden," I whisper.

"You're not," he says firmly. "You're the example. Happy eightieth birthday."

"I love you."

"I love you too, Mom. Now go celebrate. You've earned it."

"Hold on." I walk over to the others and switch my call to camera mode. "It's Karl."

Ashley and Karen crowd around the camera and include him in the celebration with a chorus of "Love you and see you soon." I hang up the phone and hug my girls.

Sydney comes running across the plaza, grinning ear-to-ear. "Dot, you made it! I never doubted you for a minute."

"What are you doing here?"

"I told you that I wouldn't miss your birthday party. I really wanted to be here for your party. I've been following you on the Camigas Facebook page and knew you were about a week out. I decided to walk to Finisterre while I waited. It was amazing."

Her rush of words makes me smile. She seems to have found her way, too. "We have to get a picture." I hand Ashley my phone.

"Ashley, this is Sydney. We met in Lisboa." Sydney and I pose with our arms around each other.

"And now, would you take a picture of me alone with the Scarf? I promised Valerie I would send one to her and post it on Camigas."

> POST: I arrived today—on foot, in the rain, with my pack on my back and my heart full. This Camino has given me more than I can name yet.
>
> Gratitude for the road.
>
> Gratitude for the people who walked beside me.
>
> Gratitude for the women who walked before me—and the ones who will walk after.
>
> To my Camigas: Thank you for carrying me when I didn't know I needed it.
>
> Buen Camino, always.

Luciano approaches and takes me by the shoulders. "Dot..." He kisses both my cheeks.

"Welcome to Santiago," I say, my cheeks still tingling. "I wondered when you would walk in."

"I stopped at a little restaurant I know and got reservations for dinner in their private room. How many of us will there be?"

I turn to Sydney. "How long are you staying?"

"I fly out tomorrow afternoon."

"There will be eight of us," I tell Luciano.

"I'll let them know. We'll attend mass at seven-thirty, then have dinner at nine," he announces to the group, then looks at his watch. "We have time to go get our Compostelas. Follow me."

Sydney elbows me in the ribs and nods toward Luciano.

A blush races up my cheeks. "It's not like that," I say, remembering the intention I made so long ago.

"Not like what?" Karen says.

This daughter of mine never misses a thing.

After the pictures and congratulations, we make our way to our lodging and check in. I head to my room. It's nice to be alone. I've missed myself. Karen and Ashley are together down the hall.

I check my phone.

Valerie: *Congratulations. You look fabulous. I'm so happy for you. And I just want to remind you—the scarf isn't yours to keep. You must pass it on… when the time comes.*

I text back: *Absolutely, but how will I know who to give it to?*

Valerie: *You will know. Have faith. Guess where I am?*

I answer: *Where?*

Valerie: *I'm in Kenya. My uncle got me a job at a hospital here. It's amazing. You must come visit.*

I text back and assure her that I will.

There's a knock at my door. It's only six-thirty p.m. I open the door, and it's Karen.

"Mom, we need to talk."

Oh, Scarf, I was hoping this journey would loosen her grip—not on me, but on her fear. That would allow her to let go of the apron strings, so to speak.

"Come in, darling." I step back to let her in. I take the small chair by the window as she sits on the bed.

"What is it?" I ask.

"Mom, I don't want you going off with that man."

"What?" It's all I can manage after her words, which have come out of left field.

"I can see the way he looks at you, and you are vulnerable, and I don't want him taking advantage of you. I know you must be lonely since Dad died, but you can't replace him."

Anger and sadness mix in her eyes. My poor darling.

"I have no intention of replacing your father," I say gently. "But I do have the intention of living a full life...of traveling, spending time with new and old friends, of spending time with my family. And if I find a compatible man along the way, I intend to spend time with him. But most importantly, I intend to spend time with myself—without apology."

Her tears spill over. "I miss him so much," she says.

I join her on the bed and put my arm around her. "Oh, my darling. I miss him, too."

She curls into me, and the tears come in earnest. We rock gently until she is done. She lifts her face to mine.

I smile at her. "I love you."

She smiles back. "I must look a fright. And we have a party to go to."

"You can use my bathroom to wash your face."

• • •

The service in the cathedral ends, and eight men in burgundy robes make their way up to the sanctuary, each holding the end of a rope attached to a main rope that soars to the roof of the church. A giant incense burner hangs on the other end.

"The botafumeiro is going to fly," Luciano whispers loud enough for all of us to hear him.

The men lower the silver botafumeiro. The priest separates the top from the bottom and lifts it up. He places burning incense into its massive cavity, then secures the top back to the bottom. The scented smoke starts pouring out of the vents. The men pull on the ropes, and the cauldron rises. The priest grasps the bottom, and with a strong push, he starts it swinging. The men pull down hard, then let it float up. The motion reminds me of the day I soared over the fields on the pilgrim's swing.

"Those men are called *tiraboleiros*. It's an honor to be chosen."

"Shh," I say. This is not a time for commentary.

He startles. I pat him on the knee, amused by his enthusiasm.

I withdraw my hand and follow the botafumeiro as it soars over the nave. I breathe in the richness of the scent, allowing it to fill me with love, and breathing out, I release that love to the world. Hundreds of us sitting here in this sanctuary are doing the same.

When the ceremony is over, we all solemnly leave the church and make our way to the party. We start with a *caldo gallego*, a lovely local soup made with kale, potatoes, and *chorizo*. Then come the main courses to share: octopus, scallops, pork, and *ternera gallega*, which Luciano explains is Galician beef. He offers me some from the platter. We pass the platters around and all get our fill.

Luciano raps his spoon against his wine glass to get our attention. He nods at the owner, and a waiter brings out a lovely *tarta de Santiago* with eight candles. Another waiter follows with champagne.

"My gift to you," Luciano says, meeting my gaze. "May you have many more years of health, happiness, and Caminos. *Salud*."

Everyone raises their glass of champagne to me and echoes, "Salud."

CHAPTER 24

SANTIAGO

I get up with the sun, and a bit of a headache reminds me that an eighty-year-old shouldn't indulge in too much champagne. I do my morning routine and arrange the scarf around my neck. I take a long look at myself in the mirror. I no longer see the woman I used to be, nor the girl I once was. I see someone wise, a crone.

Not too bad for an old lady, right, Scarf?

I smile and make my way down to breakfast.

We all finish breakfast and head to the Plaza del Obradoiro. The morning sun is trying to make its way over the soaring spires of the cathedral. The rain clouds seem to be taking a bit of a break this morning. We line up for our tour of the cathedral's interior and rooftop. Luciano told us last night that it's a must-do and helped us get tickets. I laugh, thinking about his desire to make our experience the best and, in doing so, he is a bit of a pest. A pleasant pest, though.

Luciano meets us at the entrance, and we join the line. It moves quickly as the tour guide passes out earphones so we can hear her speak. She leads us up a staircase and then through a door onto the balcony, overlooking the nave three stories below.

Oh, Scarf, I didn't think about this tour being full of high places. Well, I will just have to get over it. I'm not going to go through the rest of my life in fear. Not of heights. Not of desire. Not of change. Maybe it took turning eighty to loosen my grip on fear.

After the tour guide tells us about the church's interior, she takes us up a spiral staircase to the rooftop. Luciano offers me his arm. I smile and step confidently out upon the rooftop. We move forward to the ridge. I catch him watching me—not with expectation, but with recognition and love. The kind of love Luz taught me. The love we give ourselves and share with others.

I hold Luciano's gaze. He nods slightly, as if acknowledging the crone I have become—strong and capable.

There is no promise in the moment, no claim, just a quiet understanding that something could unfold—or not. A future held lightly. An openness without demand.

We turn and follow the group onto the rooftop, taking in the view of Santiago, reveling in the church's history.

We descend into the museum. The riches on display

are mesmerizing. The centuries represented are mind-boggling. Karen and Ashley are ogling the fine embroidery on an ancient tapestry. I stop in front of a simple statue of St. James as a pilgrim. I like this depiction of him. I like the simplicity.

"Mom, Gran, come here."

"What is it, Ashley?" Karen asks.

"This is what's left of the original rose window in the cathedral from about 1211. Can you imagine?"

"It's beautiful." I step closer to get a better look. The museum has backed it with an image of what the original would have looked like, and they have superimposed what remains of the stone on top.

"Yes, it's beautiful, but look at the design. Do you notice anything?" Ashley can barely contain her excitement.

"Well, that image looks like an eight-pointed star. Interesting. And those three images sort of look like the phases of the moon. You know, there was ancient worship of the heavenly bodies. And it's so interesting to find it in a church," I say.

"Yes, the phases of the moon. But it's also the same symbol for the triple goddess."

"Triple goddess?"

"Yes, Gran. The triple goddess shows the three stages of womanhood. The waxing moon on the left is the maiden, the full moon is the mother, and the waning moon is the crone. That's you, Gran. I'm the maiden, and Mom, the mother. It's us."

I slip my arm around the waists of my daughter and granddaughter and hug them tight. We stand together like living pieces of a great rose window—maiden, mother, crone, and each a fragment of light joined in a pattern that turns and returns, never truly ending.

Ashley touches the fabric of the scarf around my neck. It too continues. What began before us will continue long after us—like the scarf passed from one woman to the next.

EPILOGUE

California — One Month Later

Dear Dot,

I was enthralled by your journey on Facebook. My name is Carrie, and I'm planning to walk the Camino next spring. I saw your post on the Camigas page asking who might feel called to carry the scarf next, and I haven't been able to stop thinking about it. If you feel it's right, I would be honored to carry it on my Camino.
I live in Wisconsin, so we'll need to connect by phone. By the way, we have a pilgrimage here called the Wisconsin Way. Come walk it sometime.

Please let me know what works for you.

Buen Camino,
Carrie

I read the message twice.
I smile.
I know.
I fold the scarf carefully, smoothing the soft fabric as I go. Three Caminos before me. Now another.
I press the soft fabric to my lips and whisper, "Buen Camino, Camiga."

I place it into the box addressed to Carrie and close the lid.

Alder stands before a restored fragment of the original rose window from the façade of the Portico of Glory at the Cathedral of Santiago de Compostela. Carved in granite by Master Mateo around 1200, this Romanesque tracery once held stained glass and formed part of the cathedral's earlier outer façade before the Baroque Obradoiro front was built. Its intertwined bands and star shaped openings reflect a precise, ordered design rooted in both craft and symbolism. That sense of structure and continuity echoes through Alder's trilogy, where the stages of Maiden, Mother, and Crone are not separate paths but part of a single unfolding life. In this image, the layered geometry of the rose quietly mirrors that arc, each phase connected, each held within the whole, pointing toward the deeper integration that comes forward in *Crone.*

ALDER ALLENSWORTH

Alder Allensworth began her career as a therapist and continues her work in healing as a nurse, helping people navigate life's challenges.

In 2017, she walked her first Camino, the Camino Francés. While in Burgos, she received news that her manuscript, *Prevail: Celebrate the Journey,* had won a publishing contract with Richter Publishing; it was released in 2018.

She returned to the Camino in 2022 for a writer's retreat, where the seeds of this trilogy took shape. In a moment of serendipity, a long-lost scarf found its way back to her—one she carried to the top of O Cebreiro, capturing the image that now graces the cover of Book One.

Alder continued her pilgrimage in 2024 on the Camino del Norte and in 2025 on the Camino Portugués from Lisboa to Santiago. Her journeys—both personal and professional—center on healing, resilience, and transformation.

She coauthored *Mackenzie Meets Alzheimer's Disease* with Brenda Freed and helped develop the Mackenzie Meets Alzheimer's Awareness Program to support families navigating dementia. She is an active member of the Tampa Writers Alliance, an advocate for Alzheimer's awareness, and is involved with *American Pilgrims on the Camino.* She lives in Tampa, Florida.

email: aldertree0720@gmail.com

www.alderallensworth.com

If you'd like to learn more about LifeWave patches
and how they have supported this journey, you can visit:
https://liveyounger.com/Alder07
Scan the code to learn more.

www.ingramcontent.com/pod-product-compliance
Lightning Source LLC
LaVergne TN
LVHW091249110826
845146LV00002BA/577

* 9 7 9 8 9 9 0 0 1 8 9 4 5 *